"Are you trying to drive people away?"

"Just you," Parker said.

He thought he heard Carly's breath catch. And her voice was entirely different when she said, very quietly, "Why?"

"Because you... What happens between us...scares the hell out of me."

"Funny. It intrigues the hell out of me."

"Intrigues?"

"Because I've never felt anything like that so fast—" She stopped, gave him a wry smile. "Because I've never felt anything like it at all."

He sucked in the deepest breath he could and let it out slowly. "Neither have I."

"So that leaves us with one question."

"Only one?"

"One big one. What do we do about it?"

"Don't you mean, do we do anything about it?"

"Splitting hairs now?"

"No. Because the problem with what do we do is... I don't think there's any halfway here for me. Not when just a kiss about put me under."

The smile she suddenly gave him then was blinding. "Whew. Glad that wasn't just me."

* * *

Dear Reader,

Ten or so years ago, I had an idea for a story. This is not at all unusual, mind you. It happens all the time. I made a few notes and set it aside to let it perk because I was in the middle of writing another book. About a year later, as I was pondering my next project, I was going through my notes trying to find something that leaped out and said "Now! My turn!" I can't really explain it any better than to say that some ideas need to stew in that pot on the back burner for a long time before they're ready to cooperate (looking at you, Rafer Crawford!).

In this case, the notes I'd made the year before suddenly sparked a new idea about a special couple and their even more special dog. The couple had yet to find each other, but when they did, they found not only love but a life calling. And out of that was born the Cutter's Code series, with that furry rapscallion Cutter playing a major and continuing role. And now, after twelve books, I finally came back to that original idea and found it was more than ready to cooperate. So in that weird way that things happen in my fictional worlds, book number lucky thirteen in the series is in fact the idea that started it all, finally come to fruition.

I hope you enjoy reading it as much as I enjoyed finally getting to tell the story!

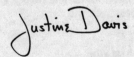

OPERATION WHISTLEBLOWER

Justine Davis

HARLEQUIN

ROMANTIC
SUSPENSE

HARLEQUIN®
ROMANTIC SUSPENSE™

Recycling programs
for this product may
not exist in your area.

ISBN-13: 978-1-335-75947-4

Operation Whistleblower

Copyright © 2021 by Janice Davis Smith

This edition published by arrangement with Harlequin Books S.A.

For questions and comments about the quality of this book,
please contact us at CustomerService@Harlequin.com.

Harlequin Enterprises ULC
22 Adelaide St. West, 40th Floor
Toronto, Ontario M5H 4E3, Canada
www.Harlequin.com

Printed in U.S.A.

Justine Davis lives on Puget Sound in Washington State, watching big ships and the occasional submarine go by and sharing the neighborhood with assorted wildlife, including a pair of bald eagles, deer, a bear or two, and a tailless raccoon. In the few hours when she's not planning, plotting or writing her next book, her favorite things are photography, knitting her way through a huge yarn stash and driving her restored 1967 Corvette roadster—top down, of course.

Connect with Justine on her website, justinedavis.com, at Twitter.com/justine_d_davis or on Facebook at Facebook.com/justinedaredavis.

Books by Justine Davis

Harlequin Romantic Suspense

The Coltons of Grave Gulch

Colton K-9 Target

Cutter's Code

Operation Midnight
Operation Reunion
Operation Blind Date
Operation Unleashed
Operation Power Play
Operation Homecoming
Operation Soldier Next Door
Operation Alpha
Operation Notorious
Operation Hero's Watch
Operation Second Chance
Operation Mountain Recovery
Operation Whistleblower

Visit the Author Profile page at Harlequin.com,
or justinedavis.com, for more titles.

I have loved all my dogs who have passed over the rainbow bridge. And I adore my current dog, Coco, who is a rescue. But one of my dogs holds a special place in my heart, and I suspect he always will.

Maverick was my big, goofy, beautiful golden retriever. We got him as a puppy, and he grew up to be a beautiful cream color that got reddish gold as he grew older. He was mischievous, hardheaded, smart (no matter what the rest of the family says) and the sweetest dog I've ever had. Maverick loved to swim. Every summer he'd swim in the pool until he was so tired he was ready to drop. He loved to eat everything in sight. Especially sticks and twigs. Then he'd hide under the kitchen table where I couldn't reach him and throw up on the carpet. Come to think of it, all my dogs have done that!

We took obedience classes, but Maverick always thought that "come" meant to run away as fast as he could.

Maverick loved to be petted. He'd lie on the couch in his spot and let my ninety-two-year-old father-in-law pet him. Or anyone else who wanted to. He loved to go on a walk. After he passed, I didn't go on a walk alone for years. My next dog was old when I got her, so I couldn't walk her and it just wasn't the same without Maverick. I've finally started again with Coco, who's a sweetheart. But I still miss Maverick. I'm sure I always will.

—Eve, Maverick's mom

Chapter 1

Nowhere on Parker Ward's résumé did it say dog sitter. No, his job history was a bit more impressive than that—on the surface, anyway. Yet here he was, doing just that, with no end in sight. On that same surface, anyone would say his life had gone to hell, but the truth was Parker was more content than he'd been in a very long time.

"Woof," he said to the animal who sat looking up at him expectantly, "you're more trouble than a kid, y'know?"

The aptly named dog gave him a woof and a tongue-lolling grin. Since he'd ended up sharing quarters with the black—except for the clownish white spot around one eye—bouncy critter, he'd realized he should never under-estimate the devious mind behind that silly expression. He was learning fast. Desperately fast.

"You're a sneaky, counter-surfing thief, that's what you are," he muttered, looking rather glumly at the empty box that had moments ago housed his lunch. "And if you get sick on that pizza, don't come crying to me."

Instead of crying, Woof let out a happy little yip, then rose up on his hind legs and gave Parker a doggy hug, wrapping his forelegs around him and resting his head serenely on his stomach.

"He's sensitive," Ray had said. "It's easy to hurt his feelings."

Sensitive like a fox, Parker thought. Darn dog knew exactly what he was doing. Parker knew exactly what he was doing.

"So what does that make me for falling for it?" he asked the dog wryly as he gave in and stroked the soft, floppy ears, eliciting a happy sigh from the blissful animal. "I ought to tell Ray on you," he warned, knowing he wouldn't. The old man had enough to worry about without adding his dog to the list. No, it was better if Ray thought Parker and Woof were getting along famously.

And it wasn't that they weren't; it was just that Parker had never known a dog could be so adept at stealing food. Like absconding with and opening a pizza box. And even that would be merely cause for bemusement, were it not for the fact that the dog was so darn smug about it.

As usual, he ended up smiling at the animal. And that alone was rare enough these days that he was once more grateful that things had worked out as they had. Because were it not for the clever, ever-entertaining Woof, he'd probably be mired in the wreckage of what had once been a good, productive life, and sinking fast. He'd lost the most prestigious job he'd ever had or would have, at a level he'd never expected to reach. He'd lost the home he'd never expected to be able to afford, a sleek place in the city on the other side of Puget Sound. And he was back living someplace he'd never expected to be, not just the quiet little town he'd left behind, but one house removed from the house he'd grown up in.

Of course, he'd never expected to end up a whistleblower, either.

Parker was glumly thinking yet again he should have stayed a simple carpenter when his cell phone—the one he wouldn't be able to afford much longer—rang. When he saw the caller ID, the nursing home where Ray was rehabbing his badly dislocated shoulder, he jumped at it.

"Mr. Ward?"

"Yes. Is he all right?"

"Physically, yes," the woman said. "He insists on talking to you."

Parker wondered what she meant by "physically." And what made her sound so cautious, as if she were warning him.

Within two minutes of talking to Ray, Parker understood why she'd been wary. Because what he was saying sounded crazy. But he was insistent, and given that Ray was as mentally sharp as anyone half his age, Parker refused to entertain even the thought that he was slipping into some kind of dementia. Besides, that happened gradually, didn't it? Not all of a sudden, while out on a walk.

It was almost time for his daily trek anyway, so he loaded Woof into Ray's small SUV and was there in fifteen minutes. Ray was outside waiting in the courtyard, wearing the gray sweats that matched his short military-cut hair and the beginnings of a beard, since shaving was difficult for him right now and they'd told him to focus on recovery rather than keeping his usual clean-shaven jaw. Out here was where the visits with Woof happened, since the animal wasn't certified as a therapy dog and therefore wasn't welcome inside. Woof greeted his owner with his usual delirious joy, as if it had been weeks since he'd seen him, not less than twenty-four hours.

Odd, Parker thought, that this simple task, this daily reuniting of his mentor with his precious furry friend, gave him more satisfaction than his big-time job had in a year.

Careful what you wish for.

The old warning flitted through his mind again. He'd once wished, more than anything, to be a success at Witner Associates. And he thought he'd done it; not a corner office, but definitely one with a window, and close to the boss.

And idiot that he was, he'd never realized he'd gotten it for reasons that had nothing to do with his work.

He shook off the fruitless ponderings and focused on Ray, who seemed to be giving the aide who had insisted on following him outside the side-eye. Then he looked at Parker and indicated the aide with a short nod. Parker finally got it.

"I'll bring him back in, Art, if you need to see to other things," he told the young man.

The man in scrubs nodded and gave him a thankful look that told Parker it hadn't been an easy afternoon with Ray. Clearly they'd decided that they needed to keep a closer eye on him, and Parker assumed it was because of what he'd come back from his solo walk claiming to have seen.

"Finally," Ray muttered. "The way they're acting, you'd think I'd lost my mind in the space of half an hour."

"Well, you have to admit, it sounds kind of crazy. I mean, this isn't the sort of town where that kind of thing usually happens."

Ray glared at him. "Don't you start. I know what I saw, Parker Ward."

"A kidnapping," Parker said, very neutrally.

"Yes."

Parker smothered a sigh as they sat on one of the outside benches, Woof at Ray's feet. Medication, he thought. It had to be medication. Ray couldn't be losing it. Couldn't be losing his grip on that keen engineer's mind of his. Parker couldn't handle that, not Ray, the sole sane light in his life.

But if it was medication, he'd be groggy, wouldn't he? Or maybe it was something else. Maybe when he'd fallen and severely dislocated his shoulder, he'd hit his head, too, and they'd missed it. But could that be only now showing up, all this time later? Wouldn't it—

"Listen up, kid! And don't give me that look. I'm not drugged up. I won't take that crap. NSAIDs only."

Parker snapped out of his thoughts. He should have known he'd refuse anything stronger, because he treasured his clearheadedness too much. The man barely drank a beer on Independence Day, let alone anything stronger.

"All right, Ray. What do you want to do?"

"Call the cops, of course!"

He frowned. "They didn't do that?" He would have thought even a questionable claim of a kidnapping would have warranted a call to the authorities.

"Oh, they said they would. When they got around to it. They're good at what they do here, but don't throw them any curveballs."

Parker stared at his old friend. Who, damn it, was as sharp as ever. "I'll call right now," he said and pulled out his phone. The smile that got him made it worth the small effort.

The facility was in county territory, so he called the sheriff's office. A deputy arrived within ten minutes, which he gathered from Ray was quick, given the territory they had to cover. The young man listened and took notes of Ray's descriptions of the location and the victim and kidnapper, sketchy though they were. But Parker was watching him carefully, and he apparently hadn't quite perfected hiding his thoughts; Parker could tell he was leaning toward that same assumption, that Ray was having mental issues.

Parker walked with the man back to his marked unit.

"I know what you're thinking, so I should tell you, that man is sharp as a tack. There's no way he imagined this."

"I'll need a list of any medications he's on," the man said carefully.

"He's stubborn as a bulldog. He won't take any narcotics."

"All right," the deputy said, "I'll look into it."

That, at least, sounded sincere. Whether "look into it" meant going to the scene, checking for a missing person report or just asking on the radio if anybody had seen or heard anything, Parker had no idea.

"He thinks I'm a senile old man, doesn't he?" Ray said angrily when Parker came back to the bench.

"Ray—"

"You kids never believe it until you get there and it happens to you. Once they categorize you as old, you get treated like the opposite, a stupid child."

"You're the smartest guy I know. That I've ever known."

Ray blinked. "Well. All right, then." He said it gruffly, but he was smiling. And Parker knew he'd somehow found the right thing to say.

It was a quiet night after that, when he'd gathered Woof and headed back to the house. It felt more like coming home than he'd felt in a long time. Certainly more than his metal-and-glass condo in the city, where even week-nights were full of activity. And definitely more than the house next door, where he'd grown up.

He might not know what would come next, but this was a comforting place to figure it out. This was the kind of place he'd always wanted to build himself, comfortable, homey, warm, functional… No, he never should have put down that hammer.

He yawned as he poured his second cup of coffee the next morning. He supposed it was significant that he was sleeping like a log here in the quiet, semirural neighborhood, without the ever-present noise of the city. He'd thought he might have trouble being back in this neighborhood, given the chaos he'd grown up with here as his family fed on its own discord.

He walked back out on the back deck. Looked up at the sky, already gray with impending rain. Looked around the backyard. And set down his mug on the arm of the nearest Adirondack chair when he realized Woof was nowhere in sight. The yard wasn't fenced, but Ray swore the dog never went far. And he'd come inside only long enough to pour that coffee. But he wasn't Ray. Maybe Woof didn't think the same rules applied. Damn, if anything happened to that dog, on his watch, he'd never forgive himself.

He scanned the tree line a hundred feet or so away, but there was no sign of the goofy black dog with the white spot around his eye. He headed for the steps, skipped them and jumped the four feet to the ground. His pulse had kicked up, and he was already envisioning having to tell Ray he'd lost him. Here the man had given him a home when he'd needed it, and now trusted him with his best friend, and within a week he'd blown it. He'd—

He heard a happy yip and breathed again when Woof bounded around the corner of the house. He took a step toward the dog, then stopped. Because the animal wasn't alone. There was another dog romping along beside him.

"Found a friend, did you?" he asked, looking at the new arrival. Slightly bigger than Woof, the dog was strikingly colored, his black head and shoulders transitioning to a rich, reddish brown back to a full, plumed tail. That was all he had time to notice before the second dog seemed to fixate on him. He cocked that dark head, looking at him intently. Then, to Parker's surprise, the dog came over and sat at his feet, staring up at him.

He'd never seen eyes quite like that on a dog. Woof's were a medium brown and warm and loving, but these canine eyes were dark, intense and flecked with an amber color that looked almost gold when the light caught them. He found himself thinking about dogs controlling big flocks of sheep or herds of unruly cattle with seemingly nothing more than the power of their gaze. It suddenly seemed quite possible.

He gave a shake of his head as the dog nudged his hand. "And who are you?" he asked the newcomer, bending to pet the dog's head. The dog let out a soft, low whuff and gave him another steady, penetrating look. It was unsettling, that look.

Parker reached for the tag, blue and seemingly in the shape of a boat, on the dog's collar. But before he could read it, the dog was on his feet and backing away, still watching him intently. Then the animal looked at Woof, barked three times, short and sharp, wheeled around on his hind legs and took off running.

And to Parker's chagrin, Woof followed, ignoring his calls to come back.

What was it someone said about trying to give someone else's dog orders?

"There's going to be a leash in your future, dog," he called out as he went after the errant duo.

At least they pretty much stayed out of the neighbors' yards even though most were also unfenced; he didn't want to get caught trampling somebody's garden. An elderly man a couple of houses down was out on his deck with a cup of coffee and turned as Parker jumped a fallen tree trunk. The man looked at the dogs, then back at Parker. He was grinning.

"Good luck!" he called out.

Parker, seeing how it must look, grinned back and gave

a wry shake of his head as he kept on. At the corner of the next yard, the strange dog—and he was thinking he meant that in more than one way—cut right and headed toward the water, Woof close behind. Just as Parker was vowing to up his fitness game, given he was starting to feel this, the leader dodged down a long, sloped driveway.

There was a man in the garage at the end of the driveway, putting something in the back of a large, dark blue SUV. The instant Parker stepped on the gravel of the driveway, the man straightened and turned to look directly at him. Parker blinked. Could he really have heard that faint sound from this distance? Or was he just hyper-attuned to his surroundings? Instinctively he slowed to a walk.

The closer he got, walking down the drive after the dogs, the more he thought it was the latter. The guy had the look of a man who didn't miss much. And he was studying Parker's approach intently. Assessingly. One hand out of sight, still in the back of the SUV, as if he were holding something, Parker suddenly realized. And he had the crazy thought that if this quiet neighborhood was ever hit by a burglar, they would be wise to avoid this house.

With the sudden idea that maybe he should signal benign intent, he rather ruefully gestured at the dogs in front of him. Woof's newfound friend bounded up to the man, who now closed the back of the SUV and stepped out of the garage. The man looked like he topped out at about six feet and had that way of moving Parker had always associated with the police or military men. Ray had it, even now. Strong, powerful, trained…and intense.

Like his dog.

That it was his dog was instantly clear as he gave the dog a scratch behind one ear. Woof bounced right up to the man as well, clearly unafraid, but then, Ray had always said that while no one would ever get into the house unannounced by a trumpeting bark, once in they were more likely to get licked to death than bitten. Woof, quite simply, loved people.

The man said something to Woof that Parker wasn't quite close enough to hear, and Woof yipped happily at him, tongue lolling after the merry jaunt through the neighborhood. Then the man reached down and stroked Woof's head, and the dog wiggled in delight.

"Sorry," Parker said when he got close enough. "That's Woof. He followed your guy home, apparently."

"It happens," the man said, and Parker had the strangest feeling he meant more than his pet bringing home other dogs.

"I'm Parker Ward. I'm watching Woof for Ray Lowry. He lives a couple of blocks up and over on Cedar View." He wasn't sure why he was explaining so much, except that something in this man's steady gaze seemed to compel it.

"Quinn Foxworth," the man said after a moment and held out a hand. Parker shook it—no death grip here, just firm, strong, solid, a man with nothing to prove—and tried to think about where he'd heard the name before. "And this," the man went on, gesturing at the dog now sitting politely at his owner's side, "is Cutter."

The dog rose and walked back over to Parker, and he found himself smiling, as if the dog he'd chased about a half a mile were going to come say hello now that they'd been introduced. He reached out with the intent of simply patting the dog's head. But something about the soft fur was…soothing, in a way quite different from the simple comfort Woof gave him, and he ended up stroking him. And then, oddly, the dog turned his back on him and sat. Parker could tell from the angle of his head he was staring up at the other man, who lifted a brow at the animal.

"Oh?" Foxworth said, but it was to the dog, not Parker.

Puzzled, Parker looked down at the animal. Then at Woof, who was trying to entice the dog named Cutter into playing some more. But his new friend never moved. He just kept staring at his owner.

When Parker looked up again, Quinn Foxworth's disconcertingly steady gaze was fastened on him. "Well, you might as well come in."

Parker blinked. "What?"

Foxworth gave him a wry smile as he nodded at the dog who was practically sitting at attention. "Trust me, it's best not to fight him."

"About…?"

"It's a long story. Digest version, you've got a problem he thinks we can fix."

The first thing that popped into his mind was Ray.

The second thing was to wonder if the guy was crazy. He'd learned to be wary—very wary—since his life had blown up, almost three years ago.

The dog—Cutter—nudged his hand. Instinctively he stroked the soft fur again. His edginess eased. His suspiciousness faded a little, although he didn't let go of it entirely.

"Look, Mr. Foxworth—"

"Quinn, please. Coffee?" he suggested.

Parker thought of the steaming mug he'd left behind. Made a rather impulsive decision.

"Okay. Sure. Thanks."

The instant he spoke, Cutter was on his feet, giving a quick bark that sounded like some kind of acknowledgment.

"Got it, boy," Quinn said.

And as he followed Quinn and the dogs inside, Parker was inwardly—with a smile—wondering who exactly ran this house.

Chapter 2

"Woof!"

Parker stopped short at the delighted greeting, delivered in a decidedly female voice. And Woof bounded over to a woman who was seated on a comfortable-looking sofa next to a sandy-haired man who had the same air as Quinn Foxworth. Tough, strong, steady. The woman herself was pretty, looked long and tall even seated, with dark brown hair pulled back in a ponytail. Woof was greeting her happily. Obviously the delight was mutual.

"Parker Ward, meet Laney Adams and Teague Johnson." Then, to the woman, "A client, I gather?" Quinn looked back at Parker. "Laney's the groomer here in town."

"Yes," the woman said with a laugh as Woof swiped her cheek with a pink tongue. "One of my favorites." Then, brow furrowed, she looked at Parker. "Where's Ray?"

There was concern in her voice, in her warm brown eyes, and Parker liked her for that. "He's in rehab. He fell off a ladder a while ago and dislocated his shoulder pretty severely."

"Oh, no! But he's all right?"

"He will be. He'd be home now if it wasn't his dominant arm. He's pretty stubborn."

Laney grinned. "I hadn't noticed."

"Parker's watching the dog," Foxworth explained.

"And the house," Parker added, feeling much more relaxed now with this obvious connection.

"How long will Ray be there?" Laney asked.

"Depends who you ask," Parker said dryly. "The doctors, a couple more weeks. Ray, tomorrow."

She laughed again. The man beside her smiled. Lovingly. Parker noticed the engagement ring on her left hand. *Lucky guy.*

"Bring Woof in the day before he comes home," Laney said, "and I'll make sure he's all clean and pretty for him. On me."

A little taken aback at her generosity, Parker blinked. "Wow. I've been fixing some things at the house for when he gets home, but I never thought of that. Thanks."

"Least I can do. I got poor Woof ready for three adoption fairs, and he was always so sad when he had to go back to the shelter. Broke my heart."

Parker was curious. "I never understood how this lovable clown went so long without somebody taking him."

"He didn't use to be like this," Laney explained. "He was quiet, mopey, didn't interact with people at all. Then Ray came along and it was love at first sight. And once Ray convinced him it was forever, he decided it was safe to love everybody. It's all in finding the right match."

Teague Johnson put his arm around his fiancée and brushed a kiss over her cheek. *Definitely lucky guy.*

Parker was quashing a pang of not envy, exactly—wistfulness, maybe—that he'd never felt that way about someone, when the Foxworth dog came and once more sat at his feet with his back to him. The animal looked at his owner and gave a quiet whuff that sounded oddly like a human saying "Ahem," to get everyone's attention.

Quinn grinned at the dog. "You sure about this, dog, or are you just missing Hayley?" At Parker's glance, he added, "My wife, who's out of town. He was her dog first."

"And little did we know," Teague put in with a grin, the first thing he'd said, "that he'd end up running the show."

Parker smiled. "They do take over, don't they?"

"This guy," Teague said with a nod at Cutter, "in ways I never imagined possible. Including signaling that you—" he shifted his gaze to Parker "—have a problem."

"What?" Parker drew back sharply. Him, too? Quinn outside, and now this guy? Was he wearing a freaking sign or something?

Teague laughed. He glanced at Quinn, who had taken a seat in the armchair across from Parker. "I still think you need to have Dane Burdette make a video explaining it all. It would save a lot of time and energy."

"I'm starting to think you're right," Quinn said with a wry grimace. "But for now, let's start with what we've got. What it boils down to, Parker, is you have a problem. And the Foxworth Foundation's specialty is solving them."

It suddenly clicked. *Foxworth Foundation.*

"Wait… You're those Foxworths? The whole thing with the governor going down last year?"

"That was our friend Detective Brett Dunbar's doing. We were only peripherally involved," Quinn said.

"Well, except for Cutter, who literally dug up the evidence—and the body," Teague said.

Parker blinked. Looked down at the dog who, still with his back to him, tilted his head back so far he could see the dark, intense eyes, although the silliness of the position almost made him laugh. And he had the strangest feeling that was intentional. Then laughed at himself for imputing human motivations to a dog.

Woof, who was nothing if not pure dog, came over and nudged Cutter with his nose, clearly eager to go outside and play some more. That was one thing Parker had learned about the clownish dog. He knew when rain was on the way and was always eager to get outside before it hit. And then, of course, after it had cleared, to go find the nearest muddy spot to play in. Maybe that was why Laney had been so generous. Ray kept her business going with frequent visits.

He gave a shake of his head, stopping the urge to veer down that path of suspecting everyone of ulterior motives. It was hard. He'd seen so much of it before he'd left the city, but he didn't want to be one of those who assumed the worst about everyone. He—

"Go ahead, boy. We've got it now, I promise."

Parker snapped out of it at the quiet words, then realized Quinn had been talking to the dog. Cutter gave a short, sharp yip again, got up and trotted off happily with Woof, leading the way to a doggy door set into the door to what was apparently the back deck and yard.

"Rain coming in," Parker said, for lack of anything else to say.

"Safe bet this time of year," Quinn agreed.

"Yeah, but Woof always knows when it's getting close. Wants to get outside for those last few minutes to play."

"Well, then," Quinn said, leaning back in his chair, "maybe it won't be so hard for you to understand that like Woof's talent, Cutter has his own. One of which is sensing when someone's in trouble or has a problem. So what's yours?"

Now that he knew whom he was dealing with, he could only laugh. "Minuscule, compared to the kind of thing you do."

"Don't count on it," Teague said. "We handle a lot of stuff."

He glanced at the other man. "You work for Foxworth, too?"

"I work for Foxworth, yes," Teague said. Then, nodding toward Quinn, added, "But he *is* Foxworth."

"We all are," Quinn said. "And our criteria for helping are actually pretty broad. You just have to be in the right and have fought as far as you could on your own."

Parker thought of his self-righteous former boss. "In the right...according to who?"

Quinn grinned at him. "That's the fun part. We get to decide. So what's the problem?"

"I... It's not mine, really. It's Ray's, although it's not directly his, either." Well, that was garbled enough. "Look, it's nothing you'd get involved in, not that either of us could afford you anyway." *Once, I could have. Six months ago, I could have. I could bankroll anything Ray wanted or needed.*

"That's not an issue," Quinn said. "If we take it on, we don't charge a fee."

Parker blinked again. "You do this for...free?"

"Not exactly. But we'll get to that."

"But... This isn't that kind of thing. Actually, it's a police thing."

"We've got friends there, too."

"Your detective... Dunbar, you said? The guy who cracked the whole mess with the governor?"

"Yes."

"How's that work?"

"He knows if we find anything he should know, we tell him. And we've been able to help him in turn with some things where people wouldn't be as forthcoming with law enforcement as they are with us."

Fascinating as this was—and, Parker thought, rather wistfully again, as uplifting, given the kind of slime he'd spent far too long dealing with—it still didn't have anything to do with Ray's situation. Unless...

"Detective Dunbar doesn't happen to investigate kidnappings, does he?"

Quinn went very still. "Is that what it is?"

"Not Ray?" Laney asked, and Parker couldn't doubt her concern was genuine again. "That's not really where he is, is it?"

"No," he assured her. "But he thinks he saw one."

"You don't think so?" Teague asked.

"No, I believe him, but... I don't think they do. The people at the rehab center or the sheriff's deputy who came out when I called them. And Ray's angry because he thinks they're all blowing him off because he's older, even though he's as with it as you or I are." Parker's mouth twisted wryly. "More than I am, sometimes."

"He is very sharp," Laney agreed. "And funny. Quick-witted, in an old-fashioned, charming sort of way."

Parker couldn't help it. He smiled widely at her. "He'd be delighted to know you think that. Especially right now. He says it's driving him nuts to be cooped up with people younger than him who have surrendered to being old without fighting."

"I'll be sure to tell him, then," she said with an answering smile.

"What, exactly," Quinn asked, "did Ray see?"

"He takes a long walk every day, so his legs don't get weak while he's working on his shoulder. Yesterday he was passing the entrance to an alley, glanced down to check for traffic, and saw a guy grabbing a kid and shoving him into the trunk of a car."

"A kid? They usually take even the possibility of a child abduction pretty seriously."

"Ray's words. Sorry, I should have explained. Ray calls anybody under forty *kid*."

Quinn nodded, easing back a little. "Ray didn't recognize…the kid or the guy?"

"No."

"Or the car?"

Parker shook his head. "And it was a silver sedan. He couldn't see the plate because they were in front of it as he tossed the guy in the trunk."

"Couldn't get more generic, then," Teague said.

"The deputy did take a report?" Quinn asked.

"He took notes. Where it went from there…" Parker shrugged.

Quinn and Teague exchanged a look. Then Quinn nodded. Teague excused himself and walked out of the room, pulling his phone out as he went.

"I'd believe Ray over most people," Laney said staunchly.

"So would I." Parker hesitated, but she was being so supportive of Ray he couldn't hold back. "Ray's kind of my mentor. Has been since I was a kid." He glanced at Quinn. "That 'in the right' bit you spoke of? What I know of it came from Ray."

Something changed in Quinn Foxworth's expression then. Went from considering to set. As if he'd moved from thinking to deciding.

Teague came back then, replacing his phone in his pocket. "Brett's still down in Vancouver," he said. "But Detective Devon is covering for him until he gets back. She ran a check and couldn't find a report."

Parker's mouth tightened. *Figures.*

Teague kept going. "She's actually here in the area, though, and offered to stop by."

"And you said?" Quinn asked with a lifted eyebrow.

Teague grinned. "Yes. I knew we were in the minute Cutter sat on his feet," he finished, still grinning as he shifted his gaze to Parker. "She'll be here in about five."

Parker blinked. "You've got a sheriff's detective coming to your house on something another deputy didn't even think worth reporting, all on the say-so of…your dog?"

"Ah, but what a dog!" Laney said, laughing.

What followed was a string of tales, each one seeming more impossible than the last, that composed the track record of the dog who was currently out being very normally doglike with Woof. And when the doorbell rang, Teague laughingly said he hadn't heard the half of it yet as he got up to go answer it, since he'd made the call.

"Rain's here," Laney said to Parker. "Let's get the dogs in. Hayley's always got towels by the door."

They were wiping down both Woof and Cutter when Teague came back with the woman Parker assumed was the detective.

And that was all he assumed. It was all he had time to assume before his brain shut down completely as he stared at the most beautiful woman he'd seen in a very long time.

Chapter 3

Carly Devon had met Quinn and the other Foxworth man, Teague Johnson, through Brett. Her fellow detective had a stellar reputation for, among many other things, his judgment, and she had little doubt his assessment of the Foxworths and the work they did was accurate. More than once he'd told her they gave him back faith in humanity.

She was a little iffy on his assessment of their dog, Cutter, but she couldn't deny the results, even if her logical brain wanted to write it off to coincidence or the human tendency to credit the animals they loved with more than animal intelligence.

She'd never been here to the Foxworth home, though, and she had to admit it surprised her. It was a simple, solid house, older but well-kept. Hardly the fancier kind of place she might have expected, given Foxworth's standing. No, this was above all else a home, warm and welcoming.

Quinn introduced her to Teague's fiancée, who, with another man, was wiping down the two dogs they had apparently called inside as the rain had started in earnest. The one with the silly expression—no doubt because of the big blotch of white fur around one eye, standing out like clown makeup against the rest of him—greeted her as if she were an old friend. The other dog came over rather more calmly and sat at her feet looking up at her.

"So you're the famous Cutter?" she asked. And would have sworn the dog nodded, although she was certain he'd just cocked his head to look at her in a way that appeared to be that gesture. "I see what Brett means when he said you could stare down anything on four legs or two," she said, half smiling at her own unexpected reaction to that dark, gold-flecked gaze. It seemed the thing to do, so she reached out and stroked the dog's head. An odd sensation of calm seemed to spread from the touch, although she hadn't been particularly wound up, just feeling a bit harried as she tried to keep up with Brett's job on top of her own. Fortunately, juvenile cases were light at the moment.

Still, she'd be glad when Brett got back from that seminar. As would his wife, Sloane, she thought with an inward sigh. Those two were so perfect together, each having come through their own hell to find the light that now practically glowed from them. She liked them both too much to be envious, but it did make her feel a bit...wistful.

"And this," Quinn said as she straightened, "is Parker Ward, who just got led here by these two mutts."

She turned to look at the third man in the room, who was still holding the towel he'd been using on the clownish dog. He looked young, maybe early twenties, although when she got a look at his eyes she thought she might be a bit low on that. Within a hair either way of six feet tall, she estimated with the ease of long experience. Kind of rangy, but he looked fit and strong. Hazel eyes, she noticed, a mix of green and brown and gold that seemed vivid with his dark brown hair. Hair that seemed determined to tickle his eyebrows with a few long strands that kicked forward over his forehead. Nice hair. Nice eyes. Nice face.

"Hi," he said, staring at her a little oddly and sounding just a bit wary.

Nice voice to go with...the rest of him. He didn't say anything more. His jaw was so tight she doubted he could get another word out. Nice jaw, too. She was startled at her reaction. Even to just the way he moved. She'd seen plenty of men built as nicely as this one—there were a couple in this room right now—so she didn't understand the little frisson that went through her.

Going in for cradle robbing now, Devon?

She made herself focus. "You're the one whose friend witnessed a kidnapping?"

He looked a little surprised. "You believe it?"

She shrugged. "I'd rather believe it and be proven wrong than the other way around."

He smiled then. And said softly, "Thank you." And *nice* was far too tame a word for either the smile or the voice then.

Good grief, Devon, get your head in the game.

"So tell me what he saw." She listened as he explained. Smiled when he explained his friend's interpretation of age.

"He calls me *kid*," he said. She found herself liking the way he stood up for his friend Ray, refused to let him be dismissed as a foolish or worse old man. "He's not senile or confused or on medications. He's clearheaded and clever. He was an engineer for decades, and he hasn't lost a step."

"Then I'd best go see him," she said, smiling.

For an instant it seemed as if he was gaping at her, and she wondered what he'd expected her to say. She made a mental note to check into which deputy—although she had an idea, since she knew who was assigned to the area—had responded yesterday and determine what, if anything, he'd done. And if the answer was nothing, she was going to find out why. She wasn't the sort to rat out a colleague, but darned if she'd let it slide unnoticed if this turned into something.

"I…I take Woof in to see Ray every day." Okay, now she was even more impressed. "I could go now, introduce you. I want to be there anyway. Not," he added hastily, "that I don't trust you—"

"You don't know me," she said easily. "And after it appears he was blown off yesterday, I understand. But I'll need some time with him without the dog."

A short, sharp bark from Cutter drew their attention. The Foxworth dog had gotten up and gone over to sit beside Woof, who was leaning adoringly on Laney. "I think you have a volunteer for that," Teague said with a laugh.

"He'll be welcome," Quinn said. "Hayley got him certified as a therapy dog, and he's been there before."

"Great," Parker said wryly. "Now all we need is a dog wrangler for both of them."

"I can do that," Laney said lightly. "Woof trusts me."

Teague glanced at Quinn, who nodded. "Then I'll go along and make a futile effort at getting Cutter to do anything other than what he already intends to do," the man said with a grin. "Besides," he said to his fiancée, "where you go, I go."

The pretty brunette just looked at Teague for a moment. Then she whispered, "I know," and the two words were so full of love Carly felt her throat tighten. She glanced at Parker, saw him watching the couple. And then she heard him suck in a deep breath and lower his gaze and give a barely perceptible shake of his head. As if the sight and sound of the obvious connection between those two had hit him the same way it had her.

Points for being aware, for seeing it.

She stopped herself again, thinking she was awarding a lot of points to a guy she'd met all of half an hour ago.

They took Quinn's big SUV, since it had room for all of them and both dogs. Although Carly had said she had no problem with transporting the animals in her sheriff's unit.

"After some of the humans I've had in this car, dogs are an improvement," she said, making him grin all over again. "Even wet ones."

At Parker's request, they stopped at Ray's. "I kind of took off after the dogs and left everything open," he said ruefully.

But luckily this was a very quiet, safe neighborhood and everything was as he'd left it. He retrieved his mug of now rain-watered-down coffee, locked the back door on his way back inside, dumped the cold liquid in the sink and put the mug in the dishwasher, grabbed his jacket from the rack by the front door as he went out, locked up, then headed back to the SUV in the driveway.

Fifteen minutes later they were pulling into the parking lot on the rehab center's inpatient therapy side of the complex. The rain, fortunately, hadn't yet reached this far, so Ray was able to come outside. And as he watched her with the older man, Parker decided Detective Carly Devon was the kind of cop who made guys fantasize about getting handcuffed. An odd idea to pop into his head, since that wasn't his thing at all. But as he surreptitiously eyed the woman, he could almost understand it. Four or five inches shorter than his own six feet, she seemed almost delicately thin until you noticed the curve of taut muscle…along with other curves. She had short, thick blond hair in a tousled sort of cut and a pair of eyes so vivid they made him think of the bright blue shade of Ray's truck. Another odd thing to think. But that seemed to have been all he could do ever since he'd looked up from drying Woof and seen her.

And as if that wasn't enough, he liked her. He had liked her answer about believing Ray, and he liked even more the way she had approached him now, with kindness and, more important, respect. Ray was clearly delighted with all the company, and more, appreciative of Carly.

"You're a lot better-looking than the guy who was here yesterday," he said.

Carly didn't take offense, even laughed. "I have an idea who that was, and if I'm right, that's not a huge compliment."

Ray laughed, which made Parker laugh in turn. The mild flirting the older man indulged in kept him smiling, and the easy way Carly handled it impressed him. And he could hardly blame Ray; he'd probably be flirting with her himself, were he not homeless, jobless and with no prospects.

They watched the two dogs, who had started a kind of game of tag with Laney and Teague, Ray looking a bit wistful then.

"I imagine keeping up with that one keeps you in good shape," Carly said, gesturing at Woof. "And by the way, love the name."

The shadow that Parker knew too well descended over Ray's expression. "My late wife named him."

Parker waited for the inevitable condolences, meaningless expressions that Ray had told him he'd come to hate. But instead, Carly smiled. "I already know I would have liked her, just because she picked that name." After that Ray was smiling again, and Parker thought he could have hugged the woman.

Like you don't want to hug her—and more—anyway?

He reminded himself he was in no position to even be

thinking things like that. Then made himself settle in quietly, watching and listening as Carly led Ray through a description of not just what he'd seen but the entire walk, asking him if that was his usual route, what else he'd seen on the way and a few other questions Parker couldn't see the reason for but that Ray answered thoughtfully.

She was thorough and professional, and she listened. She was, Parker could see, taking him very seriously, which was all Ray had wanted.

It was only when she got to one last question that Parker's gut knotted.

"Is there any chance the man saw you, Ray?"

He hadn't even thought of that. He stared at his old friend, horrified.

"No," Ray said certainly. "As soon as I realized what I was seeing, I dodged back—well," he amended with a grimace, "as fast as I can with this bum shoulder—behind the corner of the end building. I could still see down the alley, though, but he'd have had to know I was there to see me."

Parker breathed again.

"Good thinking," Carly said.

"I'm good at thinking," Ray said with a smile at her.

"Obviously," Carly returned with a matching smile.

Again Parker wanted to hug her. And again he fought it down. And laughed at himself. Because it just figured that when life was at its lowest point, when he had nothing to recommend him except what some called a foolish sense of ethics, when his future would have to brighten some to look bleak, he'd meet the first woman who sparked this kind of interest in years.

Maybe in his whole life.

Chapter 4

Carly ended her phone call and turned to walk back to where Ray was still sitting, Parker next to him, with Laney and Teague standing behind the bench. Her interview completed, Ray was now communing with Woof, who sat with his chin on his knee, looking up at him adoringly as the man stroked him. Parker was watching them both, a slight smile on his face.

They both looked up as she approached. "Deputy Borden did check to see if there were any missing persons reports—none from that time period forward, at least not yet—and he did go by the scene and did a cursory check, but found nothing."

"More than I thought he'd do," Ray admitted.

"It's only a few blocks from here, right?" Carly asked.

Ray nodded and pointed with his good arm. "Straight down the street, the alley that runs behind the bakery." The older man grimaced. "Sorry I can't tell you exactly how far down the alley it was."

"You were focused on what was happening more. Understandable," she said. She'd encountered that often enough to know it was commonplace; people focused on what had drawn their attention in the first place. She was more concerned that Ray couldn't really guess as to how old the victim was. Because if it truly had been a juvenile, that made this an entirely different kind of case.

"You get to be my age and anyone under thirty looks like a teenager. These days some over thirty." He smiled at her. "You, now, you're like Parker. You'll look like a teenager until you're fifty."

"And you," she teased right back, "are a flirt."

"If I was twenty years younger, I'd show you flirting."

"If I was twenty years older, I'd be flirting back," she promised him, making Ray grin.

Then she looked at Teague, who'd been driving. "If you don't mind, I'd like to go by the scene myself."

"I was just thinking we should," Teague agreed.

Parker immediately stood up, obviously intending to go with them. "We can leave Woof here for his visit and come back to pick him up, since it's on the way," he suggested.

Teague nodded. "Then we'll drop you off at Ray's place on the way back to Quinn's." He grinned. "Save you another trek through the woods."

Somewhat to her surprise, Cutter chose not to stay with his furry friend, but walked as politely as if on a leash next to Parker as they headed for the SUV. She realized she had no idea what the man did for a living, but he was certainly in good shape for it, whatever it was.

And you've got no business staring at his backside.

Because she needed to say something, to distract herself, she nodded toward Cutter and Parker and said to Teague, "Looks like they hit it off."

"He's the focus right now," the former—were they ever?—marine with the rather steely blue eyes said. "The one with the problem. And that's how Cutter works."

"I have to say, even after all I've heard from Brett, seeing it firsthand is…"

"Different?" Laney suggested with a grin.

"Very," Carly agreed.

"I love dogs," the groomer said, "and have often been accused of anthropomorphizing them too much, but Cutter? Nope. He's a different breed, and I don't mean the American Kennel Club kind."

Carly smiled back at the woman. Brett was right. These Foxworth folks were good people.

Parker and the dog were far enough ahead of them that she said to Teague, "His name seems familiar, but I can't pin it down."

"Quinn had the same thought. He'll probably have it by the time we get back there."

Carly nodded; that fit with what Brett had told her of the man and the Foxworth operation.

She knew this stop would likely be a futile effort, even if the rain hadn't arrived there yet, but she would make it just the same. There had been just enough cases in the past where it had seemed futile, but she'd followed her instincts anyway and had turned up something.

They got back to the SUV and climbed in. Unexpectedly, Cutter insisted on following her into the back seat, rather than getting in the wayback where he'd ridden with Woof on the way over here. Maybe he was missing his canine companion. She barely had time to think that before realizing that the dog's insistence meant she was going to end up sitting right next to Parker rather than a third of the expansive back seat away.

"Teague?" Laney said, very quietly, nodding toward them behind her. Teague glanced back, and his brows rose. Then he and his fiancée exchanged a rather pointed look Carly didn't understand.

"Is it okay he's here instead of in back?" Parker asked.

"He rides where he wants to," Teague said. "We've learned he always has a reason."

Carly determinedly settled back as if the new seating arrangement didn't bother her in the least. Which it didn't.

Even if she did find herself noticing a clean, woodsy scent that it took her a moment to realize was coming from the man beside her.

Great. On top of everything else, Parker Ward smells darn good.

The narrow alley was fairly clean, free of trash or debris. Also empty, except for a delivery truck off-loading what looked like enough coffee to keep a battalion going for months into the back of the bakery. Parker wasn't surprised. He knew they gave away a cup of the stuff with every purchase over ten dollars. And since their cinnamon roll cream cheese cups, a local invention, were one of Ray's—okay, and his own—favorites, he'd more than once managed to hit that level and gain the free stuff.

You'd better knock that off, kid. The coffee may be free, but the rolls aren't.

Hey, I like them, too.

When you figure out where you're going, what you're going to do, then you can buy 'em by the crate, as far as I'm concerned. Until then, watch the pennies.

That had been right after he'd moved into Ray's, and the first time he'd realized the man was worried about his finances. He'd been startled, then touched, then embarrassed, and had insisted he was fine, at least for a while. He had some savings from before and he hadn't blown them. Too much of Ray's teachings had stuck with him for that. But it had been a good reminder that now he truly did need to watch the pennies. He couldn't spend the way he had in the city.

The way he had when he'd been blind to what should have been obvious. The memory of which still left a sour taste in his mouth. He'd been so stupid…

He gave a shake of his head; dwelling on that was pointless, especially now when he needed to focus on the matter at hand. He watched as Detective Devon—he'd decided it would be best if he thought of her that way—studied the alley. He saw her crouch down, gracefully, to get a closer look at something, he guessed the scrapes in the asphalt, probably from delivery dollies like the one the guy delivering coffee was using. Then she straightened and continued her inspection, looking all directions, down, to her left and right, and up. Most of the buildings were one story; there were only a couple that were two.

He walked over to where Ray had said he'd hidden. Turned and looked down the alley. Looked back at Carly—the detective—and found her watching him, waiting.

"If he could still see it happening from here, it had to be this side of the hardware store," he called out to her.

She gave him a smile and a nod that warmed him rather disproportionately, and he was glad when she went back to her perusal. She had taken a few steps down the middle of the alley when Cutter, on a leash now that they were within the limits of a city that had a leash law, barked sharply. She stopped and looked back. Teague looked down at the animal, and the dog walked toward the detective until the leash stopped him, tugged a little farther, then looked back at Teague.

"I think he wants to go with you," Teague said to her.

"I'm not sure that's a good idea, if there is any evidence around."

"Maybe he'll find it," Parker suggested jokingly.

"If it's there to find, he will," Teague said, and there was no humor in his voice, only certainty.

"What is he, a former police dog?" Parker asked.

"We don't know. We only know he could have been one or a military K-9."

Detective Devon considered for a moment, then shrugged. "All right. I'll take him, if he's all right with that."

"He will be. He knows you're part of the team now."

Parker watched her come back and take the leash. They were once more giving a hell of a lot of credit to a dog. He'd learned a lot about how clever they could be in his time with Woof, but this was an entirely different level.

He watched as the pair moved slowly down the alley. She walked over once to look at the back door of a building, pulled out her phone and took a couple of photos. But then she went back to the slow progress, scanning all directions.

Only once did Cutter veer to one side, sniffing the asphalt intently. That was, until they got even with the next building, the one between where she'd stopped and the hardware store. Then the animal went rigidly alert, staring at the back of the building. There was nothing there but a dumpster, and visions from a hundred thriller books and movies shot through Parker's mind.

Please, do not let that kid—however old he really is—be in there.

Cutter started barking in an odd, staccato manner, still staring toward the back of that building. The detective looked back at Teague.

"Look where he's looking," the man called out. "He'll stay put as long as he knows you're going."

She looked doubtful, but she turned to the dog and said,

"Stay." To Parker's—and apparently her—surprise, Cutter sat, quiet now. She dropped the leash and walked over toward the building. Veered toward the dumpster to look over the top.

"Dumpster's empty," she called out after a moment.

Parker hadn't realized he'd been holding his breath until she said it and he breathed again.

She started toward the building, but the moment she did Cutter started that odd barking again.

"He's telling you you're moving away from it," Teague said.

She looked doubtful again, but when she took a step back toward the dumpster, the barking stopped. And when she was back where she'd been, the dog dropped down into a sphinxlike position.

A thought hit Parker. "Look underneath," he suggested. "Maybe that's what he means."

He guessed she might have been rolling her eyes at him if he was close enough to see, but she did drop down to look. And then, sharply, she looked back at him and then the dog. Cutter was back on his feet. He barked approvingly, and that plumed tail wagged. Even from here, Parker could tell she'd found what the dog had found.

He saw her give a slight shake of her head, her expression not one of disbelief but amazement. And the stories they'd told about the dog's exploits didn't seem quite so far-fetched.

She pulled out her phone again. Took several flash photos this time. Then she stood up. Walked back to Cutter and picked up the leash, saying something quiet to the dog as she did so. Then she came back to them. Looked at Teague.

"Just how well equipped is that Foxworth vehicle? Got anything like an evidence bag?"

* * *

When Brett had told her Foxworth was generally prepared for just about anything, he hadn't been kidding. They not only had a bag, it was an actual evidence bag. She took it, walked back to the dumpster and knelt down. She turned the bag inside out over her hand, reached and grabbed the crumpled knit hat that lay hidden behind one of the wheels. She never would have seen it had she simply made a cursory search.

She pulled it free, and pulled the bag right side out over the hat and sealed it. Teague had also handed her a pen designed to write on the plastic, so she was able to label the bag with the location, date and time. No case number yet, and there might never be if this turned into a waste of time.

But somehow she didn't think it would, not completely. Ray Lowry seemed to her as sharp as Parker had said he was, and certainly not given to imagining things. There might be an innocent explanation for what he'd seen, but Carly had little doubt he'd seen it. Just as she had little doubt anymore Cutter Foxworth was everything Brett had said he was. Now that she'd seen him in action, the stories she'd heard didn't seem so far-fetched.

"There were signs of a possible attempted break-in on that building the other side of the dumpster," she told them, "but no idea how old they might be. I'll check the front to see if it's secure, then track down the owner and see what he says. But right now this—" she held up the bagged hat "—is it."

When she was done, they went back to pick up Woof, who rather resignedly let Parker load him into the back of the SUV. The man then went back to talk to Ray, and she studied the pair for a moment. She had to admit she was impressed with Parker's loyalty to the man, and how he was willing to bring the dog to visit his master almost every day.

They dropped the duo off at Ray's house, then headed back to the Foxworths' so Carly could pick up her car.

"What do you think?" Teague asked as they drove the short distance between.

"I think Ray saw what he says he saw. The interpretation is up for grabs at the moment."

Teague nodded. After a moment Laney said, "Parker seems like a good guy. Taking the dog to visit every day."

"Yes."

"Cute, too," the woman added, her voice just a bit too blasé. "If you like that sweet, boy-next-door kind of thing."

"Hmm," Carly murmured noncommittally. If you'd asked her this morning, she'd have said she could take or leave the type. But now? No, she'd been a little too aware of Parker Ward to dismiss the thought.

And then there was Cutter. And his whole little trick of maneuvering them into sitting next to each other. She'd have dismissed that, too, if she wasn't working every day with the results of that other apparent knack the dog had. She had often wondered if Brett Dunbar would ever put his dark, grim past behind him, yet now he was one of the happiest people she knew. And he—and his beloved wife, Sloane, who had gone through her own hell—gave Cutter most of the credit for getting them together.

"So, did Cutter matchmake the two of you like he did Brett and Sloane?" She said it without really thinking about how it would sound, after what Laney had said. But the other woman only grinned.

"That he did," Teague said. "Although he did have some help from Hayley."

"Yes. But he was very clever about it," Laney said. "He

kept getting ridiculously dirty, enough to need grooming quite often."

Teague gave her a loving glance as he said, "And guess who got elected to go pick him up every time?"

Carly blinked. "You're saying he did it...on purpose? So you'd...see each other?"

The dog barked, albeit quietly, from behind her. It had an odd intonation, like it had had in the alley when she'd found the hat. Almost...approval. Like he was telling her she'd figured it out.

"Tell me," she said with a laugh, "does everybody who's around him start having crazy ideas about him?"

"Pretty much," Teague said.

She was still bemused by it all, and thinking about how when Brett returned she was going to have to admit he'd been right, when they got back to the Foxworths' place. She'd been going to just leave, but Teague suggested she might want to come in because he was sure his boss had been doing some research. And Carly guessed from Quinn Foxworth's expression when they came in that Teague was right.

"What did you find?" Teague asked.

Quinn looked at Carly. "Nothing that directly relates to this case, if it is one," he told her. "But...I found out why Parker Ward's name seemed familiar to me."

"It was to me, too," Carly said, realizing with a little jolt she was feeling a bit nervous about whatever he might have discovered.

"Remember the Witner case?"

"The huge Ponzi scheme bust in the city?" Teague asked. "The one where the mastermind got a zillion years in prison?"

Quinn nodded.

Carly sucked in a breath as it hit her. "It was him," she exclaimed. "He's the one who blew the whistle on it."

Quinn nodded. "And according to my source, it cost him everything."

Carly sank down into the nearest chair.

Those boy-next-door looks clearly hid a backbone of steel.

Chapter 5

Woof had already trumpeted his warning, so Parker wasn't surprised when the knock on the door came. And he wasn't really surprised when he opened the door and saw Detective Devon standing there. He was glad, in fact, because it told him she truly was taking this seriously.

The gladness had nothing to do with the fact that she was just as attractive as he'd thought she was the first time he'd looked up and seen her.

No, that wasn't quite true. She was more attractive. To him, anyway. Probably because she'd taken this all seriously. And because of how she'd treated Ray.

"I… Come in, out of the rain," he said belatedly, realizing he hadn't even spoken.

"Thank you." She stepped inside, onto the mat placed just inside the door for days like this one. Woof greeted her happily, and he liked the way she smiled when she bent to ruffle the dog's fur.

You like too much about her. Back off.

Politely, he said, "I just fixed a fresh pot of coffee, if you'd like some."

"I would, thank you."

He took the jacket she shrugged off and hung it on the rack beside the door where his own, still damp, was drying. He saw her looking around as they walked through the living area to the kitchen, where the coffee maker was. He couldn't help but notice the holstered weapon at her side. It was smaller than Ray's favored handgun but still looked plenty lethal.

Before his mind could spin off into thoughts about what it must be like to be a cop, and a woman cop, he got down a couple of mugs and poured coffee. He asked about cream and sugar and she took a small dollop of each. Then, sipping at the brew, she turned around and looked at the main room.

"This is nice. Very nice." She gestured back toward the door. "Is all the land down the drive his?"

Parker nodded. "And about an acre out back. He likes the feel of seclusion, but also had an eye on expansion when they bought it." *For the kids who never came. So they ended up with me.*

"I like the vaulted ceiling and the beams," she said.

"Ray designed it himself."

"I thought he was an engineer."

"He is." Parker smiled. "He says that's why this place will stand forever. He had to have an architect go over the plans, but he didn't let any architectural foibles mess it up."

She laughed. A great laugh. Damn.

"I suspect he has a point," she said.

Deciding he owed her this much at least, he said, "Thank you for the way you were with him."

"That could be said to you, as well."

That surprised him. "Ray's…special. To me, I mean."

"I gathered. Quinn said you grew up next door?"

He nodded. "Although I actually grew up more, in the learning sense, here. Ray and his wife let me escape over here, a lot. If it wasn't for them, I wouldn't have had any idea what a normal home could be."

"Crazy at your home?"

"In public my parents were the perfect couple. At home… Let's just say sometimes I used to wish they'd just split and get it over with. But that was before I realized they fed on each other, on the drama. And that, for them, it really was the perfect marriage." He grimaced. What was it about her that made him blab like this?

"That had to suck."

"It did. This was the place I ran to when the yelling got too loud or the sound of things breaking got too close. I found refuge here. Peace. And…something else I didn't understand until much later. A support that never wavered. Hard-won wisdom."

"A mentor?" she suggested.

"Yes. Especially that." He saw her gaze come to rest on the large framed photograph on the wall. "Ray and his wife, Laura," he said. "That was their fiftieth anniversary. She was gone a year later."

"Wow. That's a long time together. He must have been heartbroken."

"He still is. Losing her almost killed him."

He didn't think anything in particular had been in his voice, but she gave him a sideways look. "You still are, too," she said quietly.

He didn't, wouldn't, deny it. "Yes. She was more of a mother to me than mine ever was."

"Why?"

He blinked. "Because she was a kind, loving, generous woman."

"Got that part. I meant, what was up with your mother?"

"Hell if I know." He grimaced. He hadn't meant to let that out—at least, not sounding sour to the point of bitterness. "Sorry. I don't usually let that get to me anymore."

"Some people just shouldn't be parents," she said easily. "Believe me, I come across them."

He remembered then that Quinn had said her regular job was the juvenile detective, so she would indeed know. "If I hadn't had Ray and Laura to come to, I think I really would have been screwed up." *Instead of just blind.*

She set down her coffee mug and turned to face him. Her eyes seemed even bluer than he'd remembered from less than an hour ago. "Instead," she said, holding his gaze, "you turned out to be the guy who took down one of the biggest crooks and scammers I've ever heard about."

He went rigidly still. Stared at her. He shouldn't be surprised, he supposed. But he was, a little, that she'd gotten there so quickly.

"Quinn did a little homework while we were gone," she said quietly. "Brett always says they're thorough and have connections he doesn't question, since he knows they're on the side of the angels."

"Great. I keep hoping people will forget it," he muttered. He had to consciously relax his clenched jaw. Time for some reality. *Put it out there, Ward, because once she knows, maybe you'll be able to keep it on a leash.* "So. Yeah. And now I'm jobless, homeless and unemployable."

She looked startled. Then she frowned. And even then she was cute. "The first two are temporary, aren't they? And the third can't really be true."

He gave her a wry smile. "Can't it? I'm either the guy who rats out his boss or the dumbass who couldn't see what was right in front of me."

"But your boss was a criminal and you did see it."

He sighed. "Sometimes I forget how black-and-white things can be for cops."

She tilted her head as she looked at him, as if she were

intently trying to figure something out. *Don't waste the energy. No depth here.*

"Are you saying there's no one out there who'd be glad to hire a truly honest man?"

"Not when he's so stupid his former boss trusted he'd never catch on to what was happening, not once he got blinded by a plum job and a fancy office."

"Is that really how you see yourself?"

"Reality bites," he said.

She was silent for a moment, studying him in a way that made him edgy. This was not something he wanted to discuss. Especially with her.

"What this cop sees," she said softly, "is a guy who had the guts to do what was right, even at the cost of everything he had. A guy who realized innocent people were being destroyed."

That was, and always had been, the bottom line for him. Once he'd realized what the conversation he'd overheard meant, once he'd poked around enough to prove the crazy idea was true, he'd had no choice. "No choice." He repeated the thought aloud, under his breath.

"There really was a choice. You could have just gone along, reaped the benefits of turning a blind eye. But you didn't. And that took guts."

"That was Ray, too." His mouth twisted again. "My mother told me not to make waves, my dad said I was being foolish to doubt such a fine, upstanding man as my boss, and it ended with both of them telling me not to be stupid."

The fact that the only time his parents agreed was when they were criticizing him was something he'd never realized until Ray had, very tactfully, pointed it out to him. The crusty old veteran had never really criticized his parents—not his job, he always said—but he had had a way of making Parker see the truth for himself. Of course, that he gave him a haven from the never-ending chaos, a quiet place to think, was sometimes as much help as the advice.

"So Ray gave you advice?"

"That's not his way. He just…makes you see the truth for yourself. He made me see what I had to do."

"Even though it would leave your life a shambles."

He met her gaze then. "He made me see that working for slime like Witner wasn't worth it. That the big, shiny new office and the perks were a bribe to stay quiet. I hadn't earned either."

She held his gaze for a long, steady moment. Then, with quiet emphasis, she said, "There is nothing stupid about you, Parker Ward." She seemed to hesitate, then added, "My mother's best friend got sucked up into that last Ponzi scheme."

He gave her a startled look. Felt suddenly queasy. "I'm sorry."

"She's okay. My dad got suspicious fairly early and warned her. She got out without losing much, but she could have lost everything."

"Good for him." His mouth twisted wryly. "Took me nearly a year."

"Nobody goes in expecting their boss to be a crook." She gave him a smile that eased the nausea somehow. "Brett Dunbar sure didn't expect to end up taking down the governor."

"You…like him. This Dunbar guy." *Why the hell did you say that? It's pretty obvious she likes him.*

But she answered easily. "He's the kind of guy who will always have your back. Went through hell and came out shining. I admire the heck out of his wife, too."

The churning in his gut faded away. And he didn't want to think about why her answer accomplished that.

Chapter 6

Carly had told herself she'd just wanted to get a feel for the witness, in what might or might not be an actual case, and that seeing his home would help that. It had. The neat, tidy surroundings spoke of the man she'd seen at the rehab center, sharp, together and observant.

It was just a…side effect that she'd come out of that house liking Parker Ward even more.

She hadn't expected it to get so personal. She was used to hearing horrible stories of abusive parenting, and his was much less horrific than many she'd seen, apparently never having turned physical. But still, it had left scars, and if he hadn't had Ray Lowry to turn to, he could have turned out, as he'd said, really screwed up.

She was a little surprised he'd told her so much. She hadn't really been trying to pry his own story out of him, as she sometimes had to do with suspects and victims, since he was neither. And she had the feeling he was even more surprised at how much he'd told her.

As she drove back to the office, she found herself remembering Cutter's little maneuver in the back seat of the Foxworth SUV. And Brett's joking reminiscences of how the dog had seemed to constantly be doing just that kind of thing to him, maneuvering so that he and Sloane had always seemed to end up closer together.

She had to admit the idea had a certain appeal. Parker Ward was a good man. A little down on himself right now, it seemed, for not guessing immediately that Witner was a con man. Never mind that to be a con man at that level required being able to fool just about anyone except maybe another con man. Like the politician he'd bribed to get his building code violations overlooked by hiring the man's son, who knew zip about construction, zoning, codes or anything else helpful.

She spent until nearly the end of her shift winding up some loose ends on cases that were closed. A burglary that the area deputy had solved, two runaways returned home and, the saddest, a child orphaned by a traffic accident now placed in the care of the aunt who had flown in from Iowa to get her.

Then she sat back in her chair, tapping her thumb idly on the desk as she thought. She'd turned the knit hat in to the lab, but told them not to make it a priority until—unless—she came up with more evidence that a crime had actually occurred. Right now there were only her notes on a field interview form, classified as suspicious circumstances. Which could be the start of a case or simply a dead end signifying nothing.

There were still no missing persons reports, so she made another check for anyone who might have called the county jail about someone they'd lost track of. Nothing. She did a quick check for any reports on the building on that alley that looked as if someone had at least tried to break in. Nothing, except the fact that it had been vacant for over a month. Then she took her last few minutes officially on duty to call the cities in the county that had their own police departments, but turned up no new MPs, only one lost little girl they were actively searching for. She told them to call her if the sheriff's office could help or they needed more resources, then shut down for the day. All the while acknowledging that if what Ray had seen was truly a kidnapping, it was very possible the victim's family or the targeted people had been told not to report it.

She went through her routine when she got to her apartment, setting her bag on the table by the door, hanging her keys on the rack above it, removing her SIG P365 and securing it in the fingerprint-activated case fastened to the side of the table. She'd developed the system long ago, so she could be up, armed and ready to go in mere moments. Of course, that had been more important when she'd been down in LA, where quick responses—and the 10 + 1 capacity—were often needed. Back here where she'd grown up, in this mostly peaceful place, the need was much less. She once again said a mental thanks to Brett for letting her know when the opening had come up four years ago when she'd been desperate to get out and come home.

Once that was done, she turned around and was face-to-face with what she laughingly called home. She'd never intended this apartment to be forever; it had just been what was available when she'd needed a place after she'd gotten here. She'd thought she'd find a house or cabin somewhere, with a little space for a garden maybe, but time seemed to have gotten away from her and here she still was.

It wasn't that it was a bad place, and the managers were responsive enough if she had a problem. It just felt… temporary to her. Looking at it now, it felt even more so. Because when she'd thought about that home she wanted, she'd thought about someplace exactly like Ray Lowry's house. Warm, homey, welcoming.

And far, far from the taste of her ex-fiancé. James had been much more a chrome-and-glass and sharp-edges kind of guy. Nice enough, but not her style at all.

Of course, in the end, she hadn't been his style, either. She knew her friends and family assumed he couldn't handle her being a cop, and in a way, it was true. Except they assumed it was her life being in danger that bothered him, when in fact it was that her work too often interfered with his plans for their social life.

That's what you get when you fall for a guy determined to become a mover and shaker.

She gave a sharp shake of her head; she didn't often think of James anymore and preferred it that way. It only reminded her of her own foolishness in thinking that was what she wanted.

Later, as she sat not watching some police drama, not even to pick it apart for violations of standard operating procedures or the magical swiftness of lab results, it occurred to her having a dog would be nice. One like Cutter—if there were any more like him—would be a bit unnerving, but one like the sweet, endearing Woof would be nice. She shut off the screen and leaned her head back, yawning sleepily. Yes, a dog like Woof would be nice. Maybe he'd be willing to curl up on the couch with her, another living being, warm and alive, to share some quiet time with.

She woke up with a start and was instantly rattled to realize that she'd dreamed of sharing time on this couch with another living being, but it hadn't been Woof. It had been Parker Ward.

And the time had been anything but quiet.

"Whoa, girl," she said to the empty room. "You know it's been too long when you start having dreams like *that*."

She went to bed still shaking her head at herself.

* * *

Woof whined, sounding worried. Parker didn't blame him; he'd been up pacing for almost an hour now. But he couldn't seem to settle, and he wasn't sure why.

Up until today, it would have been worry about his future—or lack of one—but this felt different. He wasn't really worried about Ray for the moment. He was doing well, the doctors said, considering the complexity of the damage.

After he got home he'd have to stick around and see how he did on his own. He'd often thought about what would happen if Ray got to the point where he couldn't live by himself anymore. But as Ray always said, when the time came they'd deal.

Then he laughed at himself. He'd thought about sticking around as if he had any other options.

He dropped wearily back down into Ray's favorite chair, as if somehow the man's wisdom could be transferred that way. Woof walked over and plopped his chin on Parker's knee, looking up at him with that worried gaze. With a sigh, he reached out to stroke the dog's head.

"It'll be all right, boy. I'm not sure how, but don't worry. Just be glad you're a dog." Woof gave a little whine, as if he weren't convinced. "How about we go see Ray early tomorrow, huh?"

The dog's ears perked up at the sound of his most beloved human's name. Parker smiled. Yep, being a dog was the ticket. If people were half as loving, half as forgiving, the world would be a better place.

When he awoke the next morning, it was to find the dog curled up on the bed at his feet. Woof usually stayed in his bed in Ray's room, so this was a change. Maybe he'd been more down than even he'd realized, but the dog had sensed it. Or maybe he was just lonely, missing Ray.

Or maybe he was just reminding him of the promise to go see Ray early today. He found himself grinning at that, already feeling better.

"Okay, mutt, shower, coffee— No, make that coffee, shower, some breakfast, and we're off. Maybe we can take that walk with Ray."

The dog yipped happily, leaped off the bed and stood looking at him expectantly. He laughed and got up. Remembered his thought last night about dogs making the world a better place, decided he'd been right and headed for the kitchen. He let Woof out the back, cautioned the dog to stay close this time, and the memories of yesterday came back in a rush.

Carly.

Detective Devon, he corrected.

What this cop sees is a guy who had the guts to do what was right.

He supposed it wasn't much to cling to, one woman's opinion, but that didn't stop her words from playing back in his head. Often.

And then there was Foxworth. He'd done a little research after she'd gone last night. He'd needed the distraction and he wanted to know anyway. Their website was slick but fairly minimal. Most of what he'd found had been secondhand. Mentions in news articles, more in various blogs and comments, all of which praised them for helping when no one else would, even the people who should have. From helping someone in the proverbial fight against city hall to recovering a precious memento to taking down that corrupt, murderous governor, it seemed they'd always been the good guys.

Especially, Parker had thought with a grin, if you judged by the people they'd gone up against along the way. From crooked politicians to missing mementos to protected witnesses to murder, they'd run the gamut.

Including a couple of kidnappings.

Ray was pleased to see them both when they arrived, and Art indicated he'd been in a much better mood since their visit yesterday. Ray also insisted a little rain, if you could call this heavy mist actual rain, wasn't about to stop him from escaping this place for a while.

"I'll go with him on his walk today," Parker walked over and told the man as Ray greeted Woof happily. "If that's all right."

Art gave him a smile. "No problem. You're in his file."

Parker blinked. "What?"

"You're in his file. As emergency notification and for release of information, plus the medical power of attorney, of course. Besides, he told us all as far as he's concerned, you're his son."

Parker drew back. Glanced at Ray, who was grinning at his goofy dog. He swallowed tightly. "I... Thanks."

He wanted to say something, thank Ray for his trust, even though he was a little uneasy about the responsibility. He knew Laura had never been able to have children, something he'd once, as a kid, selfishly counted as a blessing for himself. But as he'd grown older, he'd come to realize that it would have made no difference; even with children of their own, they would have seen to Parker, provided that same refuge. Their hearts had been more than big enough.

But he knew the man would just shrug it off if he did say something. So he simply renewed his silent vow to return that trust and love in kind. Whatever Ray needed, whenever he needed it, he'd do his best to provide.

When he had Woof on the leash, they started out. And

it didn't take long for Parker to realize they were again retracing the walk he'd taken two days ago. He'd expected that.

What he hadn't expected was to reach that alley and see Detective Devon already there.

Chapter 7

Carly sensed rather than heard the approaching trio. When she looked and saw the black dog with the funny white patch, she smiled. And Mr. Lowry looked good, was walking well, although she supposed his shoulder didn't interfere with that much.

As for Parker Ward… Yes, darn it, he was as cute as she remembered. He really rocked that boy-next-door look, especially today, wearing a bright green-and-gray-striped knit hat that was much nicer-looking than the grubby mess she—or rather Cutter—had found here yesterday. In fact, both men wore them.

She saw them spot her, and they turned down the alley. She started toward them, smiling at the sight.

"You match," she teased, looking at the hats.

"My wife made them," Ray said.

He didn't say it sadly, so she didn't offer any of the standard condolences that to her had always seemed meaningless from strangers. The requisite line when they had the grim duty of delivering a death notification was "I'm sorry for your loss," and it was true in the sense that most cops by nature felt, if they'd been at all involved, it was a failure of sorts on their part not to have saved the person. But unless it was one of their own, there was nothing personal in it, and both sides knew it.

Instead she went with the truth. "They're very nice. I always wanted to learn to knit."

"She could have taught you in an afternoon," Ray said. Then, with a grin, he nodded at Parker. "She taught him, after all."

Parker groaned. She blinked. "You knit?"

He sighed. "She taught me because I was curious about how it worked. How she took that long string and turned it into fabric. But it ended there, once I figured it out."

"A bit too female?"

He frowned. "No. Lack of patience with tangled yarn."

She smiled. And then, as if he realized she'd set him up, he smiled back, ruefully. "Did I pass?" he asked, one brow raised.

"You did," she said, not denying it. Then she looked back at Ray, who was smiling. The older man winked at her, as if in appreciation of the ruse, and she found herself smiling back at him. "How's the walk going?"

"More interesting these days," Ray said.

"Indeed," Parker muttered.

When she looked back at him, he was glaring at her. It took her a moment to see the slight twitch at the corners of his mouth that told her it was a mock glare. Although why she wasn't staring at that beautiful mouth all the time, she wasn't sure, because it certainly was—

Whoa. Again.

She coughed, gestured back at the alley behind her. "I'm waiting for the owner of that building with the pry marks on the door."

Ray looked pleasantly surprised, Parker pleased sans the surprise. Which pleased her in turn.

Talk about tangled yarn...

"You think it's connected?" Ray asked.

She didn't want to mislead him. "More in the nature of eliminating possibilities," she said.

Parker nodded slowly. "I guess disproving is just as important as proving, sometimes."

"Exactly," she said with a wide smile. "More than once I've seen people get so focused, so intent on proving their theory, they walk right past something that completely disproves it."

"Then what happens?" Ray asked.

"They've wasted a lot of time," she said. "Worst case, during that time the real bad guys get away. Or they don't realize it until they're in court and some Gavin de Marco–level lawyer tears it apart."

She'd had the chance during Brett's takedown of the governor to briefly meet the internationally famous attorney, who had walked away from a career most people could only dream of, vanished for a while, then turned up working with Foxworth. She didn't know the whole story; all Brett would say was that it had been a moral dilemma that had precipitated the change.

Like Parker's dilemma?

She had spent too much of those lying-awake hours last night pondering just that. What would it be like to discover, say, that the sheriff himself was taking bribes to influence cases, or directing investigations away from the true culprit toward an innocent party? Or payoffs to focus safety enforcement in one area while neglecting another? And what would it be like if she was the only one who could prove it?

She couldn't imagine anything more...isolating. Or more likely to put a target on your back. And yet he'd done it. Knowing—he had to have known—what it would cost him, he had done it. Because the corruption was like a sewer running beneath his world and his life. Because innocent people were being hurt.

Because it was the right thing to do.

She wondered if he had any idea how rare that was these days.

The sound of a vehicle approaching snapped her out of the reverie, and she saw Parker looking at her curiously. She had the oddest feeling he was about to ask her what she'd been thinking about—wouldn't that be fun to answer?—and quickly turned toward the newcomer.

Newcomers, she corrected in some surprise as she recognized the dark blue SUV from yesterday. What were the Foxworth people doing back here? Including, judging by Woof's excited bark and tail wagging, Cutter.

Even as she thought it, the vehicle came to a halt and the back hatch started to rise. The moment it was up far enough, the clever Foxworth dog was out and headed for them. He greeted Woof with an energetic tail wag and sniff, Ray the same way plus a swipe of pink tongue over his fingers, making the man smile again. Parker he looked at consideringly, then gave a nudge of his hand with his nose. Finally he came over to sit at Carly's feet.

All this was accomplished before Teague Johnson got out and over to them.

"Didn't expect to see you back here," Carly said.

"Didn't expect to be here," the man said with a grin. "But Cutter said we needed to come, and since Hayley just got home after a week away, there was no way Quinn was leaving."

She blinked. "Cutter said…?"

"Yep. In his own inimitable way. Which consists of going out and sitting by the car and raising a ruckus until you get it and give in. Kind of like his driving directions.

Peace and quiet as long as you're going the right way, but he'll bust an eardrum for you if you miss a turn."

Parker was staring at the man. "You're saying he... wanted to come here, specifically?"

Teague nodded, his eyes twinkling to match his grin. "I know. Believe me, I took some convincing. But how do you argue with a track record of a hundred percent?"

"That's crazy," Parker said, but he sounded as if at least some part of him wanted to believe it. Carly did believe it, because Brett had told her exactly the same thing.

"Brett said he had to quit thinking about it and just go with it," she said.

"Pretty much our SOP since he came along," Teague said cheerfully. The former marine seemed perfectly content with the idea, and from what she knew, Carly couldn't blame him. "So why are we here?"

She explained she was waiting to talk to the owner of the building with the pry marks on the back door, right next to where she—or rather the estimable Cutter—had found the knit hat.

"No report on file, I assume?" Teague asked.

Carly shook her head. "Building's vacant, though, and from what the neighboring businesses said, it has been for nearly a month, so the owner might not be checking it regularly."

"You mean he might not even know somebody tried to break in?" Ray said.

"That is what I hope to find out," Carly said as another vehicle pulled into the alley. She noted it was a silver sedan. Matching what description they had. But she also knew she could walk out to the main street here and probably find a half dozen cars that also matched. She looked back at the others. "Let's play you just being passersby out walking your dogs for the moment, all right?"

Parker and Ray exchanged glances, but only nodded, and she noted Teague looked as if he'd expected just that.

The man who got out of the silver sedan looked quite startled to see the four-person, two-dog welcoming committee. Carly was sure she would have been, too, so when she introduced herself, she went out of her way to assure the man it was merely happenstance.

"You're Mr. Charles Turner?" she asked. "And you own this building?"

"I'm Chuck Turner, yes," he said, still looking at them all warily. Woof seemed more than willing to greet him as he did any person, it seemed, as if they were long-lost buddies. The man seemed not to even notice. She made a mental note of that, although she wasn't sure it told her anything about the man, really.

Then Teague's slight cough drew her attention, and he looked pointedly at Cutter, who was staring at the newcomer intently, on alert in the same way she'd seen police K-9s react when onto something. He wasn't growling, but his ears were up, his tail up and level with his back, all rigidly still. And those too-wise amber-flecked eyes were fastened on Mr. Turner with an intensity that would have—or at least should have—rattled anyone paying attention.

Turner was not paying attention. Not to the dog, at least.

"I wanted to ask you about the pry marks on the back door of your building. Did you have a break-in?"

"Oh." The man grimaced. "Yes, a couple of weeks ago. I replaced the lock, but haven't gotten around to refinishing the door."

"Or reporting it?"

The man went as still as Cutter for an instant, but then shrugged casually. "The place is vacant. It seemed a waste of time. It's still pretty cold at night, so I thought it might be someone needing shelter."

Magnanimous answer. But that frozen instant before he answered...

And Cutter's stare.

But she smiled at him, as if she appreciated his concern for those less fortunate. "Well, hopefully you'll have a new tenant in there soon."

The hesitation again, this time accompanied by a glance at the others as if he was wondering why they were hanging around, before he repeated, neutrally, "Hopefully."

"Anything of concern happening in the area? Something keeping tenants away?"

He blinked. "No. Not that I know of. It's generally very quiet." Again he looked at the others. "Lots of dog walkers, though. If that's all, I have…an appointment."

She nodded. "Sorry to make you come out on a false alarm."

When the man had gotten back into his car, she turned to look at Teague. "You want to translate that?" she asked, nodding at Cutter.

"Yeah," Parker said. "He was zeroed in on that guy pretty intently."

Teague nodded and leaned to scratch behind the dog's right ear. "I think Mr. Turner was just declared a person of interest."

Chapter 8

"Unfortunately," Detective Devon said, "a dog's instinct isn't quite enough for us to officially go on."

Parker's gaze shifted from Cutter, who had relaxed as the silver car had pulled away, to her. Funny, he'd always thought he preferred long hair, but that short, tousled haircut, and the way it bared that gorgeous neck, could change his mind.

He yanked his unruly brain off paths it had no business following and made himself focus. It didn't help much, because it put him in the conundrum of completely understanding the insanity of trusting a dog—even one as apparently clever as this one—on something like this, and yet knowing Ray hadn't been wrong.

At least she sounded like she meant the *unfortunately* part. Small comfort, but telling, somehow.

"So you're saying you don't believe me?" Ray said sharply. "It could even be the same car."

"Not at all. I'm just saying that despite Cutter's stellar reputation, my bosses aren't likely to take his word—or stare—as evidence." She'd said it briskly, as if she'd somehow understood Ray would take a gentler, soothing tone as condescension. "But you saw what you saw, so I'll do what I can."

She didn't sound particularly hopeful, either, and Parker could tell the man was not happy. All the way back to the rehab center—they'd declined the ride offer from Teague because Ray wanted to keep walking—he was fuming. Even Woof was behaving, as if he knew this was not the time to push his luck.

"I believe you, Ray. You know that. And I'll keep pushing, I promise. I won't let it drop."

It placated the older man a little, but he was clearly still in a mood when they reached their destination. They ran into Art near the doorway as Ray and Woof said their temporary goodbyes, and Parker gave him a glance of warning. The attendant scuttled away hastily.

"Ray—"

"If I had one damned wish to come true, besides having Laura back, I swear it would be for every person under forty to have to spend a month being treated the way seniors are treated."

Parker trod carefully. Counted on the man's innate sense of humor. "Couldn't you make it under thirty? Then I wouldn't have to spend a month being tortured to learn something I already know." Ray glared at him, but he saw one corner of the man's mouth twitch. He shrugged. "What can I say—I'm selfish."

Ray reached out and put a hand on his shoulder. "That," he said with quiet emphasis, "couldn't be further from the truth. And if I haven't told you, I'm proud of you, boy."

Parker's throat was suddenly tight. "You have. But say it as often as you want." He managed a smile. "Like I said—selfish."

Ray's fingers curled into a fist and he gave him a light, manly slug on the arm. When Parker saw Art hovering a few feet away, he gave him a nod. The man mouthed, "Thank you," as he came to see Ray safely back to his room.

"It's my dog who needs a walker, not me," Ray was grumbling as they went, but it was no worse than his normal complaining tone about being here at all.

The next day dawned to steady rain. Parker had resorted to toast with peanut butter this morning and was sitting in front of his laptop at Ray's dining table, grimacing as he looked at his dwindling bank account. The real one, the one that was his, not fat with money pilfered and swindled from innocent people.

Woof, who had been soaked after his romp outside but was almost dry after a vigorous toweling he seemed to love, was plopped sedately on his bed by the fireplace, as if he'd never done a day's mischief in his life. Parker glanced over at the dog, pondering again whether to start a fire to take the chill off. He was still a bit sketchy on the intricacies of getting a good fire going, but he was learning. They'd had a fireplace at the house next door, but neither of his parents had wanted the hassle of dealing with actual wood, so it had been mostly unused. Unless his mother had been having one of her parties and thought it added to the ambience.

He smiled rather wistfully as he remembered telling Ray this once when he'd been about ten.

"So she'll do it for others, but not for her own family," he had said. It hadn't been a question, and so hadn't required an answer, but it had planted the seed in his ten-year-old mind, and it hadn't been long after that that Parker had realized that was the way of most things in the Ward household.

Deciding that staring at the depressing numbers wasn't

going to change them, and that he couldn't face another fruitless round of job hunting just now, he shut down the laptop and stood up. Ray had appointments with the doctor and a full slate of therapy sessions today, so he wouldn't take Woof over until tonight. He'd done every little chore he could find around the house, he'd made a grocery store stop on the way back yesterday, and he'd run Woof ragged this morning. That didn't leave him much. Except maybe more reading. He'd done a lot of that lately.

But first he'd start that fire. Maybe the practice would help. "Pickle," he muttered, smiling again as he remembered the fire-building acronym Ray had taught him as a kid. PCKL. Paper, cardboard, kindling, logs.

He was pleased when the fire caught and seemed to hold. Then he walked over to peruse Ray's well-stocked bookcase. He'd gotten out of the habit of reading print books, relying mostly on his e-reader, which fortunately had been well stocked before the roof had fallen in. But surprisingly he'd found a different kind of pleasure in reading actual dead-tree books.

He smiled as he scanned titles, remembering the first time he'd used that term in front of Ray. The man had given him that level look and said, "The thing about trees is, you can grow new ones." And left Parker to figure out his point, just as he had since he'd been a kid and had discovered that a haven of sanity bordered on his personal chaos.

He passed over a legal thriller—lawyers weren't real high on his favorite-people list at the moment—and a mystery he'd already read, then lingered for a moment over a title that had to be one of Laura's favored romances. He knew Ray had kept all of her books, but this one was in the midst of Ray's shelves. And another memory shot through his mind, of Ray telling his cocky teenage self with a wink not to get snooty about those books, that he'd learned an awful lot about women—and his wife—by reading some of her best-loved ones.

He thought about it for a moment, but the way the image of a certain sheriff's detective crept into his mind made him veer away. The last thing he needed was to have her taking up permanent residence in his head. He settled on a science fiction classic he remembered reading as a kid and loving, and silently thanked Ray for having such eclectic tastes.

He read until almost noon, thinking there was tremendous peace to be found in this simple scenario, the sound of rain, a fire, a book and a dog at your feet. Ray was really onto something here. But now the rain had eased up for the moment, and he was restless. He let Woof outside and threw the ball for him for a good half hour, until the goofy animal plopped down in a puddle to rest. It took him a while to get him dry and de-mudded enough to go back in the house. Content, the dog settled down with his favorite chew bone and went to work.

When he found himself pacing the floor, Parker knew he had to do something. He made sure Woof had water, then grabbed up his keys. The dog's head came up, and he told him, "Not this time." As if he'd understood perfectly, as perhaps he had, Woof went back to his bone.

He wasn't sure what he could do, but he headed back to the alley anyway. If law enforcement couldn't do anything, it was up to him to do at least something to keep the promise he'd made to Ray. Even if it was only sit and watch the place for a while. Not that he expected anything to happen, not like a kidnapper would return to the scene of the crime, but it was all he could think of.

He found a parking place near the alley entrance, where he could actually see from inside the vehicle. Maybe he should have brought Woof along for the company. It was a lot easier to indulge a tendency to talk to yourself if you had the dog around to blame it on. Of course, he hadn't had that tendency until he'd realized the truth of where his obliviousness had landed him. Then he'd spent time— far too much—trying to talk himself out of what he deep down knew to be true. He really hadn't wanted to believe he'd been, even unknowingly, a part of something that had hurt so many.

He got out and started walking; he wasn't sure why. Rather than head straight for the alley, he walked around the block to come at it from the other end. He wasn't sure why that, either, except it was different from what they'd already done. And Ray had said that was the way the car had gone.

He paused on the front side of the empty building that had had the pry marks. The windows were masked off so you couldn't see inside, and there was no sign of any tampering at the front door.

At the other end of the alley, he looked around. The side street connected directly with one of the main streets that could have taken them anywhere. West to the bay, which had some grim possibilities. Or north to the highway, which could take them either to the Hood Canal Bridge and a national park where it would be easy to dump a body, or south toward Tacoma, where it would be easy to vanish into the city. All of which was useless speculation, since they had no idea which way they'd gone, and this small town didn't run to traffic cameras at every stoplight.

He kept going. The alley was deserted this afternoon, no delivery truck. He walked slowly, looking, although he had no idea for what. There didn't seem to be anything different, and there was nothing new in or near the dumpster except a bunch of cardboard boxes, flattened and stacked neatly. He pushed one back and saw the label that indicated they were from the coffee delivery they'd seen.

He never heard a thing until the words came from close behind him.

"And just what are you doing, Mr. Ward?"

Chapter 9

Carly had anticipated he'd be startled, so was clear when he spun around. He was surprised, yes, but he did it steadily, no wobble. But then, she'd already noticed he was in good shape.

In great shape.

And she hadn't imagined—or embroidered upon—the color of his eyes, the green mixed with a light brown she could call only golden, especially here in the sunlight that seemed even brighter after the rain had cleared out.

"Just looking around," he said, obviously disconcerted.

"Because?"

He gave a one-shouldered shrug. "Because somebody should. And I promised Ray."

I promised Ray.

Did he have any idea how rare that was these days, at least in her world, to have those simple words be as binding as an oath? Unless it was one of her fellow deputies—and not all of them—or her family, she didn't trust many who threw out promises. Too often they were like confetti, pretty when thrown but debris when they hit the ground.

"And what," she said carefully, "do you suppose I'm doing here?"

He blinked as if he hadn't gotten to that yet. "You said there wasn't enough evidence to go on."

"Cutter. Officially."

"What?"

"I said Cutter's instinct about Mr. Turner wasn't enough to go on, officially. I didn't say anything about dropping it. I just can't devote a lot of department resources to it."

He had the grace to look abashed. "I'm sorry. I… misinterpreted." He grimaced. "I'm good at that, it seems."

"Good to know," she said neutrally.

"So… You're here unofficially?"

"I'm here because I trust Brett Dunbar, and he says trust Cutter."

This morning's conversation with Brett Dunbar ran through her head.

The wit seems like a pretty sharp guy.

Then take him at his word. Something happened, even if it might not be what he thinks.

She'd described the encounter with the building owner to him, and Cutter's interesting reaction to him. Brett immediately told her to trust the dog's instincts.

If Cutter zeroed in on the owner, he's probably connected, somehow.

You've got that much faith in a dog?

I've got that much faith in that dog.

And Brett Dunbar was nobody's fool. He hadn't built the reputation that had spread far beyond their little county— even before he'd taken down their murderous governor— by being stupid. If he said trust the dog, she'd trust the dog. Crazy as it sounded.

"So, did you find anything?" she asked.

"No." Again he grimaced. "But I'm good at looking right past what's in front of me, too."

It didn't take any detective intuition to read the meaning behind that, given what she now knew. "For somebody who did the right, the honorable and a very brave thing, you're awfully hard on yourself."

"I…" He stopped and simply stared at her.

"I talked to some people, and they universally said without you Witner would be going on his merry way, bilking more innocent people out of every penny they have."

He let out an audible breath. "That's why I had to do it. I'm not brave, Detective. I just couldn't stomach it once I finally realized the truth."

She smiled at him then, and his eyes widened. "And just what do you think bravery is, Mr. Ward?"

Her point made—she could see it in the half smile he gave her, in an almost shy way that made her insides take an odd tumble—she proceeded to do her own reinspection of the area. It felt like a wasted effort, but it was part of due diligence, so she did it. Especially since this wasn't normally her bailiwick.

At the same time she felt a buzz of excitement because of just that; this wasn't her usual. Unless it really had been a kid, not Ray Lowry's idea of a kid. But if he called Parker Ward a kid—because despite his youthful looks, the guy was pure adult male, no matter the vibe he put out, or at least that she seemed determined to get from him—the range was wide open.

She found nothing new, and nothing that tickled her suspicions on this third scouting of the area, not that she'd expected to. Mr. Ward's presence made concentrating a bit more difficult, but she told herself anyone's presence would. And that she had made a conscious decision to think of him as Mr. Ward had everything to do with protocol and nothing to do with the odd effect he had on her.

The rain—evidence-destroying stuff, although she doubted there was any more to find here—started again. Absently she flipped up the hood on her jacket as she turned around to look back toward where Mr. Lowry had said he'd been standing.

"Ray said he wished he could pin it down better than 'past the dumpster,'" Mr. Ward said.

"Especially since dumpsters can be moved."

He nodded. "Takes some doing, though."

"Yes. They tend to be left alone as long as they're not in the way of something."

"Or…you need to move it for other reasons?"

She turned to look at him. He seemed unbothered by the rain, or that his hair was getting wet. That seemed significant somehow. The return of the rain clouds had also shifted the color of his eyes, to where they were more green than anything now.

She had to think for a second to formulate a response, and yet again chastised herself for getting…distracted. "Like to hide or retrieve something? Yes."

"Maybe those scrapes on the asphalt are from that, not a delivery cart."

That made sense. "And that hat was the tiniest bit under the wheel it was hidden by, so it's possible the owner tried to get to it and ended up pinning it down."

"And decided to cut his losses?"

"If he had a kidnap victim to control, he might not have had any choice."

She gave the area a final glance, grimaced in frustration as the rain got even heavier. Then she looked at him again. His hair was soaked now, longer strands falling down over his forehead, the rest clinging to his head. It looked like he'd just gotten out of the shower.

Whoa. Do not *go there, girl.*

"You need to get out of the rain. And so do I. I want to keep an eye on the place for a while, just to see if anybody comes or goes, but I'll find a drier place."

"Where are you parked?"

"Down by the post office."

He blinked. "That's a ways."

"It's an 'oh, look, an undercover cop' car, so I kept my distance just in case."

One corner of his mouth lifted in that rather endearing smile. He nodded toward the street. "I'm parked right there, if you want immediate shelter. And it's a good spot for seeing the back of the building, if you're assuming nobody connected to this would go to the front door."

She hesitated. Then a trickle of water found its way past her ear and down the back of her neck. "Thanks," she said, meaning it even as she contemplated the wisdom of being in the same vehicle with this guy. "But you have to promise you'll stay put if something happens."

He let out a low chuckle. "I'm no hero. You're the one with the gun and the badge."

Many would dispute that first assessment with him, especially those who had been caught up in Witner's schemes. But he clearly didn't see himself that way. *Part of his charm.*

And again she had to divert her own thoughts.

He led her over to an SUV she'd seen before. Once they were inside, he glanced at her.

"This is Ray's," he said simply. "I…don't own a car anymore."

She studied him as he reached back to a small stack of towels on the back seat. Wondered what kind of financial mess his honesty and sense of justice had left him in. He straightened and handed her a towel.

"It's clean, honest. We keep them in here for Woof, but he hasn't used these yet."

She smiled at him. "Either way, it's better than dripping. And I have no aversion to a little dog hair."

"You have a dog?"

"No, sadly." She wiped up most of the rain, then refolded the towel. "I grew up with them, and I'd love to, but…apartment, sometimes crazy hours. It wouldn't be fair."

He nodded. "I wasn't allowed one as a kid. Until I started taking care of Woof, I never realized how much company they could be."

Interesting way to put it. *Wasn't allowed one.* Her parents hadn't been thrilled at the idea, either, but she'd pleaded, and they'd given in and found they adored the puppy they'd adopted from a neighbor's unexpected litter. Carly had wanted to take all of them, but they'd managed to curb that. Barely.

He'd used his towel on his hair, and it was now a damp mass that all seemed to kick forward in a way she liked. Maybe too much.

Dogs. Stick to the dogs.

"It's a good thing you're doing. Ray clearly loves that dog, and it would slow down his recovery if he was worried about him all the time."

"I'd do anything for Ray," he said simply. "But it's helping me out, too, staying there."

It was sad that it was remarkable to meet someone so honest, and someone who, when they said something like that, you were utterly certain they meant it completely and would follow through. Whatever his parents had been or not been, he'd clearly managed to become the kind of man you couldn't not admire.

She glanced down the alley again; all quiet.

"Going to get a dog of your own now?" she asked rather hastily, wary of where her mind kept going.

One corner of his mouth turned down in a wry expression. "Life's a little too in flux at the moment."

"I can only imagine." She didn't really have to imagine because she knew that he'd lost a pretty cushy life. And that he could have kept it, simply by keeping his mouth shut. He shifted uncomfortably, and she saw one finger was tapping against the steering wheel as he watched the alley. "Do you regret doing what you did?"

"What I regret," he said flatly, "is ever believing any of it was real."

"From what I've seen, read and been told, Witner was very, very good. A lot of supposedly brilliant people were sucked in by him. Don't blame yourself."

He looked at her then, gave her that wry smile again. "At least I never claimed to be brilliant." Then his expression changed again. "About the hat…" he began.

"Nothing yet," she said. "Since we don't have a case to match it up to, and we can't even be positive it's connected, the lab isn't in a hurry."

"I appreciate you coming back out here," he said.

"My job," she answered.

"But you don't have much to go on."

"No. But I'll keep checking the missing persons reports, for anything in the area. But a male Caucasian maybe a kid but anywhere under forty in jeans and a blue shirt doesn't narrow the victim pool down much."

He let out a breath. "I know. And a big guy in a hoodie isn't much help, either."

His finger was tapping again as he looked back toward the alley, where another delivery truck had pulled in, this time behind the video game store. Carly watched the driver, a young female in the company uniform carrying a couple of boxes, go in the back door.

"These Foxworth people… I read some stuff. They're for real?"

The abrupt question came out of the blue as he watched the truck. "Yes, they are," she answered. "Brett swears by them." Then her mouth quirked. "Their dog, I'm not so sure about. Like whether he's really a dog or some sort of disguised alien with a nose for bad guys."

He looked at her then, and that slight grin did the same damned thing it had done before, made her insides take a tumble. And brought back the recurring memory of what Cutter had done, maneuvering so that she'd ended up sitting next to the endearing Mr. Ward in the back seat of the Foxworth SUV.

She looked away quickly, back toward the delivery truck. She was not going to start thinking that way. It had been merely a whim on the dog's part, that change from the wayback to the back seat. He probably just wasn't used to having people back there. That was all it was.

She was certain that was all it was.

Chapter 10

"So, what did you do before all this?"

Parker took the chance, now that her head was turned again, to study her profile. Yep, it was as nice as the rest, with that cute nose and delicate jawline. But the unexpected question and the way she'd so quickly looked away from him warned him he'd probably let too much of what he was feeling show.

You've got no business even thinking that way. Your life's a disaster.

"I was in construction. Where I should have stayed," he added, unable to quite keep the bitter note out of his voice.

"Everything's clear in retrospect," she said simply.

"Yeah," he muttered. "And everything was clear when I had a hammer in my hand. Simple."

"Satisfying?"

That surprised him. And when he glanced at her he saw she was looking at him again. "Yes. Yes, it was. Less… glamorous, less mover and shaker, but definitely more satisfying."

Something in her expression shifted, but she only said, "That says a lot about you."

"Yeah, I know. Says I'm a simpleton."

"I did not say that," she said with some emphasis. "You do not think or act or speak like a fool, Mr. Ward. And I've already told you what I think of what you did. I might add that *simple* can also mean down-to-earth, straightforward and unpretentious, and those are qualities to be admired, not looked down upon."

He stared at her. Swallowed. "Wow. Nice speech."

She held his gaze. "My late father was a truck driver who put taking care of his family above all else, and I get very, very tired of the people who think they're so much better than those who do an honest day's work for a living because they work in some fancy office in a high-rise or some ritzy campus or government office somewhere."

He wondered, for a moment, what it must have been like, to have had a father like that. He quashed a pang of envy and focused instead on the result. "He clearly did a great job." She smiled at that. "And your mom?"

"Well, she doesn't approve of my job choice. It makes her worry. But other than that, she's great."

"It would be tough, being the parent of someone in law enforcement."

Something shifted in her gaze, made him wonder what she was thinking. But half the time he was with her, he was wondering that. But "Better here than in the city" was all she said.

His mouth quirked at that. "I'm starting to think that's true in a lot of ways."

She sat silently for a while. He noticed that she wasn't just watching the alley, though. She looked around and occasionally watched the rearview mirror for a while. He wondered what it must be like, a life spent always on watch, trained to see what others overlooked. What they could safely overlook because there were those like Detective Carly Devon around to look out for them.

Eventually the downpour began to lessen to just steady rain, then gradually fade until it was down to a mere drizzle. He wondered how long she'd stick this out. She must have other cases to work, solid ones. Other things to do besides sitting here with him, staring at a nearly empty alley.

"I wonder," she said, "if we're dealing with something slightly different. Maybe the timeline's off. Maybe what Ray saw was an escape attempt. Or a previously reported runaway or missing person who's still tangled up in something, or maybe a street kid who got into a mess."

She'd clearly not been sitting here idly. And despite the subject matter, he almost smiled; she was taking Ray's report with utter seriousness, and that warmed him more than he ever would have expected. Then his brow furrowed as he thought about what she'd said.

"Are there a lot of street kids around here now?" There hadn't been when he'd lived here, but that had been over a decade ago.

"Only those smart enough to realize it's often safer in a smaller town."

"But wouldn't they stand out more, in a place that doesn't have many?"

She turned to look at him then, and she was smiling. And, damn it, he was still reacting, like it was some gut-level thing he couldn't control. Maybe it was.

"Life's a trade-off, for a lot of people." Then her expression changed, became more serious. But it was tinged with something that made his chest constrict. "But then, you know that better than most."

Admiration. She really meant what she'd said, about what he'd done. He had no words for how that made him feel. And he had to look away before he did or said something utterly stupid. He looked back down the alley, trying to focus on why they were here.

He thought about what she'd said, about street kids or some previously reported runaway. Then the driver came back out of the video game store and got back on her truck. A moment later the alley was empty again. And Parker frowned as something occurred to him. He didn't realize he'd made an audible sound until she spoke.

"What?" she asked.

"Nothing. Just a crazy thought."

"We're down to crazy thoughts here," she pointed out, and when he turned to look at her, she was smiling. That sweet, encouraging smile that made him think of doing whatever it took to impress her.

"I just… I used to go in there, when I was into gaming for a while."

"And?"

"And sometimes, people would get really, really wound up about stuff. A couple of times I heard about somebody hunting down someone they'd been playing against in real life."

Her gaze narrowed instantly. She looked back toward the store. "Now, that is an angle that didn't occur to me."

"Told you it was crazy."

"Like a fox," she said. "And it's something more to actually check on. Now that the rain's letting up a bit."

He smiled at the admission that she'd been as restless as he about just sitting here. Not that he'd minded sitting here with her. In fact, it had been the most pleasant time he'd spent with a woman in recent memory.

"I wonder if Mr. Sutter still owns the place? I got along okay with him. But that was a long time ago."

"How long?"

"Since I was into games? It was only from when I was twelve to about fifteen."

"So, what, five years ago?"

He blinked. He was used to people thinking he was younger than he was, but really... "You think I'm only twenty?" Then he caught the glint in those vivid blue eyes. "You set me up."

"Guilty," she said easily, but with another one of those killer smiles.

He tried to scowl at her and failed utterly. She'd played it perfectly, as if she'd guessed it bugged him. Or—it hit him with a jolt—as if she wanted to find out how old he was without really asking.

"Try fifteen years ago." She looked genuinely surprised now. "Yeah, yeah, I know. I look like a kid. It's a pain."

"Ten years from now it'll be a blessing," she said.

"Maybe." Then his brow furrowed. "But I could use it, right now. If it's still the same, I could go in, blend in a little, maybe see if anything weird has happened or if any regulars have dropped out of sight."

"Regulars?"

"He's got—or at least he had—a nice setup in the back, with a big screen and test consoles, so people could try out games. People were always coming in to try the latest greatest version of whatever had just been released."

"I was thinking of just going in and asking," she said, rather dryly.

He looked at her rather intently. "Lots of teenage guys in there, usually. No way they wouldn't talk to a woman who looks like you."

She drew back slightly. And was staring at him. Had he offended her with that simple truth? Surely she knew the effect she had. He scrambled for the rest of what he'd been going to say.

"But they'd also be tempted to brag, claim to know things they don't."

"That's an astute observation," she said. "I've dealt with enough juvenile boys to know about the temptation to brag, especially around their peers."

He shrugged, feeling a little relieved. "I can only claim to have been one."

"And I'll bet you were adorable."

She said it with an utterly straight face, and he had no idea how to take it.

She was losing it. She needed some time to talk some sense into herself. She was sitting here trading compliments with a guy she'd known for all of three days. She just didn't do that.

And he was connected to a case, a big no-no. Maybe. The case, not the no-no.

But he was also the first guy in longer than she cared to admit who made her want to...proceed.

She thought about what he'd said, and the derisive tone of his voice when he'd said "mover and shaker." Exactly what James had wanted to be. Was that what she was reacting to? Sure, he was cute—she'd meant that "adorable," because he still was, in a very grown-up way—but she ran into lots of good-looking guys. Maybe it was just her admiration for the stand he'd taken that was messing up her mind. Maybe she was mistaking that for something else.

"You must be glad the Witner case is over."

"Very." He grimaced. "Living under guard for a year was no fun."

"At least they kept you safe."

"Sometimes it felt like I was in jail as much as Witner was. It was just a nicer one. I'd much rather have just come here until the trial."

"But you had to be protected. Witner wasn't going to go down easy. You had to be somewhere safe. And you used to live here, so his associates could have found you."

"Fourteen years ago," he said. "I've been on the other side ever since." She registered the local appellation for the city side of Puget Sound. "Witner would never believe anybody would voluntarily go back to Podunk, as he called it. Besides," he added, "I'd trust Ray more than any hired security, if anybody had come after me."

That startled her. "Ray?"

"He's an Army vet. He's got a ton of medals, and half of them are shooting medals." He gave her a wry smile. "But I did officially announce to everyone I could that I'd never, ever commit suicide."

So he'd done it facing reality. He'd known exactly what he was risking.

That made her admire him even more.

Chapter 11

Parker's venture into the video game store accomplished nothing but to catapult him back to the days when this had been his refuge, when he couldn't hide out at Ray's. The game systems in the test area in the back were new, and the flat screen was bigger, but the rest of the place had the same vibe it had always had.

Mr. Sutter, on the other hand, was looking a bit older, hair a little grayer, and a little thinner. But he seemed just as enthusiastic as he'd ever been, and to Parker's surprise, he recognized him. And seemed quite willing to chat.

"I worried about you, kid, after you vanished. Knew your home life wasn't the best."

Parker was surprised and touched. "It got better," he said, thinking of Ray. "But thanks for even thinking about me." He decided he'd never get a better way in. "Anybody else vanish lately?"

Sutter laughed. "Not lately. Got a team of regulars, and they don't seem to change much."

"Nobody getting a little too invested in winning? Maybe getting into fights over it?"

Sutter frowned. "No more so than usual."

Eventually he went over to the game test area, and although he had to earn his way in by showing he at least had an idea what he was doing, Mr. Sutter showing them his name on the all-time-high scores plaque on the wall helped that along. But nobody knew anything about anyone suddenly disappearing. And all he managed to do was feel old. And rusty.

Then he heard the front door open, and one of the boys made a sound he thought would have been a whistle if the kid could have gotten it out. And he wasn't in the least surprised when he looked over and saw Carly had come in.

He left the gaming crew to the blistering lecture from the two females among them and walked toward her. She looked around and smiled when she spotted him, and changed course. He heard the speculative whispers from the gamers—male and female this time—and felt a tug of extremely juvenile and very male satisfaction. Sort of like that bragging he'd thought of earlier. True, none of what they were speculating was true, or likely to ever be, but they didn't have to know that, did they?

"Nothing," he said quietly. "Nobody that stopped turning up suddenly, and no new people hanging around in the last week." He grimaced. "A stupid idea anyway."

"It was not," she said firmly. "It was an excellent idea, and I never thought of it."

He felt a little embarrassed when, as he paused to thank Mr. Sutter, the man eyed Carly appreciatively, then raised a brow at him as he said, "You went and grew up, didn't you? With good taste, too."

He opened his mouth to explain it wasn't like that, but Carly spoke first. "Thank you," she said with a smile.

"Sorry about that," he said to her once they were back outside.

"He seems nice."

Parker glanced back at the store. "He is." *And has good taste, too.* "He said he worried about me. Back then."

"You sound surprised."

"I am. I had no idea," he said, with no small amount of wonder. She gave him a considering look, and he wondered what she was thinking. Hell, he was always wondering what she was thinking.

But when she spoke again it was back to business, and he told himself he should be glad they'd gotten off the personal before he said something even more stupid.

"While you were in there, I checked for any earlier missing persons reports. Only one I found in the last month was an eleven-year-old female, blonde and only four feet tall. Not likely to be mistaken for male unless they've done a complete makeover on her."

Eleven was awfully young. He frowned, feeling unsettled as horror stories tumbled through his head. "She's still missing?"

"They suspect it's a parental abduction, but yes."

"I guess that's a little better than other possibilities. At least she'd be with someone who wanted her." He frowned. "Unless the one parent took her to slap at the other."

She gave him an odd look then. "It happens," she said.

He shrugged, glanced at his watch and realized just how long he'd been gone. "I need to get back and check on Woof, then get him over to see Ray. Want that ride to your car?"

"No, thanks. I'll walk it, now that the rain's let up. I need to think about this some more."

He watched her go, thought about that missing little girl and wondered how a woman with such an obviously kind heart survived doing the work she did.

* * *

Carly wasn't sure why she gave in to the urge, but when she was back in her plain-wrap detective vehicle, she headed back to the rehab center. Ray's doctor was just coming out of his room, and to her surprise, she recognized him as the orthopedist who often worked with the department when someone was injured on duty. Including Lieutenant Carter when she'd broken her ankle. But then she remembered the man often worked with veterans, and Parker had said Ray had been in the Army.

"Detective Devon, isn't it?" the man said before she even spoke. "I gather you're the 'lovely young lady detective' Ray was talking about?"

She laughed. "How is he?"

"He's doing well. Stubborn enough I think he'll be out of here sooner than I thought."

"But later than he wants, I'm guessing?"

Dr. Masters smiled. "You already know him, I see."

"I admire him. He doesn't quit."

"No, he does not."

"And," she said carefully, "he seems razor-sharp mentally, too."

"He is." He gave her a nod. "He told me what he saw. And that you were at least one who took him seriously."

"I did. Do you?"

He nodded. "I believe he saw what he saw."

"Yes. It's the interpretation I'm trying to resolve."

He had another appointment, so they left it at that, and she went on to see Ray, still not quite sure why. But he greeted her with a wide smile that she decided was reason enough. And when she told him where she'd found Parker, watching the alley, that smile widened.

"I knew I could count on that boy."

"He thinks the world of you," she said, smiling back at him.

"That kid saved me," he said, and there was nothing of the gruff exterior in his expression or his voice. "When my wife died, when everyone else only offered platitudes, that boy took a month off and moved in with me. He made me stay active when all I wanted to do was curl up and cry. He made me eat, sleep, and even though he loved her, too, he took care of all the crap that would have broken my heart all over again. Who the hell knew you'd need a dozen copies of a damned death certificate?"

Emotion was rising in the old man's voice, and Carly felt a tangle of feelings ranging from sympathy for his loss to acknowledging Ray had apparently had that rarest of things, true love, to admiration—again—for what Parker Ward had done.

"All that makes it even harder, doesn't it? I'm glad he was there for you. And he feels the same about you."

Ray snorted, and a bit of the gruffness was back. "That kid needed somebody to be on his side."

"I get the feeling I'm glad not to know his parents."

Ray studied her for a moment. She wasn't sure what he was looking for, but apparently he found it, because he said, "His parents had never intended to have kids. Ask me, they were too selfish. Ironic, huh? We wanted children and couldn't. They never did and got one by accident. But when she got pregnant, he was at a place in his career where the image of a family man would help, so they kept him. And that's all it was. An image. Not real."

She held the older man's steady gaze as she said softly, "Then it's a very good thing he found his real family next door, with you and your wife."

He gave her a smile then, approving, but tinged with the lingering sadness of his loss. "I couldn't be prouder of him even if he was my own. And Laura loved him as if he were."

"I know." She smiled back. "And so does he."

Again he studied her for a moment before saying, back to his gruff tone, "Do you know what he did? That swindler case?" She nodded. "Heroic, if you ask me."

"I agree. And then some."

There was approval in his gaze again, and it warmed her all over again. "Too bad those parents of his don't see it that way. They called him a fool and a failure, because he was on easy street and blew it all up for reasons they don't understand."

Anger sparked in her, anger at people she'd never even met. And hopefully never would. "Reasons like honesty, integrity, honor and seeing past his own interests?"

Again Ray smiled and nodded approvingly. But this time there was something else in his steady gaze, something more…speculative?

A bark from outside drew her attention. "Sounds like my mutt," Ray said.

"He said he was going to get him."

He gave her yet another considering look. "Not many who'd do that for an old man."

She gave an exaggerated look around the room. "Is there an old man here somewhere?"

Ray laughed. "You'll do, Detective. You'll do."

When the attendant appeared in the doorway, Carly gave him a smile and said, "I'll go out with him, if that's all right?"

The woman smiled. "From what Dr. Masters said, he couldn't be safer."

"You know Doc Masters?" Ray asked as she helped him settle the sling to support his arm after the examination that had made his shoulder a bit sore.

"He's our go-to at the sheriff's office for injuries like yours. And," she added with a grin at him, "he says you'll be out of here sooner than he expected."

"Hallelujah," Ray muttered.

They headed outside, and Carly was startled to see not just Parker—his first name seemed to be stuck in her head now—and Woof, but the newly arrived Foxworths and Cutter.

Chapter 12

"Let me guess," Carly said with a wry smile and a nod at Cutter, who Parker had already decided looked rather smugly satisfied. "He made you come?"

"He did," the woman with Quinn Foxworth said cheerfully. Parker guessed she must be the wife who had recently returned home. And judging by the happy glow on her face and the smile on her husband's, he could guess how they'd been getting reacquainted. "Quinn explained everything on the way."

Carly turned to Ray and said, "Ray, these are the Foxworths, Hayley and Quinn." Parker liked the way she introduced them to Ray first, before adding with a look at the other woman, "And, Hayley, this is Parker Ward."

Ray's gaze had sharpened at the introduction. "So. You're those Foxworths, huh? The ones who took down that slimy governor of ours last year?"

"We only helped," Quinn said. "Her colleague," he said with a nod at Carly, "Brett Dunbar did the heavy lifting."

"Well, and Cutter," Hayley added with a grin that lit eyes that reminded Parker of the fresh green of a spring meadow. That made Ray smile. Then Hayley looked at Carly. "Working late?"

Parker saw her glance at her watch, a big chronograph-style thing that made her wrist seem practically delicate. "Technically, I've been off duty for twenty minutes."

"You're about as on the clock as Brett, when you're on a case," Quinn said, and there was no mistaking the approval in his tone.

Carly smiled, as if she'd heard it, too. "Where do you think I learned it?"

"Anything new?" Hayley asked. "Quinn said there was no missing person report yet?"

Carly shook her head. "Not yet. So," she added with a regretful glance at Ray, "there's only so much I can do."

"Officially," Parker said, remembering what she'd told him when she'd found him watching the alley.

"You know, we're fairly good at unofficially poking around," Quinn said neutrally.

Carly looked at the other man, brows raised. "Foxworth really wants into this?"

"Cutter seems to have decided we already are," Quinn said, and Parker noticed he didn't even crack a smile; it was not a joke. "I know the resources you can devote to this are limited, until you have a report to justify it. But ours aren't."

Judging by what he'd read when he'd done that bit of research on the Foxworth Foundation, Parker could only imagine what resources they had to call upon.

"And," Hayley added with a warm smile at Ray, "we're always ready to help a neighbor."

Ray practically blossomed at either the words or the warmth, and in that instant Parker decided he really liked these people. All of them.

"Come by the office," Quinn suggested. "We have a

party to drop in at tonight, but I'll have Liam—he's our resident tech guy," he explained with a glance at Ray and Parker, "—start digging, and if we don't come up with anything, we'll contact HQ in St. Louis and turn Ty lose on it. If he can't find it, it's not there to be found."

"All right," Carly said.

"You better go with them, boy," Ray said to Parker. "You can tell 'em I'm not a crazy old man."

"He's welcome," Quinn said, but then, with a steady look at Ray, added, "but I would never believe you're a crazy old man. Sir."

There was enough emphasis on that last word that Ray straightened. He studied the other man for a moment before saying, "You're a vet, aren't you?"

"Second Ranger Battalion."

Ray nodded in satisfaction. "You've got the look. Me, I was just a grunt. The Big Red One."

"Nothing *just* about the Fighting First."

Ray smiled widely. Then his gaze shifted to Parker, who had been watching the exchange with both pride in his mentor and gratitude for the respect Quinn Foxworth was showing him. "You go with them, boy. They'll do this right."

And so he found himself back in Ray's car, along with Woof, and following the Foxworth SUV and Detective Devon's unmarked unit back toward Redwood Cove. They went through the little town—although Ray had always joked it was barely a village, and that was what he liked about it—and made a turn at the newest of its two stoplights.

If he hadn't been following them, he probably wouldn't have found the place on his first try even if he'd had the address. There was no signage, and it was almost completely masked from the road by the surrounding stand of evergreens. Carly obviously knew where it was, however, since her brake lights came on in the same instant as the Foxworths', as they slowed to make the turn onto a long, fairly narrow drive that curved through the thick trees.

They came out into a gravel parking area in front of a three-story building painted the same green as the trees. Off to one side was another building that looked as if it were storage or a warehouse of some sort. And in between was…a helicopter pad? It really was, he saw as he pulled up to park. Complete with a wind sock, which was barely moving now that the storm had moved on.

Talk about resources…

He opened the door and got out, still scanning the area. It looked as if there was a large clearing behind the green building, and then the trees began again, thick and looking almost impenetrable.

Quinn had walked over to him, and he couldn't resist asking, "A helicopter pad?"

"Yep. She's in the warehouse." Quinn grinned.

"Igor, you mean?" Hayley said as she came up beside them. Quinn rolled his eyes, and his wife laughed. "Liam named it. After the guy who practically invented helicopters, Igor Sikorsky."

Parker couldn't help smiling back at her. "If you don't count da Vinci."

"Exactly. Guess what he named Quinn's pet airplane?"

A plane, too? Foxworth was obviously quite an organization. But then, it would take quite an organization to do some of the things they'd done. He thought for a moment about her question. "Um… Wilbur or Orville?"

She laughed delightedly. "Wilbur it is."

"Can we dispense with Liam's habit of naming mechanical objects?" Quinn said rather sourly. Then he nodded at Woof, who was looking anxiously out the window of the back seat. "Let him out. He and Cutter can play out back while we figure out what we've got."

"He plays?" Parker asked wryly as he released Woof and the canine duo ran toward the building. "Like a normal dog?"

Quinn smiled. "When he's not running this place or ordering us around, yes. It's the only thing that keeps us thinking he's really a dog and not some alien being trapped in a dog body."

Parker laughed as he glanced at the dogs in time to see Cutter reach the front door, rear up on his hind legs and bat at a square button beside the door handle. His laugh stopped when he saw the door swing open on its own and the two animals disappeared inside.

"Whoa."

"Like I said," Quinn said with a grin. And Parker thought again that, despite his rather intimidating demeanor, he could really get to like this guy.

Which reminded him of something, and as they walked into the building, he said, "Thank you, for how you were with Ray. Respectful, I mean."

"He deserves it." Quinn eyed him for a moment. "And that you feel that way says a lot about you."

Parker let out a breath and spoke the truth once more. "He saved me. Then and now."

"Funny," Carly said from behind him. "He said the same thing about you."

His gaze shot to her face, and the warmth of her smile and the shine of approval in her blue eyes made him feel almost deserving again. Crazy, he'd felt better around these people—and their dog—than he had around anyone but Ray in months.

Quinn hung his keys on a hook near the door. The entry was tiled, with a row of coat hooks on one wall, and on the floor a basket full of folded towels he guessed were for drying off, either person or dog. Under the coat hooks Parker spotted a small drain and suspected the floor was slanted there just enough to channel any runoff. The place looked solidly built. Built to last. The kind of work he'd once done, before he let his ego and his parents' expectations send him on that twisted road.

The rest of the place surprised him. He'd expected an office-style building, but instead it was as if he'd walked into the welcoming living room of a spacious, open-concept home. There was a large gas fireplace on one wall, a flat screen above it, and couches and chairs arranged facing those, with a large square coffee table in between. In one back corner, he could see a compact, modern kitchen, and in the other, two doors, one to a bathroom that was open, another adjacent to that that was closed.

Cutter appeared for all the world to be showing Woof around, leading the visiting dog to the water bowl in the kitchen and the basket of tennis balls by what was apparently a door out onto a covered patio and access to the big meadow out back. But then Cutter's head came up sharply, and he let out a short, staccato pair of barks.

"Yes," Hayley said to the animal, "he's here." Parker turned to look at her, and she smiled. "He's got different barks for everyone. That's Liam's. He's upstairs."

He'd noticed the stairway in the back, and as he looked, a man came trotting down. He looked young, but with the wariness of personal experience, he didn't assume the man with sandy-blond hair cut shorter on the sides was as young as he looked. Parker guessed he must be the object-naming tech guy they'd talked about. Cutter trotted over to greet him, tail up and wagging, so obviously he was familiar.

"Well, hi there, you rascal," the man said as he scratched behind the dog's right ear, and Parker thought he heard a bit of a drawl in his voice. "You found us a Foxworthy one, huh?"

"Foxworthy?" Parker asked.

Quinn's mouth quirked. "Liam's got a Texas way with words." Then, as the newcomer approached, he introduced him. "Parker Ward, Liam Burnett."

They shook hands. Then Liam looked at Carly. As if any man breathing could stop himself from looking at her.

"Detective," Liam said with a nod.

"How's Ria?" she asked, bringing out a wide grin on the man's face.

"She's great," he said. He glanced at Parker. "My lady. We met on a case Detective Devon helped on, with some kids in a bad situation."

A murderous politician. Potential kidnapping. Kids in a bad situation. Foxworthy?

In the right, Quinn had said. So it wasn't just crimes people got away with?

"What, exactly," Parker asked as they walked into the seating area and Hayley walked over and turned on the fire, "is your criteria?" He wondered what the official version of their mission was.

"What you did would qualify," Liam drawled, looking at him steadily. "That Witner needed taking down. Man thinks he glows when he walks."

Parker blinked. Smiled at the description.

"Well, that fits," the detective said with a grin.

And Parker became aware once more what an effort it was to keep thinking of her that way. As he thought it he started to sit in one of the upholstered chairs, but the Foxworth dog somehow got in his way, bumping hard against his legs, and he ended up on the couch facing the fire. Next to the woman he was trying so hard not to think about. Thankfully not too close, but still.

When he looked up again, he saw Quinn and Hayley exchanging a rather pointed glance, and Liam Burnett was grinning again.

"Hey, Mr. Poker Face," Quinn said dryly, "let those two outside before you head back up to your toys."

The man clearly took no offense and did as asked. Ordered? Yeah, that, too.

When they were settled, Quinn looked at Parker and said, "Liam was right. You did the right thing no matter how hard it was, and that's what Foxworth is all about."

"So you what, just find things and volunteer to help?"

"Used to," Quinn said with a wry smile. "Now we just try to keep up with what Cutter brings us."

Parker drew back slightly. "I…thought you were kidding about that."

"Nope," Hayley said cheerfully. "He keeps us quite busy. If we could duplicate him, every branch of Foxworth would have a dog like him."

"Every branch?"

"We're up to five now. Have most of the country covered, generally," Quinn said.

"And they all do what you do?" Quinn nodded. "For free? How the heck do you manage that?"

Quinn smiled, and Parker heard Hayley laugh. "In part because while we don't take money from the people we help, we do ask them for help down the line, for someone else. And it doesn't hurt that we have a financial genius at the helm," she said. She glanced at her husband. "Has she ever made an investment that didn't pay off a hundredfold?"

"Once," Quinn said. "When she was nineteen."

Parker blinked at that. But before he could think of a thing to say, Quinn had turned back to him, focused now with an intensity that was a bit unnerving.

"Elizabeth Reed sends her best and asked if there was anything she could do."

Parker went still as he mentioned the name of the DA who'd handled the Witner case. "I... You talked to her?"

"We've had dealings before. With several of the people involved on your side of that mess."

"That's...quite a network you've got."

"It's the foundation of our foundation," Liam said brightly as he came back from shepherding the dogs outside to play.

"You were just waiting for that opening, weren't you?" Hayley said with a grin.

"Yep," Liam admitted easily.

"They'll be okay out there?" Parker asked.

Liam, who had started toward the stairs, turned back to look at Parker. "Cutter won't let him wander off. There's lots of adventuring to do out there. He'll be tired enough to snore tonight."

Then he was gone, back upstairs to the digging Quinn had mentioned, Parker guessed. And Parker sighed, still a little boggled at the faith these people had in a dog. And cringing anew at the idea of something happening to Ray's beloved companion. At the way that would betray Ray's trust.

He swallowed tightly. He'd sometimes wondered what else life could possibly take away from him.

Don't even ask. Don't tempt life to show you.

Because the only thing he had left to lose was Ray, and that would already happen far too soon, simply by the numbers.

And he didn't think he could take it when it did.

Chapter 13

Parker still looked a bit wary, as if he couldn't quite believe what was happening. As if he couldn't quite believe he had help. And Carly wondered how many people he'd thought were friends had turned on him. Anyone who had known what was going on with Witner's scheme and done nothing, she guessed.

"DA Reed also mentioned," Quinn said, "that you'd surrendered all your assets, voluntarily, before the court even froze everything connected to the case."

"I didn't want that money."

"What did you think they should do with it, then?" Carly asked, curious to see what he'd say.

He didn't look up, but said without hesitation, in the tone of someone who'd made the decision long ago, "Give it back to the people who lost it. I know it's nothing compared to the total he swindled people out of, but it's something."

"It is," Carly said quietly. She was a little surprised—or maybe amazed—that he'd noticed anything outside of his own misery. But then thought she shouldn't be, not after she'd seen how he took care of Ray amid that misery. But even with his life in chaos, he cared about those who had been victimized. Parker Ward was the real deal.

She glanced at Quinn, who nodded, as if he'd expected nothing less. "Especially since your own world crumbled along with theirs, in essence," he said.

Parker grimaced. "Except I was on the wrong side."

"How'd you end up in that position?" Parker winced at Quinn's question. "Not judging, just curious. I always like to know how scum like Witner pull it off. Besides knowing what politicians to make big donations to."

Parker let out a long breath, and for a moment Carly thought he wouldn't answer. And wasn't sure she'd blame him if he didn't. But then he said, "It's a long, pitiful story. And if I tell you—" he looked up at Quinn then "—you may want to change your mind about helping."

Quinn looked steadily at Parker, and Carly remembered Brett saying he would not ever want to have to face down this man. She understood why, now. "The only time we pull out once we've committed," Quinn said evenly, "is if we learn someone has lied to us. Have you?"

Parker held his gaze, didn't look away. "No. Sir. I have not. Nor has Ray."

"I didn't think so," Hayley said quietly.

She saw Parker draw in a deep breath. "I fell for his pitch when he said my not having a college degree didn't matter, he wanted a guy like me." He grimaced. "He was offering things I never imagined I'd have. And I bought it, hook, line and sinker."

"He's very, very smooth," Carly said, the undertone of pain in his voice tugging at her in a way that made her chest tighten.

"And I was very stupid," he said, glancing at her for a moment before he went back to Quinn. "Because it took me a long time to realize he was counting on that. Me being stupid, I mean."

Carly's eyebrows lowered. "But you're not. You're far, far from stupid."

A faint smile curved his lips for a moment, but it faded quickly. And then Quinn said quietly, "I think he means that Witner assumed he was, because of that lack of degree. From what I've read, he's the type."

She saw Parker's jaw clench for a moment. Wondered if her presence was making this harder for him, then chastised herself. *Because it's all about you, Carly, right?* She purposefully made her voice light, teasing.

"I get it. He wanted that innocent, all-American-boy face of yours. I'll bet you get away with a lot because of that."

Parker blinked. Stared at her. She gave him a crooked smile and a teasing wink. And suddenly the tension in him seemed to ebb. And when he did speak again, his voice sounded, if not relaxed, at least less on edge.

"I think he also assumed I'd look the other way because I'd never have been where he put me without him."

"A lot of people would have," Hayley pointed out.

"I couldn't," Parker said, his voice and gaze lowering as he gave a slow shake of his head. "Not once I realized how many people were going to get really hurt. Not just the rich ones, but people who'd put their life savings, their retirement funds, into it. I kept thinking, what if it was Ray? And I couldn't."

"Thank you," Carly said softly.

He looked up at her again. "I'm glad your mom's friend got out early."

"Me, too. But that's not what I meant. I meant thank you for restoring some of my sometimes shaky faith in the human race."

"Amen," Quinn and Hayley chorused together.

"And contrary to what you said before, that makes you a hero in my book," Carly said firmly.

"Amen again," Quinn said.

Parker looked disconcerted and more than a little uncomfortable. And Carly guessed he was grateful when there was a faint noise from the back door.

"That'll be the furry ones," Hayley said cheerfully.

"No automatic door back there?" Carly asked with a smile.

"Not yet," Quinn said as he got up. "But he's working on convincing us."

Parker stood up abruptly. "I'll let them in. I...need to move."

Quinn nodded. "You can help. I suspect the rain is back, and drying two of them off is going to be an effort."

"Especially Woof," Parker said with a grimace. "He has no concept of wet dog."

Carly laughed, and he shot her a glance that she couldn't categorize. The two men headed over to the alcove leading outside to the patio. The moment the door opened, Carly heard the rain and knew Quinn had been right. There was a second basket of towels there, and the two started on the thoroughly drenched animals.

She looked back at Hayley, remembering what Brett had told her when he'd first met the woman, that she was one of the best assessors of people he'd ever encountered. So it would be foolish not to take advantage of that, wouldn't it?

"What's your take on him?" Carly asked with a nod toward Parker.

"I think he's exactly what he presents as. A good guy who innocently got sucked into something crooked, and who blew the whistle on it as soon as he realized. You?"

Carly nodded. "The way he looks out for Ray..."

Hayley nodded in turn. "Exactly."

"Ray told me that when his wife died, Parker took a month off work and moved in with him. Did all the nasty stuff that had to be done and took care of him, made him eat, all that."

"That," Hayley said with certainty, "is worth more than any amount of money. Dealing with my mother's death was bad enough. If I hadn't had my friend Amy to help, I wouldn't have made it."

Quinn and Parker came back. Parker sat back where he'd been, giving Carly a glance she would have called almost shy, but decided it just had to be his unease about this whole situation. Quinn stayed on his feet and glanced at his watch. With that silent communication she'd observed tightly connected couples seemed to have, Hayley understood immediately and stood up herself. In almost the same moment, Carly heard Cutter give out a quick series of barks.

Hayley smiled. "Teague's here."

Parker blinked. "You're going to tell me that's his bark?"

"And Laney's, too, now."

Carly smiled. "Brett told me he felt honored when you told him he had his own bark. But he recognizes cars, too?"

"That's what we thought," Quinn said, "until we realized he got the right bark no matter what car the person is driving. But the minute they hit the driveway, we know who's coming. Or if we don't know them."

"How does he manage that?" Parker asked.

"No idea," Hayley said blithely. "He just knows."

Carly shifted her gaze to Quinn, who shrugged. "I've learned to just accept, when it comes to Cutter." Then he looked toward the stairway and called out, "Liam! Teague's here. If you're coming with us, time to roll."

Parker started to stand back up, but Hayley shook her

head. "Stay put. We're still running checks, but we have an engagement party to go to, for a former client. And Liam helped work Tate and Lacy's case, so he's coming, too."

"Is that another Cutter match?" Carly asked wryly.

Hayley smiled. "Absolutely." And she gave Carly a look that told her she hadn't missed Cutter maneuvering her to sit next to Parker in the car, or Parker to sit next to her on the couch.

"Oh, no," she said. "No, no and no."

Hayley's smile became a grin. "That's what they all say."

"Who all?" Parker asked, clearly puzzled by the exchange. But thankfully Liam came down the stairs just then, and at the same time Carly heard the front door open. Cutter trotted over, Woof close behind him. Teague Johnson came in, pulling off his dripping jacket and hanging it on one of the hooks by the door. He greeted Parker and Carly before looking at Liam.

"Check's still running, nothing that looks significant yet," Liam said.

Teague nodded. "I'll monitor it."

"Just don't break my baby."

"Watch it, or I'll do it just to spite you."

The exchange was clearly teasing, almost brotherly, Carly thought. She glanced at Parker and saw he was watching the two men as well, with an odd sort of expression. She remembered what he'd told her about his family and wondered if he was pondering what his life would have been like in a normal family.

And she made a mental note to congratulate Ray the next time she saw him, for having somehow molded this man out of what had to have been a neglected and forlorn kid.

Chapter 14

Parker watched Woof as he worked at enticing Carly to pet him. He envied the blatant ease with which the dog did it. Much as he'd like to try to entice her to pet him, he had neither the nerve nor, at the moment, the right to even try. And watching the two Foxworth men verbally spar, like he would imagine brothers did, had caused a strange sort of feeling in him. Not a wish that he'd had siblings—he wouldn't wish his parents on anyone else—but a sort of curious nostalgia for something that had never been.

He felt a nudge and realized Cutter had come over to him and was sitting practically on his feet. Automatically he reached out to stroke the animal's dark head. He'd meant to ask what kind of dog he was. His coloring, with the black head and shoulders shifting to a reddish brown over his body and plumed tail, was like a police dog he'd seen once. But Cutter's fur was much longer and softer. And—

Okay, that was weird. The moment he'd stroked that fur, he'd felt…better. Calmer. Or at least less stirred up. Just as it had that first time, when Cutter had led him—them—to the Foxworth house. Petting Woof felt good, sometimes even calming, but not like this. He stared down at the dog, who looked up at him with amber-flecked dark eyes. And somehow even that seemed to help.

He heard Carly laugh quietly and looked up to see Woof giving her his best, most charming tongue-lolling, head-tilting look.

"He's a goofball, but a lovable one," he said, able, thanks to Cutter's apparent knack for spreading calm, to say it normally.

"He's a darling." She gave Cutter a sideways glance. "Whereas he is scary."

"I can't argue that, and I've only known him three days."

"Did Quinn or Hayley tell you he's how they met?"

"No," he said, but he could understand that. He was getting the feeling this dog could accomplish pretty much anything he wanted to. It would be a challenge to keep up with him.

"He romped up to Quinn while he was in the middle of moving a witness in a big drug cartel case. And wouldn't leave him."

"And now they're in the middle of this, and I'm not even sure how it happened."

"From what I know, I'd say you can blame him," she said with a nod at Cutter. "Given he brought you to them."

He drew back slightly at that. "Brought me?"

"Isn't that what happened?"

"I was just following Woof."

"Who was following him, right?"

"Well, yes, but…"

"You think a dog who can get someone like Teague Johnson in the car and make him drive to meet you in that alley—not to mention getting the best detective around to go completely off his running route to find the body that ended up taking down a governor—couldn't make that happen?"

"I didn't think about it like that," he admitted.

"That's because you're used to a normal dog. A sweet, lovable, darling dog." With a smile that stirred up those urges again, she leaned forward and planted a kiss on Woof's head. The dog grinned blissfully.

Lucky dog.

"Best detective around, huh? I would have thought that was you." *Oh, subtle, Ward...*

She leaned back and simply looked at him for a moment. He'd never realized how intense blue eyes could be before. "I'm good," she said easily. "I'm focused, and I know the territory I deal with, which is usually kids and families. But Brett is amazing. He's the big-picture guy, and he sees threads and connections unlike anyone I've ever known." She grinned then, and it took his breath away. "Except maybe that guy," she said, pointing to Cutter.

She had him half believing it. And when Cutter dropped his chin down on Parker's knee and looked up at him with those dark eyes, he almost went the rest of the way. He settled on the dog being a very clever, very unique animal, and left it at that before he got really stupid.

"What made you want to do what you do?" he asked. He'd just been grabbing for something to say, but once it was out he found he really wanted to know.

She studied him for a moment again, as if deciding what or how much to say, and he remembered what she'd said about being focused. And it was a bit unsettling to have her focused on him. At least like this, as part of a case.

Don't even think about what it would be like to have her focused on you personally.

"I had a brother," she said finally, and he didn't miss

the tense. "Will was the brain of the family, the one we all expected would run the world someday."

"But it didn't go that way," he said quietly, seeing in her eyes the echo of a pain he guessed would never go away.

"No. He died at sixteen. In a car crash, in a car he'd just stolen."

He winced. Not just at the awful words, but at the way she'd said them. In short bits, as if that was the only way she could get it out. And he knew he'd been right about the pain. And felt oddly privileged that she was telling him.

"Ouch." It was all he could think of to say.

"Yes. He started getting in serious trouble right after our father died. By the time he was fourteen, he'd been in juvie a dozen times, and every cop in town knew him. One of them took an interest, because he could see how smart Will was. And that man tried so damned hard to save him. On duty, off duty, all hours, he tried. And I don't think he's ever forgiven himself that he couldn't."

"So he's what inspired you to go into law enforcement?"

She nodded. "I'd never thought about cops like that before, but watching him try so hard was just…inspiring."

"Do you ever talk to him?"

Unexpectedly, she smiled. "Oh, yes. Often. Because afterward, he came to check on us now and then. Comfort my mom. She's a tough lady—she's a teacher, so just ask any of her students—but dealing with that double loss was devastating. And eventually, that comfort turned into something else. He's my stepdad now. I'll never forget my father. That's why my legal name is Carly Clark Devon. But Dave Devon is my dad, and I'm crazy about him."

Parker blinked and slowly smiled. He hadn't expected that. But it explained her expression when he'd said it must be tough for her mother to have her in law enforcement. "Wow. He must be really proud of you."

"He is," she said, "and I of him. It was a horrible loss, but the best possible thing came out of it. I'm lucky to have him in my life." She spent a moment acceding to Woof's demand for more attention—and he spent it watching her—before she looked back at him again. "And you were lucky to have Ray and his wife next door."

"Yes." His mouth quirked wryly. "The summer after we'd moved to the other side when my father got the job he'd been after, I snuck away, hitchhiked down to the ferry and went back to see Ray. I was there for three days before they noticed I was gone."

Her brows rose. "How old were you?"

"Sixteen. They didn't care, as long as I did my job."

"Your job?"

He shrugged. "Put in an appearance when they needed the image. Like in front of a client who was into the family thing. Pretend I was polite and well-mannered and that they were the best parents in the world. After that, I was on my own."

She stared at him. Then, slowly, she said, "Do not even tell me their names. Because if I ever accidentally came across them I would probably do something unforgivable."

Her expression was so fierce it made him feel... He wasn't sure how it made him feel. Something like when Ray had always defended him, gotten angry on his behalf, but yet different. As if her reaction mattered just as much, but in a very different way.

"It could have been worse," he said. "Not like they hit me or anything."

"Physical abuse isn't the only kind."

And she would know. He'd almost forgotten for a moment what her job was. But that thought made him wonder if she was thinking of him like that, one of her cases, part of her job, even though he was an adult. He didn't like that idea.

"It doesn't matter anymore. They don't matter."

"No, they don't."

The smile she gave him when she said it erased any qualms. He wanted to say something deep, meaningful, but looking into the deep blue of her eyes, he forgot most of the words he knew.

Carly heard Teague coming down the stairs and made herself look away from the man on the couch with her. There was a good foot between them, and she couldn't decide if he was too far away or too close.

She'd sensed his tension earlier, and for the first time seen the Cutter effect firsthand, the way simply petting the dog seemed to calm him. Woof was adorable, and made her go all silly over him, but he didn't quite get the same result; Woof made her want to forget her problems and play, while Cutter seemed to somehow convince people whatever the problem was, it would be all right.

Now you're getting as crazy as they are about that dog.

"Afraid I don't have much news," Teague said as he came in and took a seat in one of the chairs opposite the couch. "I sent what we had on to Ty in St. Louis, at our headquarters. He'll take it to the next level, but we're pretty much done for tonight. Right now, the only thing that turned up was that the building we were looking at, the one with the pry marks, is up for sale."

Almost instantly, Parker asked exactly what she'd been about to ask. "When, do you know?"

Teague smiled. "Yesterday."

"Funny he didn't mention that," she said.

"But not necessarily suspicious," Parker said. "Some people are just more private."

"And some people don't volunteer anything to a cop," she said.

"But it's a blip on the radar, so we'll dig," Teague said.

Carly raised a brow at the man. "Is this the part where Brett says don't think about it too much?"

Teague grinned. "Yep. Look, we know you need more evidence before you go digging, because if you do it it's official. So we do it. And I swear, Ty is the absolute best at not leaving a trail."

She quashed what misgivings she had, knowing Foxworth hadn't built the reputation they had—and earned the trust of the best detective she'd ever known—by making mistakes. And if it would help Parker…

"All right," she said. Then, her mouth quirking, she added, "I have to admit, nearly limitless resources are not something I'm used to on a case."

Teague's grin widened. "We do have that. All the tools to do the job."

"And a few toys, too?" she asked, grinning back at him.

"You mean Igor and Wilbur?" He was laughing now. "Yeah, those, too."

She glanced at Parker and saw a fleeting smile, no doubt at the nicknames. Teague stood up then, and instinctively Carly looked at her watch. And was startled to see how late it was. Had she and Parker really been sitting here just talking—and petting dogs—for that long?

She noticed him glancing at his wrist, which was sans any timepiece. He grimaced. "Left the Rolex with everything else," he muttered when he saw her looking at him.

For some reason, that more than anything pounded home to her how deeply he believed in what he'd done. Even if he'd worked for the money he'd earned, to him it was now all ill-gotten gains, as the old saying went. And he didn't want any part of it.

Parker Ward wasn't just honest and compassionate and full of integrity. He was...practically noble.

And she knew enough about him now to know he would laugh his throat raw if she were to say such a thing to him. She stood up, and Parker followed suit. Along with the two dogs, Woof happily, Cutter alertly.

"I need to get going," she said and told herself she had not sounded as reluctant as she thought she had.

"Me, too," Parker said. He looked at Teague. "Thanks. All of you."

"What we do," Teague said cheerfully.

Parker walked out beside her, escorted by the polite Cutter while Woof wandered about like a normal dog.

"Shouldn't I be escorting you to your car?" she asked teasingly as he turned toward her unmarked car. "I am the one armed, after all."

"Depends. You any good?"

That startled her. Her brows lowered. "Darned good," she said. Then she saw the twitch at the corners of his mouth. And laughed. "Walked right into that one, didn't I?"

"I figured you were." He smiled, and it did that crazy thing to her again. But it faded away all too quickly, and she imagined dragging all that painful history out again hadn't been pleasant for him.

On impulse, she pulled out one of her department business cards, turned it over, grabbed her pen and wrote her private number on the back. "If there's anything I can do, even if it's just talk, call. Whenever."

He gave her a quizzical look. "Worried about my state of mind?"

"Worried about you," she admitted. "I don't run into so many genuinely good, brave people that I want to see one suffering for doing the right thing."

He stared at her. His lips—damn, he had a great mouth—parted as if he were going to speak, but then closed again. And then, driven by an urge she didn't even try to fight, she stretched up and kissed his cheek. She felt the snap of tension that instantly went through him. She started to pull back, just as he turned his head. Their lips brushed, and suddenly it was an entirely different kind of kiss. And the feel of his mouth on hers, his lips practically caressing hers, sent so much heat rippling through her that she felt overdressed for this chilly, early spring night.

She heard the front door of the building open, and in the same instant he jerked back. Stared down at her. It couldn't be clearer that he hadn't planned that; he looked as if he were as startled as she had been.

The question was, had it been as…hot for him as it had been for her?

Chapter 15

Parker continued to pace the floor, even though Woof had gotten bored with this silly human game and settled down with his chew bone.

He pondered the information that the building where Ray had seen the kidnapping had been put up for sale two days afterward. The strangeness of having an organization the size and power of Foxworth behind him. And the amazing fact that even after he'd told them the truth about his own foolishness, they were sticking by him, although it was more for Ray.

He pondered everything but Detective Carly Devon. Whose business card with her personal phone number on it was practically burning up his pocket.

Like kissing her had burned up...several places?

He called himself a few names, the kindest of which was *fool*. He had no business doing that. That it had been hotter than he'd ever imagined only made it worse, because it would make it harder not to think about it and her. And he had no business doing that, either, not in the position he was in. His long-term prospects would have to brighten up quite a bit to be gloomy.

He had one of the most restless evenings since this had all begun, since that day he'd stared at the documents he'd inadvertently accessed that had shown him what was truly going on, that it was a scam, that the energy system people thought they were investing in didn't really exist.

Then he caught himself with his phone in his hand. He tried to focus on the fact that he'd forgotten to undo the forwarding. He forwarded the house phone to it anytime he left, just in case. Ray had a smartphone, one with more bells and whistles than his own economy model, but he wasn't about to give up his landline. Not just because cell reception was spotty here but because it also gave him the fastest internet he could get here without bundling it all into one provider. A choice Ray had pronounced idiotic in that "lived long enough to learn" tone he had.

Parker went through the undo process with far more concentration than was necessary for the simple function. He knew he was thinking about that to stop himself from dialing that damned number. Because while there was probably something stupider than calling her—because texting wouldn't be enough—at nearly midnight just because he wanted to hear her voice, he couldn't think of it at the moment. He stuffed the phone in a drawer and slammed it shut.

His night wasn't much more restful than the pacing had been. And when he blearily made his way to the kitchen late the next morning, he put on a full pot of coffee instead of the half he'd been doing since Ray had been gone.

When he heard a faint scratch at the back kitchen door to the yard, he thought it was Woof telling him that letting him out should have come before coffee. But when he turned around, the happy dog was just then trotting toward the door, letting out a bark. Not a warning bark, but a delighted one.

Cutter, he thought suddenly, and went to open the door. It was indeed the Foxworths' clever dog. Cutter greeted the excited Woof with a tail wag, but then he came over and nosed Parker's hand.

"Polite of you," he told the dog, who sat at his feet.

Cutter tilted his head and fastened those intense eyes on him. It was the strangest experience he'd ever had with an animal. Except maybe that mountain lion he and Ray had encountered hiking in the Cascades that time. He stroked the dog's head and again felt that odd easing of his inner turmoil.

Parker had just noticed the dog's ears were twitching as if he were hearing something when Cutter got up and trotted across the kitchen. He sat down in front of a cupboard and looked back at Parker.

"That ain't the treat cupboard, if that's what you're looking for," Parker told him.

He got a short bark in answer. Woof watched curiously, as if puzzled why his new friend didn't want to immediately get to the business of playing. And then Cutter turned his head and stared at the cupboard. No, wait—not the cupboard. The drawer above it. The drawer he'd put his phone in last night, to keep himself from doing something very stupid.

Parker's brow furrowed. He couldn't hear anything, like the phone signaling a call or text, but then, he didn't have a dog's hearing. Still… He walked over and pulled the drawer open. His phone lay there, facedown and silent. Not even the faint buzz of a vibration.

Another short bark from Cutter that sounded oddly like encouragement. He gave the dog a side-eye as he reached for the phone and turned it over. And saw the notifications of both an incoming text and a missed call.

Carly?

His pulse leaped in the same instant his gut knotted, and it was a bizarre sensation. But the number was not the one she'd written on her card, nor was it the one with the sheriff's department prefix.

Calmer now—and feeling more than a little silly—he opened the texting app.

Foxworth. He should have realized that; they were the only ones he'd given his number to that he wouldn't recognize. There weren't a lot of people calling him these days anyway.

He read the text, which asked him to meet up at the Foxworth headquarters at noon. It was initialed *H*, so he presumed Hayley Foxworth had sent it. He shifted his gaze to Cutter, who was now giving him an approving look and a tail wag. And for a moment he actually considered texting her back and asking if she'd sent her dog to get him to answer.

Losing it, Ward.

He glanced at the phone again and saw that the text had been sent nearly an hour ago. He sent back an apologetic explanation that the phone had been in another room. He decided not to mention that it had been shut in a drawer. And most especially why.

No problem, Hayley responded in less than a minute.

And Cutter's here.

I suspected as much.

She suspected her dog was here? Nearly half a mile from their house? Good thing this was a quiet, low-traffic area. Although now that he thought about the initial chase that had led him to the Foxworth house, they hadn't set foot on an actual paved street.

Bring Woof. They can play, she added.

Thanks.

He sent the reply, then noticed Cutter was at the back door again. "Mission accomplished, huh, dog?"

This time he stayed outside to watch as the dogs gamboled around for a bit, before Cutter unexpectedly led Woof back to the back steps. He sat, and Woof again looked at him curiously. Cutter gave a soft whuff of sound, and acting more on instinct than anything, Parker leaned over and grasped Woof's collar. Cutter gave him that approving look again—yes, he was definitely losing it—let out a single bark, turned and trotted off.

And left Parker holding the dog who was merely a sweet, silly dog as he watched the dog he wasn't at all sure was just a dog head toward home.

Carly had expected the Foxworths and Cutter. She wasn't surprised at Liam's presence and wouldn't have been surprised at any of the other Foxworth operatives being at their headquarters, although she was kind of glad Rafe Crawford wasn't there; the man made her the tiniest bit nervous. Not because of his lethality, which she knew about from Brett, but because of the shadows in his eyes. They reminded her too much of cases that had not turned out well, and she'd wondered if she was seeing her future, if she, too, would one day see everything through ghosts of the past.

But she hadn't expected Parker to be there, which in retrospect she realized had been silly of her; to Foxworth this was his case, after all. Or perhaps she'd just so forcefully put him out of her mind last night when, at about 2:00 a.m., she'd quit thinking he might actually call or text and had made herself rest.

Four hours of sleep qualifies as rest, right?

But at least she'd had warning, when she'd pulled up and Cutter had raced around from the back of the building to greet her, because he'd been followed by his now familiar clown-spotted companion. And if Woof was here, Parker was here. So she was mentally prepared when she went inside and saw him sitting there by the fire. Mentally prepared and totally not thinking about that unexpected, crazy-making kiss.

So if you're so prepared, why did your heart make that little jump when he looked up at you? And kick up the pace of your pulse when he stood up?

She told herself it was some old-fashioned appreciation of manners, and not the way his tall, rangy yet muscular body moved. She even liked the way he jammed his fingers through his hair. And she was not going to stare at his mouth, remembering what it had felt like to have those lips on hers.

Once inside, she was abandoned by Cutter, who apparently decided escorting her to the door was the extent of his duties this morning and returned to his play outside with Woof, but greeted by the others by name. Except Parker, who gave her a half smile before he looked away. Embarrassed? Or regretful? He waited until she was seated before he also sat. And shoved back those unruly strands of hair again.

"I really need a haircut," he muttered under his breath.

"I have Laney do mine," Liam said with a grin.

Carly blinked at that. "You have a dog groomer cut your hair?"

"Better than driving fifteen miles. And she does a good job."

"She does," Carly agreed. "I never would have guessed."

"And she's a lot cheaper," he added.

"Don't let him kid you," Hayley said as she brought a tray of mugs of coffee and the accoutrements over and put it on the coffee table. "He just likes telling people a dog groomer cuts his hair."

"That, too," Liam admitted easily.

Even Parker smiled at that. And then, in the same lighter tone as Liam had used—Carly belatedly realized the man had probably done it intentionally—he said, "No such thing as a weekend around here?"

"Not on a case," Quinn said. "In between, we're the most relaxed bunch you'll ever see."

"Ha," Carly said. "You mean when you're not out doing all that community service stuff Brett told me about? Like building that veterans memorial at the park?"

Parker stared at Quinn. "You guys built that?"

"Helped," Quinn said.

Parker could imagine what Quinn's idea of helping was, judging by what he was doing for him and Ray. "I'll have to tell Ray. It really pleased him when that went in."

"Men like him are why we did it," Hayley said.

Quinn's gaze shifted to Carly. "So, you found something?"

She sensed rather than saw Parker go still, since she wasn't—didn't dare?—looking at him. "It's not much," she cautioned. "Just a blip on the radar I want to check out, but I wanted you to be aware."

"What is it?" Parker asked. His voice, edgy again, so clearly wanting something to make this real, for Ray, grabbed at her. And her discipline broke and she turned her head. Quinn had all the command presence in the room, yet it was Parker she found herself looking at.

"I did a little more digging this morning," she said.

"No weekend for you, either?" he asked, his voice steadier now.

She hadn't expected that and smiled. "Sometimes weekends are the best time to get anything done in my office." *Especially if you don't want the brass hanging over your shoulder and seeing what you're doing.* "I had some things to catch up on anyway."

"Because you've spent so much time on this," Parker said and lowered his gaze again.

That had, in fact, been the reason she'd gotten behind, but she wasn't about to blame him or Ray. "Doesn't matter. But while I was doing that, I thought I'd run a search on our building owner, just to see if we'd had any official encounters with him." She glanced at Quinn. "The kind of thing no one else *should* have access to."

Quinn barely smiled. "It would take Ty a long time and get him in trouble if he got caught, so we try not to do it."

Her mouth quirked wryly at that *try.* It was a good thing Brett swore these people were on the side of the angels.

"And you found something?" Hayley asked.

"Not on him. But a variation on his name popped up— not Charles or Chuck, but Chas—so I dug a little deeper. Turns out it's his son. And that son has a drug problem."

Quinn raised a brow. "A serious problem?"

She nodded. "I can't discuss his juvenile record," she said, "but he turned eighteen ten months ago and has been arrested three times since then."

"Possession?" Quinn guessed.

She nodded. "But the last time was for grand theft."

"To support the habit," Hayley said, her voice sad.

"Hints he needed the cash more than the drugs at that moment," Quinn said.

"Exactly," Carly said. "So he could be in trouble with his dealer."

"Or a father who finally had enough," Hayley put in.

"Eighteen," Parker said slowly. "That would definitely be a kid to Ray."

"Yes," she said. "And that opens up a whole new range of possibilities."

Chapter 16

Parker shifted in the passenger seat of the dark green, compact SUV. Unlike what she called her "plain wrap" official car, Carly's personal vehicle was much less blatant. And it pounded home to him that she was doing this mostly on her own, unofficially, albeit with the help of Foxworth.

And he was even more amazed that she allowed him to tag along. They'd left his—or rather Ray's—vehicle at the rehab center, where they'd dropped off Woof for his daily visit. Parker had intended to stay, but when Ray found out she was headed over to talk again to the building owner, who had grudgingly agreed to meet with her there, the man had prodded Parker into going with her. And once she'd secured his promise to stay out of it—"If this turns into something, having a civilian witnessing an interview could cause some problems" had convinced him—she'd agreed he could at least watch from a distance.

So now he sat in her car, waiting. They had gone inside the empty building at least ten minutes ago. He tapped a finger on the armrest nervously, wondering when he should start worrying about how long she was alone in there with the guy. Sure, it was her job, and she was well trained—

she could probably put him on the mat with one try—but Turner was still a big guy. If he was more involved in this than they'd thought—if, for instance, he was the guy Ray had seen, maybe throwing his troublemaking son into the trunk of his car—then he might panic, and if he got the jump on her...

He got out of the car. She'd told him to stay out of it, but that didn't mean he couldn't at least go listen at the door, did it? He'd go around to the front, where the doors were glass, where it was perfectly reasonable he might be walking down the street, and he'd be able to hear better anyway. He'd just make sure there were no sounds of a struggle, that was all.

He rounded the corner and spotted the vehicle Turner had arrived in on Thursday. He could watch that, too, just in case. Visions of the man pretending to help an injured Carly into the vehicle to cart her away just as he had his son flashed through his mind.

Rein in the imagination, Ward.

He knew the father/son scenario was just one possibility and the odds were she was fine, but he just couldn't sit there and wait when there was the slightest chance she might be in trouble.

He leaned in and put an ear to the front door. Silence. Not even the sound of a conversation, but if they were talking in normal tones it probably wouldn't get through the heavy glass anyway. But more important, there were no other sounds, either. At least, there weren't until he heard steps approaching on the inside.

He backed up, keeping himself on the side of the door where it wouldn't block them from him. He wasn't sure what he would do; he was fit enough, ran and worked out fairly regularly—track and field had been his sport in school—but physical fighting wasn't in his repertoire.

Maybe he should rectify that. The door started to open, and he heard Carly thanking the man for his time. He hastily backed up several more steps, since it sounded like things were fine and he suddenly felt a little foolish. He didn't want to cause her any trouble by sticking his nose in when she'd told him to stay out of it.

Turner stepped outside, then turned back. Parker backed up a little farther, so he could turn and look into the window of the shop next door, although when he realized he was looking at baby clothes and gear, he was a little startled. And then he heard Carly's lighter, quicker steps. The door swung closed and Turner locked it after them. The man didn't even glance at Carly or anywhere else, just hurried to the driver's door of the silver sedan. In fact, Parker saw out of the corner of his eye that he didn't even check for oncoming traffic when he yanked the door open. And when he pulled away from the curb, it was a lot faster than Parker would have done with a sheriff's deputy standing right there.

Carly stood on the sidewalk watching him go, looking thoughtful. And without a glance or change in expression, she said, loud enough for him to hear, "Something I don't know? You have a sudden need for baby shoes?"

Parker had thought the last couple of years had crushed any capacity he'd ever had for blushing, but he felt his cheeks heat now. She hadn't even looked his way, but obviously she'd known he was there. That was the source of his embarrassment, he was sure. Nothing to do with the juxtaposition of Carly and…baby shoes.

He sucked in a steadying breath and walked over to where she was standing. "I just…wanted to be sure everything was okay." *That you were okay.*

She glanced at him as if she'd heard his thought. "It wasn't necessary, but I appreciate the thought."

She hadn't, as he'd half expected, criticized him for sticking his nose in when she clearly had things completely under control. "He probably wouldn't have recognized me, but I don't think he saw me."

"Mr. Turner didn't see anything, he was in such a hurry," she said, going back to watching the silver car as it proceeded up the street.

"I know I'm no expert, but there's something up with him," Parker said.

"You're right." That gratified him far more than it should have. He was glad she was still watching the car, because he could only imagine what was showing in his face. She went on. "I just don't know what. I call it my itchy feeling."

"Maybe he's embezzling, or cheating people in his business," he said sourly.

"Maybe. Or he could have blown off a parking ticket. People react differently." She was still watching as the man's car made a left turn several blocks up. Then she reached for her phone and pulled up a map program, tapped the screen a few times. Looked at the result and murmured, "Interesting."

"What's interesting?"

For the first time she actually looked at him. "His home is that way." She pointed to the right. "His office is that way." She jabbed a thumb over her shoulder.

So he wasn't headed for either. "Maybe he's got business or an appointment elsewhere." His mouth quirked. "Or he's off to play a round of golf."

"Possibly." She gave him a sideways glance. "Play a lot of golf, do you?"

"No. Tried it, didn't like it much."

She tilted her head slightly. It made her bangs shift, drawing even more attention to those vivid blue eyes.

As if you needed something to make you look at them...

"Didn't like the game?"

He shrugged. "And the attitudes. Or, in my case, the people I was playing it with." He let out a compressed, unamused laugh. "Should have been a clue early on, huh? They barely suffered my presence anyway."

"Their loss," she said easily, and he thought he might flush all over again.

"He have anything to say about his son?" he asked hastily, before he said something he'd regret.

"He said he's living in San Francisco now, with his mother. Trying to get straight."

Parker blinked. "He went from here to San Francisco because...what, he thought it would be easier to clean up his act there?"

"No accounting for some people's perceptions. Maybe Mom's a disciplinarian."

Parker spent a useless moment wondering if that meant Mom cared, or simply didn't like anything disrupting her life, decided he was letting his past color his own perceptions and kept his mouth shut.

"He also has," Carly said, "if it checks out, an iron-clad alibi for the time in question. With multiple witnesses."

"Don't tell me he was playing golf," Parker said dryly.

Carly gave him a grin that sucked every last bit of air out of his lungs. "Nice one. But no. Chamber of commerce luncheon."

Her expression went back to thoughtful. And Parker wondered how many cases had been solved by the agile brain behind that expression. He was guessing a lot. A whole lot. "What?" he finally asked.

"He said it was at the Sound View Inn. They've got security cameras. And I'd like to know if he was there the whole time."

Every one of those he'd ever been to in the city—as an observer, certainly not a contributor, told he was there only to eat and schmooze—had gone on for what seemed like forever. Plenty of time for someone to make an excuse, leave and come back without anybody really noticing how long they'd been gone.

"It's close enough," he said; he knew the new, small hotel that had become a popular destination was barely a mile from the alley.

"Yes." She spoke rather absently, as if she were still focused on something else.

"What are you thinking?"

She focused on him then. The change was evident. The effect it had on him was absurd. "That for me to ask for that video from a private business, I need an official case. Plus, saying I need to verify an alibi could start something I don't want to start. Yet."

He frowned. "I'm starting to hate that word, *official*."

She gave him a wry smile. "Welcome to my world."

Okay, this was getting ridiculous. She meant it only in that generic, now-you-get-it way, not in an I'd-like-you-to-be-part-of-that-world kind of way. He scrambled for something to say that would show he was focused on what was going on, not on her.

"Do you think maybe…Foxworth?"

She let out a sigh. "I'm really beginning to see what Brett Dunbar was talking about when he said to just trust and not think too much about how they get what they get."

He couldn't help his mouth quirking upward when he looked at her and said, "Is that a yes?"

She gave a rueful shake of her head, but said, "It is." Then, looking down at her phone, she added, "But maybe I shouldn't make that call on my *official* department phone."

"I'll do it," he said. "Or—" He stopped himself.

"Or what?"

He took a breath and plunged ahead. "I need to go get Woof and get him home. Ray's got a landline at home."

"Good thinking, since cell reception is sketchy out where he is. And less likely to be monitored."

"Told you he was smart."

"Lead on," she said.

And Parker realized the answer to this question was yes, too.

And he wondered if he'd get a third *yes* if he asked what he really wanted to ask her.

Chapter 17

Carly ended up making two calls, one on her official cell and one on Ray's landline phone.

Calling Turner's ex-wife she could justify as sheriff's business; determining there was no case or crime was almost as important as solving an actual one. She ended up having to leave a voice mail, which she was never happy with because it gave people time to concoct a story, if this truly was something nefarious.

The call to Foxworth—made with Woof leaning against her knee for attention—was much more pleasant. And when she hung up she was smiling. "Well, that was almost too easy."

Parker slid the soda he'd gotten from the fridge across the kitchen counter to her. She'd declined a glass and ice, but she noticed he'd opened it for her. And Woof, apparently satisfied for the moment, picked up a well-chewed bone and went to curl up on his bed by the fireplace.

"They can help?" he asked as he came around and took the bar stool next to her.

She took a long sip of the soda before she answered.

"One of those many people Foxworth has helped is the owner of the place."

He drew back slightly. "So they're…calling in the IOU? For this?"

"So it seems. Hayley called him while I was still on the line, and he said he'd be glad to help. He's over in the city tonight, but he'll go in tomorrow and pull the video for them."

"On Sunday? I wonder what they did for him."

"Brett told me back when it was happening there was a city council member who kept stopping the building permit, for specious reasons. The guy was about to give up when Foxworth stepped in." Her mouth twisted. "Turned out the councilwoman was in league with a group that had been trying to buy the land from him, but he'd refused to sell."

"Oh." He didn't sound at all surprised, and she supposed after what he'd been through, what he'd discovered about the people he was working for, that seemed pretty tame.

Then, tilting his head slightly in that way that made that strand of dark hair drop to his eyebrow, he asked, "Foxworth is really…"

She couldn't help smiling when words failed him. "Yeah, they are. I didn't believe it at first, either. Neither did Brett. Although finding out who Quinn Foxworth is shifted the narrative in his favor pretty quickly for us."

"Who he is, besides a badass?"

She laughed at his tone and nodded. "A few years back, he took down a cop killer, after being shot himself. Then last year, right before Christmas, Foxworth unraveled the real story behind that shooting."

He blinked. "Years later?"

"Apparently they also don't ever quit, unless the person they're working for tells them to. Brett says they had a leak on the mission where Quinn and Hayley met, more than two years ago, and they're still hunting down the mole."

Parker grimaced. "Remind me never to get on their bad side."

She looked again at the photo she'd noticed earlier, framed and on the wall near the old-style wall phone she'd used. At least it hadn't been one of those rotary-dial things like her grandparents had had, she'd thought then, stifling a grin.

But now she studied the picture, recognizing Ray and a younger Parker. Ray's arm was around the boy's—for that was what he looked like in the shot—shoulders. They could easily be taken for father and son. And both their smiles were blazing, which she realized probably told her who had taken the picture.

She turned back to him. "That picture says it all, doesn't it?"

Parker nodded. "Some might think he was just a neighbor who was kind to a kid in a rough spot, but it was more, really."

She smiled widely and nodded toward the wall. "Nobody who's seen that could ever think that's all it was."

Parker looked at the picture, and the soft, reminiscent smile that curved his mouth then tugged at her heart. "Thank you," he said simply.

"I know firsthand, and from my work, that family isn't always in DNA. Family is in the heart."

He turned to look at her. "You surprise me, Detective Devon."

"Carly, please," she said, suddenly hating the stiff sound of her title.

He gave her an odd look then, and she had the crazy thought that maybe he'd been using that to keep distance between them, just as she had tried to use the formality of his full name or "Mr. Ward" to do the same.

"How do you feel about pizza?" he asked suddenly.

She blinked at the non sequitur. "I… Basic food group?"

He smiled at that. "I'm starving. Plus, I missed my pizza fix when that bandit—" he jerked a thumb toward Woof, who was still innocently sprawled on his bed "—stole mine the other day."

She laughed. "Why am I not surprised?"

"So…go in or delivery?"

It appeared she'd be having dinner with him one way or another. And she wasn't quite sure what to call the feeling that gave her. Anticipation? Downright eagerness?

"Delivery," she said, adding with a glance around Ray's house, "This is a wonderful, homey place." Then, when something else hit her, she said quickly, "I'll buy."

His amusement faded, and she knew she'd hit a sore spot. "No, thank you. I can manage that much."

She hadn't meant to call attention to his financial situation, only to pay her own way. "Then I'll tip the delivery person," she said, keeping her tone light. That seemed to ease things up, and they proceeded to discussing what kind of pizza. They found that neither of them cared for pepperoni and picked one without, and Parker called it in.

"Forty-five minutes to an hour," he said when he hung up. "Saturday night."

"I'm glad they're busy. Small-town business and all."

He smiled at that. But before he could respond, Woof was suddenly on his feet, letting out a happy bark as he trotted toward the back door. She looked from the dog to him.

"Last time that happened, it was Cutter," he said with a wry smile.

"I believe that," she said with a grin.

He walked over to the door and pulled it open. And as she'd half expected—okay, maybe three-quarters; she seemed to be buying into the mythos—it was indeed the clever dog. He greeted Woof nose to nose, then came and sat at Parker's feet, looking up intently. Curious, Carly slid off the counter stool and walked over.

"Come for pizza?" Parker asked the dog with a raised brow.

Cutter grinned at him. She would swear the back corners of the animal's mouth had risen into a credible imitation of the human expression. He obviously saw it, too, because he blinked, drew back a little.

"I'd take that as a yes," Carly said. And when she did, Cutter leaned her way and nudged her hand with his nose. "Sorry," she said to the dog as she stroked his head, "was I too slow on the petting? My apologies."

It was Parker who grinned then. And when Cutter trotted into the great room, then looked back over his shoulder at them, he shrugged and said, "Might as well be comfortable while we wait to eat."

Carly smiled and went to sit on one end of the couch, near the fireplace, apparently making Parker mention starting a fire. It was chilly enough, she thought idly as he headed for a chair—a safely separate chair—if not cold.

Several things happened that made her think *That was weird*. Cutter went over to Woof and nudged him. The dog got up, Cutter nudged again, and then Woof was in the chair Parker had been headed for. So he changed course to the almost-as-safe other end of the couch. But before he could sit, Cutter was behind him, bumping the back of his knees hard enough that he took a step to get out of the way. He turned to look at the dog, who jumped up onto the very spot Parker had intended to take. The animal sprawled out, seeming utterly content. And taking up every bit of the couch except for the spot right next to Carly.

And the rest of the dog's reputation came flooding back into her mind.

Uh-oh. Serious uh-oh.

Parker was looking at Cutter with an expression she could only describe as wary. He pulled out his phone and sent a text. Glancing at her, he just said, "Letting the Foxworths know he's here."

A moment later he was frowning at the screen, reading aloud. "'He's got a plan. Send him home when he'll go'? What does that mean?"

Carly was very much afraid she knew exactly what kind of plan the Foxworths meant. But she said nothing; if they hadn't explained to him about their too-clever dog's other…talents, she wasn't about to. Not yet, anyway.

Brow furrowed, Parker went over and built that fire—which to her it seemed he did expertly, but then, she hadn't had a fireplace in years—then walked back, hesitated, then sat in the empty spot beside her.

"You're good at building a fire," she said, then groaned inwardly at her unintentional double entendre. He gave her a sideways look, and it occurred to her it would seem like a double entendre to him only if he was thinking the same way she was. Was that what that rather pointed look meant?

"Pickle," he said.

She blinked. "What?"

He explained the acronym to her. "Ray," he said. "He taught me that, along with the rest of any useful things I know."

She smiled at that. She took another sip of soda as she studied him before asking, "You said I surprised you. Why?"

He looked as if he regretted having said that. But finally, with a half shrug, he said, "I would have expected you to be...more cynical."

"Because I'm a cop?"

"A juvie cop. Don't you need a pretty thick shell for that?"

"Sometimes," she agreed, wondering what kind of juvenile officers he might have encountered. "But if you let it become more than just a shell, if the cynical goes all the way to the bone, it's time to get out."

He was quiet for a moment before asking, "How long have you been doing this?"

"I've been here at the sheriff's office for four years, the juvenile detective for two. I was with LAPD for four years before that. Now, *that* will burn you out."

"I can imagine."

"I'm grateful every day that Brett called me when they were looking for lateral hires. I wanted to come home."

"So you knew him before?"

She nodded. "He was in LA before coming here, too." She left it at that; Brett's haunting past was his story to tell, not hers. Besides, it didn't matter anymore. He'd never forget, but he had moved on.

"So you started here as a detective?"

"Doesn't work that way. I'd been gone a while, so I needed to relearn the area, the people and their way of doing things. So I was back in uniform for a while before I made detective." She smiled. "But a smaller force made that happen a lot quicker. I actually fulfilled my vow to myself to make detective by thirty."

"Two years ago?"

She raised a brow at him. "Prying at my age?"

"Um...flat-out asking?"

She liked the open admission. And figured she owed him after she'd set him up to find out his age, outside the video game store. Even if she didn't want to admit to why she'd wanted to know—or hope she knew why he did.

"Exactly two years ago this month."

"Happy anniversary…and birthday?"

"That's not for a few months yet," she said with a laugh.

"Okay. No candles on the pizza, then."

She laughed again. She liked his sense of humor, the way he thought, and it struck her that she'd laughed more with this man than any other she could remember.

Yes, there had been moments when she could see things were eating at him—her offer to pay for the pizza, for one—but that he could joke at all was a testament to the strength of his will. The strength it had taken to do what he'd done, simply because it was the right thing to do.

"I'm really, really glad you had Ray," she said quietly.

She saw him swallow. "Me, too. I don't know if I'd have made it without him."

"And I'm glad you still have him. That you're here with him and for him."

"I'd do anything for that man."

"Maybe you should just stay here with him. Doesn't seem like you'd have any trouble coexisting."

"We wouldn't. We don't. But…I can't just let him support me."

She knew instinctively it wasn't only money that made him say that. Nor was it pride. It was that same sense of right and wrong that had made him blow the whistle on Witner's con.

"I know," she said quietly. "And that makes you the best kind of person there is, Parker Ward."

For a long, silent moment he just looked at her. She saw turmoil in his eyes, but something else, too. Heat? Or was that wishful thinking? And when had she slid so far into liking him that she was hoping it was?

"Carly?"

There was no doubting the question in his voice. "Yes?" she answered, and she had to work hard not to make it a yes to anything and everything he might ask.

"I…"

He stopped. Swallowed again.

And then he leaned in and kissed her.

Chapter 18

He'd expected it to be sweet. Hell, he'd known it would be.

What he hadn't expected was conflagration. But he got it; the moment Carly threaded her fingers through his hair and began to kiss him back in earnest, he went up in flames hotter than Ray's welding torch.

He'd never felt this kind of urgency in his life. Everything else flew out of his mind, until there was nothing left except the taste of her as he probed deeper, the heat of her as he pulled her closer, then pressed her back to lie on the couch, and the joyous little shock when he realized she wasn't just letting him, she was urging him on.

The pressure of her slender form beneath him nearly sent him over the edge right then. Even the jab of what had to be her sidearm, reminding him of what she did for a living, didn't slow him down. It had been a very long time for him, since the day his world had blown up in fact, nearly three years ago. That this was the first time he'd cared. That she was the only woman to make him even think about it was something he'd deal with later. Right now what he wanted was more, what he wanted was all she would give him.

He'd noticed before the silky sort of sheen of the shirt she wore beneath the tailored jacket, but it was sandpaper compared with the silk of her skin. He found himself trailing kisses down her long, slender neck, wondering with the few brain cells still functioning why on earth he'd left her mouth but unable to stop himself. She just tasted so damned good.

And then she lifted her head to swipe her tongue at his ear and a convulsive shiver went through him. *What the hell?* When had that ever been a turn-on for him? And how had she known that, with her, it would be?

The probable answer, that with her anything would be, hovered, but those last brain cells surrendered to the overwhelming power of those nerves carrying sensation after crazed sensation through him. And in those moments everything felt right, and the rest of the world, with all the problems both large and small, fell away. Nothing mattered except this woman and this moment in time. Nothing.

Parker doubted he would have even heard the knock on the door if Woof hadn't exploded into barking fifteen seconds before it came. As it was, it took him an embarrassingly long moment to snap out of that delicious haze and remember what was happening.

Pizza.

The absolutely last thing he was hungry for now. The only thing he wanted was more of Carly, of her sweet mouth, those lithe, feminine curves. He wanted her naked beneath him, on top of him—he didn't care. He wanted to fill his hands with those soft, warm breasts, wanted to bury himself—

He stifled a groan as Woof barked again and looked at him as if to say, "There's food—move!" Cutter, oddly, hadn't stirred. As if he didn't care, or else knew perfectly well that what was outside wasn't something to concern him.

It was all he could do to stand up. His body was not happy with the interruption, and still breathing hard, he looked at Carly. And it soothed him a little that she, too, was breathing hard.

"Timing is truly everything," she muttered.

The fact that she sounded no happier at the interruption than he felt gave him what he needed to get himself moving to the door. A certain rigid body part protested every step, but he went. He took the delivered box—which smelled great and he had to admit woke up his stomach—and handed the guy at the door the tip Carly had insisted on paying. For a split second he weighed the benefits of fresh, hot pizza against going right back to what they'd been doing.

There was no contest in his mind. Warmed-over pizza was perfect. But Carly was up now, straightening the silky T-shirt he'd nearly gotten off her. The memory of her hands sliding up under his own shirt, over his bare skin, sent a shudder through him, and he had to clench his jaw to stop it. Then Cutter bestirred himself off the couch, went to nose Carly's hand, then came over to Parker and did the same. He gave Woof a sniff, then trotted unconcernedly out the door Parker was about to close.

"I guess that means he's ready," Parker muttered.

They ate in near silence, with Carly only asking if it was okay to feed Woof some sausage, and Parker telling her he'd offer her some wine but Ray wasn't much of a drinker, so there wasn't any on hand. *Not like I can afford the stuff, unless it's the kind that comes in a box.*

The pizza tasted good, but once it hit his stomach it seemed to settle there like a rock. And after two slices he'd had enough, when before he'd felt hungry enough to wipe out half of the entire thing. He sat there staring at his half-empty glass of water, noticing out of the corner of his eye Carly picking at a corner of the pizza box.

He had no idea how long they'd been sitting there in silence when Carly finally spoke.

"Parker?"

He swallowed. Turned to look at her, knowing she was going to want to talk. Women always did, didn't they? And he could see by the expression on her face, that lovely, almost delicate face, that he was right.

"If this—" she poked at the pizza box "—hadn't arrived when it did…where would that—" she glanced at the couch "—have gone?"

He drew in a deep, steadying breath. She'd always said she admired his integrity. So he gave her the truth. "If you were smart? Nowhere."

She drew back. "Nowhere? That's what you want?"

He let out a harsh laugh that was as close to bitter as he'd heard from himself in a long time. "What I want? Hell no. Unless you're blind, and I know you're far, far from it, what I wanted had to be pretty clear."

"But… Now you don't?"

He couldn't take the look in her eyes any longer and went back to staring at his glass. "Oh, I do," he said, his voice still harsh. "More than…" He shook his head sharply. Then, steeling himself, he said what had to be said. "You're not a woman for a one-time hookup, or even a casual fling."

"No, I'm not. Is that what you had in mind?"

"No!"

Even as it broke from him, he realized the truth of it. He didn't want casual sex with her, didn't want her to be like the women he'd encountered so often in the city, when he'd been someone whose position—and face it, the money he'd been making then—attracted a certain sort. A sort far different from Carly Devon. But he was so far on the opposite side of that now he couldn't even see it anymore. And he had little hope that anything would change for a long time.

If it ever did.

"Then…?" she prodded.

When he steeled himself to go on, his voice was flat. As flat as the reality he had to explain to her, when all he truly wanted to do was kiss her again. And again. And more. So much more.

"That—" he pointed at the cell phone on the counter "—is the most expensive thing I own, and it will probably be gone soon because I can't afford it. I don't have a job, or any prospects of one anytime soon, because I don't have a college degree, as I'm continually reminded. I don't have a roof of my own, a car, nothing. If it wasn't for Ray, I'd be living… I don't know where. I have nothing, nothing to offer, Carly."

She studied him for a long, silent moment. So long that he had an under-a-microscope kind of feeling. And then, her voice soft but steady, she said, "Nothing except honesty, integrity and courage. I don't know what you think I value, but I'll take that over material things any day. And if you don't realize that, then I shouldn't be here."

Then she was gone, quietly, closing the door carefully behind her after giving Woof a goodbye pat. Parker sat staring at the door, wishing fruitlessly that he'd met her at any other time in his life than now.

And yet what she'd said echoed in his ears long after the quiet of darkness settled in on him. And in the darkest hours he realized that he had, maybe, sort of insulted her. If that was how she truly felt.

Life sometimes had a bitch of a sense of humor.

Chapter 19

Carly gratefully took the cup of coffee Hayley Foxworth handed her; this was not how she'd planned to spend her Sunday afternoon. She'd intended to get out and run for a couple of miles. Maybe five. Uphill. Or whatever it took to get her mind off one Parker Ward.

But now here she was, sitting at the Foxworth headquarters, waiting for that very man.

And undergoing a rather intense scrutiny by the Foxworth dog.

When Quinn came out and headed for the second chair opposite the couch, she was about to ask him what was up with the animal now, but was diverted momentarily by the way the man casually, as if without thought, reached out and brushed his fingers over his wife's cheek as he passed. As if he needed the contact, the touch. As if it were as first nature as breathing. And as necessary.

And the way Hayley smiled up at him from her own chair seemed to indicate she felt exactly the same way.

It reminded her of Brett and Sloane. Which in turn reminded her of what Brett had said when she'd called him this morning, both to confirm he'd be on his way home in a few hours, and to get his recommendation on what to do with the information she'd acquired on her first phone call of the morning.

Take it to Foxworth. If there's something to be found, they'll do it faster and more completely than we can. Maybe they'll find enough to make it official.

Official.

I'm starting to hate that word, official.

Welcome to my world.

And there she was, back to Parker Ward again.

As if her arrival back at the very subject she'd been avoiding had triggered it, Cutter let out a bark and got up from where he'd been sitting at her feet, staring at her with those amber-flecked eyes. Staring at her in a way that had her uneasily thinking about Brett and Sloane again, and how this stubborn, clever animal had literally led Brett to the woman he now loved more than life.

Quinn rose and headed for the door, Cutter at his heels. Parker was here. It had to be him, because if it was another of the Foxworth people, they'd just come in. And the moment she thought it, Hayley confirmed it.

"That should be Parker. He'd just gotten back from taking Woof to visit Ray when we called him."

"He's…really good about that."

"He's a good man, Carly."

That seemed a bit pointed. "I know."

"Have you told him yet?" Hayley asked.

Carly shifted her gaze to the woman sitting across the coffee table from her. "Told him?"

"About Cutter's…other talent."

Carly grimaced as Hayley hit too close to her thoughts. "No. It's hard enough for me to believe, and I've seen the results firsthand."

"But he's right, isn't he." It wasn't a question, and Hayley's gaze seemed...purposeful. "You feel something for Parker."

"I admire him. What he did, despite what it cost him." Hayley just looked at her, warm understanding in her green eyes. "Okay, yes, but...I... He's..." She gave up and went with the cliché. "It's complicated."

Hayley smiled then. "It always is. But fair warning—Cutter never gives up." Her smile widened. "And having Cutter vouch for him is worth a lot. Just ask Brett."

And then Parker was there, nodding at Hayley but refusing to meet Carly's gaze. The fact that he looked about as tired as she felt almost soothed her tangled emotions. Cutter looked up at him, then shifted that intense gaze to Carly. And then the dog sat down, letting out what sounded for all the world like a disgusted sigh.

"Things not moving fast enough for your liking, eh?" Hayley asked the dog, who answered with a low whuff. Carly knew what both Hayley and the dog meant, and it was all she could do not to react visibly.

Quinn looked from Cutter to her to Parker and back to her. "You two have a...disagreement?"

At that, finally, Parker looked at her. And held her gaze when he spoke. "Yeah. I insulted her. Didn't mean to, but I did."

Carly stared at him. She hadn't expected that. At all. Cutter made a little sound that seemed almost like he was encouraging her. Pushing aside that absurd thought, she said quietly, "Only because you've been unfairly insulted yourself—sometimes, apparently, *by* yourself—for things most people would be proud of."

He visibly took in a breath. "I'm still sorry."

"Accepted," she said.

She might have been imagining the intonation of Cutter's vocalizations, but she didn't think she was imagining the combination of relief and warmth that lit those hazel eyes of Parker's.

But then the dog gave a short yip, and this time she couldn't reason away that it sounded happy.

Quinn and Hayley Foxworth reminded Parker of Ray and Laura, and that was the highest compliment he could pay any marriage. The way they looked at each other, the way they couldn't pass each other without some kind of physical contact, and especially the way they seemed to communicate without speaking.

Like now, when they looked at their dog, then each other, and grinned. Not just smiled, like two people with a dog they loved, but grinned. Almost in proud amazement. The dog was clever, and that he had a mind of his own was clear even to Parker, but there seemed to be more to it than that.

Or maybe he'd just been imagining that look of utter disgust the dog had given him when he'd arrived. Almost as if he knew that after he'd left them last night, Parker had done something stupid and needed to apologize.

Parker was laughing inwardly at his own silliness when, in a near duplication of his actions last night, Cutter adeptly maneuvered him into sitting next to Carly. And his body woke up to her closeness, clearly remembering the delightful activity that had been so rudely interrupted by the knock on the door.

He looked at her. "I didn't mean to—"

"I know," she said, with a wry look at the dog. "We'll talk about that later."

He felt cheered at the thought that she wanted to talk to him later and settled in on the couch.

"All yours, Carly," Quinn said.

Parker blinked. She'd called this meeting? When Quinn

had called this morning, he'd only said there was a development, so after dropping Woof off to visit Ray—who had thankfully progressed to where he was allowed to be out with his dog in the courtyard alone as long as he held to his promise not to try throwing a ball for him—he'd headed here. Ray had been happy that they hadn't given up, and Parker, perhaps foolishly, had promised he wouldn't until they at least found an explanation of what Ray had seen.

It wasn't like he had anything better to do anyway, just now.

"I got a call back this morning from Turner's ex-wife," she said. He remembered that she'd called and had to leave a message, which she hadn't been happy about. "She'd just heard my message. And she was not happy."

"Didn't like getting a call from the sheriff?" he asked. "Must have been a fine way to start her Sunday morning."

"That wasn't what she was upset about," Carly said, turning to look at him then. "Her son had been living with her there in San Francisco, but got into trouble. Just as you thought, it wasn't the place for a kid with a drug problem."

"Had been?" he asked.

She nodded. "She sent him to live here with his father, in the hopes he could get his life back on track."

Parker blinked. "But his father said…"

"Exactly."

He let out a breath. Suddenly this had all become much more real. "He was lying."

Chapter 20

"Yes. It seems he was indeed lying," Quinn said.

"But why would he, when it was so easy to check?" Parker asked with a frown.

"My guess," Hayley said, "is that he didn't think of that, at the time he said it. Which hints that he's not a man who is used to lying."

Carly watched Parker as he seemed to think about that for a moment. She wondered if he was comparing the demeanor of Chuck Turner with the smooth-as-silk lying and worse of his former boss. When he spoke, she knew she'd been right. "Yeah. I believe that. I should have seen it, but I'm used to…smoother liars."

"I know you are," Hayley said. "I've seen video of your former boss, and he's definitely smooth."

"For a snake oil salesman," Parker said sourly. "But that's old news."

She wondered if the people who'd been caught up in Witner's schemes had recovered enough from their shock and anger to truly appreciate the man who had put a stop to it all.

"This might explain something I saw in the vacant

building," she said. "There were signs, in the office in the back, that someone might have been hanging out there. Maybe even crashing there."

"The pry marks?" Quinn asked.

"Maybe," she said.

"Or maybe he stole a key from Dad," Parker said.

"The son," she said as she shifted her gaze to him. Smiled. Parker Ward was not slow on the uptake, despite what he might think. "Exactly what I was thinking. It would be a good place to keep his stash hidden and use." The text chime from her phone drew her attention. She pulled it out and read quickly. "Brett's on his way home. He wants to know if there's anything he can do."

Parker shifted beside her. She looked up at him. He was looking at her with raised eyebrows. "The guy who took down the governor wants to help, when we're not even sure what this is?"

Carly smiled. "If he had his way, he'd erase that line from the résumé. Notoriety is a pain, he says."

"Can't argue with him there," Parker said with a wry twist of his mouth.

"I imagine it makes it harder to do his job sometimes," Hayley said.

"But," Quinn added thoughtfully, "it also gives him some weight with the powers that be."

"It does. He gets more leeway to go with his famous gut instincts than us normal folks," Carly said with a smile.

"Which means we need to be very careful with what we ask for help with, because he'd give it when it could rebound on him."

"And now I see why he'll go to the mat for Foxworth," Carly said, appreciating Quinn's care for the man who had her full respect.

"Just for the record," Parker interjected, "there's nothing wrong with your instincts."

"Agreed," Quinn said. And then, in a decisive tone, he went on. "I think it's time to do a little more research into Mr. Turner. See if there's any innocent reason he'd lie about that."

"Ty will like that," Hayley said. "He was just saying it had been too quiet for at least three days and he was getting bored."

Quinn grinned. "We can't have that. A bored Ty gets into trouble."

Carly was still smiling inwardly at what Parker had said about her instincts when he stood up and started pacing. And after he'd admitted it was because he was restless, Quinn had tossed him a tennis ball and pointed at Cutter.

"He'll take it out of you," he said, gesturing with a thumb over his shoulder at the back door. "Throw it far and often. Or high and often."

On impulse, she followed him out the back door into the big meadow that was declaring March as the beginning of spring with an explosion of daffodils that seemed endless. He tossed the ball that she supposed had once been a neon sort of yellow but was now a bit dingy in his hand as they went. Cutter danced at their feet.

Have you told him yet?

She tried to imagine how that conversation might go. Failed utterly.

He leaned back a little and let the ball fly. The instant it left his hand, the dog was at a dead run.

"I get the feeling he's not one to be fooled by the old fake throw trick," Parker said.

"Too smart for that," she agreed. *Tell him now? Or never?* Right now she was more comfortable with option two. But then the sharp, hot memory of where they'd almost ended up, save for that pizza delivery, shot through her and made her not so sure. This was fast, very fast, for her, but… She realized suddenly, as she watched him throw the ball again and again, that this was different. On a couple of fronts, this was different. One, she knew what she most needed to know about him, simply by what he'd done in the Witner case. There would be no wondering if he was a good person, an honest person, a man of integrity, because she already knew.

And second… There was Cutter. Cutter, who had clearly decided. Cutter, whose clever manipulating and maneuvering she would have laughed off, if not for his track record.

"You're quiet," he said, startling her out of her reverie. She wondered how long she'd been lost in those thoughts.

"Oh. I…" Nope, no way she could do it. Not now, anyway. So she grabbed at the first thing she thought of. "Quinn and Hayley got married out here."

He looked at the field of flowers. "Pretty."

She managed a credible laugh. "They did it in January. And they got the stamp of approval from the weather gods, because it didn't rain and wasn't even very cold. For January."

He smiled. "You were there?"

She nodded. "I came with Brett." Hmm. Maybe she could do it. There might never be a better time to tell him. Even if it would seem impossible to him. *Yeah, like you've accepted it yourself? It's a lot different when it's you the darn dog is working on.* But she went on anyway. "Cutter hadn't introduced him to Sloane yet."

Parker blinked. "What?"

"He brought them together, while Brett was dog sitting.

He dragged him off his usual running route to her aunt's house and right up to her."

Cutter came back, and this time instead of dropping the ball for another throw, he headed past them toward the back door. Parker watched him go, but then looked back at Carly.

"And they ended up married?"

She nodded. "After bringing down the governor, yes. All in a day's work for Cutter." She took a deep breath. "He did the same thing for Teague and Laney. And Liam and Ria. Oh, the engagement party they went to? Them, too. And a bunch of others. Not to mention Quinn and Hayley themselves."

Parker was frowning. "Wait. You mean they're all…? What do you mean?"

"They're together because Cutter made it happen."

"That's…"

"Crazy? Yeah, I know. But there it is."

"You're saying he not only rounds up people with problems, he's a…"

"Matchmaker. Yep." She tried to explain, about the dog's physical maneuverings, and saw the moment when he remembered the dog making them sit together.

Parker shifted his gaze to the dog, then back to her. "You mean he's trying to matchmake…"

"Us. Yes."

He stared at her. Looked as if he were searching for words. But before he could speak, the back door opened.

"Ty's up," Quinn called.

She tried to ignore that they both took the seats they'd had before, this time without Cutter's maneuvering, and focus on what the Foxworth lead IT guy—who apparently was never off duty, given it was nearly eight o'clock where he was in St. Louis—was saying.

"I went to level three, like you asked," he said. Carly watched the young man with the spiky hair on the big flat screen over the fireplace, noticing the array of equipment visible around him and thinking if the sheriff's office had half of that they'd be light-years ahead of where they were now. And wondered just how many levels of inquiry Foxworth had.

"Go," Quinn said.

"Zip. A couple of parking tickets—one of which he fought and won because a city vehicle had blocked the entrance to the legal parking lot—and one speeding ticket years ago. No legal wranglings, lawsuits or anything like that on the business front. Besides the property in question, he owns three office supply stores, and while they've struggled a bit, he's made some changes and expanded his product lines to bring in customers for other reasons, and it's helped. Financial picture is pretty stable right now."

"So there's no obvious need for him to sell that property?" Quinn asked.

"Not financially, that I could find."

"Anything at all to indicate he's anything other than an honest, fairly smart businessman?" Hayley asked.

"Not a thing. The son, however…"

Ty's gaze shifted slightly, and she realized he was looking toward her. Carly grimaced. "Is this where I should leave? Or stay and just not think about how you got this?"

"Your choice," Quinn said neutrally. "But it'd save time if you stayed and listened. And if it's something necessary, then you can go after it your way."

"It's a darn good thing you're on the side of the angels," she muttered. But she stayed put.

"It's not really that much," Ty promised. "Just two things I don't think you knew. One, his juvie record from the city

Chapter 21

"This place," Carly said, looking around Ray's living room, "feels like a home."

"More than that place—" Parker gestured with a thumb to the house next door "—ever did."

He was nervous, even twitchy, that she'd said yes to coming back here after they'd finished at Foxworth. He was a little amazed that he'd found the nerve to even suggest it. Yet here they were.

"I don't ever have to see it to know this is a better place," she said. "And Ray is a prince."

He smiled at that. "He is."

"And also much better than the supposed adults who used to live there," she said pointedly.

Odd. The jab of pain he usually felt at any mention of his parents wasn't as sharp as it usually was. In fact, it was only a faint echo of what it had always been. He pondered that as he took another bite of the hamburger, thinking his budget couldn't handle fast food. And the only thing more embarrassing than that was letting Carly pay for it. And he didn't quite believe she'd been starving for a cheese-is huge." Carly went still. "No, I didn't hack into it—that's a level five. I just looked at the size of it."

"Okay," she said warily. "And number two?"

"I ran a cross-check up to the day he turned eighteen and found several arrests of known dealers who were picked up along with a juvenile whose ID was obviously not in the report. But four of them occurred near the landing for the ferry closest to you. It may be something, may be nothing."

Before she could stop herself, Carly asked, "You have the dates on those?"

"Sure. I'll send them."

"Good job, Ty," Quinn said. "Thanks. We'll see what we can do on this end."

He shut down the video and then looked at Carly. She shrugged. "I can at least try to get a look at the dates, see if any match up. If not, no harm, no foul. If so, then it gets trickier."

Quinn smiled. "We're good at trickier."

burger. Although she did go through it pretty fast, enough that he wondered what she did to stay as trim as she was.

He was thinking about her shape again and that needed to stop.

Good luck with that.

Searching for diversion, he said the first thing he thought. Which happened to be something he'd never told anyone.

"My parents got me the job with Witner."

She blinked at that. "They did?"

He wished he hadn't said it, but it was too late now. "They knew him. Aspired to be him, or at least the facade. And they told him about their disappointment of a son. The kid who wouldn't listen to them, had refused to even play football or baseball in school, with a view to a pro career, but only wanted to do track and field because he liked to run and jump. The son who dropped out of the fancy business college they could brag about, and worst of all, wanted to build things for a living." He grimaced. "They hated that. The idea of working with your hands was…unacceptable. But Ray got it. He understood."

"Ray has his head on straight."

"He told me to think really carefully before I took that job. I should have realized I was a pity hire."

"But it cost Witner dearly, that assumption you had no ethics, no character," she said, and something in her voice erased that last bit of pain at the subject of his parents. "As if you somehow get that installed when you get a degree."

He smiled at that. Gestured at the room they sat in. "No. I got that here."

"Why'd you take it? The job?"

He sighed. "It was a chance to make my parents proud for the first time in my life."

"That's a lot of pressure."

"I felt like I had to at least try to walk in their world, give what they wanted for me a shot. And that was their idea of success, the fancy office and house and cars, the moving in upper circles, all that."

"All of which was a lie."

"I'm not sure they cared. They could really brag at last about their son, who worked for this dynamic, money-making machine."

"They really told you to stay quiet, once you learned what was going on?"

"I think it was more they didn't believe me. Because how could I possibly know for sure. I was just a college dropout."

"I've changed my mind. I want to know your parents' first names."

He drew back slightly. "Gerald and Alexandra. Why?"

"In case I ever run into them by accident. It might be infectious, that callous stupidity." He blinked. Except for Ray, he'd never had anyone defend him the way Carly did. He didn't know what to say. And after a moment, her gaze softened. "Did you have anyone except Ray?"

He hated how pitiful that sounded, and pity was the very last thing he wanted from her, but he wouldn't lie to her, either. And if she walked away afterward, so be it. He had the vague feeling he'd just silently insulted her again, but now that he'd started, he was going to finish.

"Some old friends stuck with me. Friends from here. But over there?" He gestured toward the water, the city on the other side. "People I worked with, people I thought were friends, ghosted me so fast it took me a while to real-ize. But I get it. I brought down their world, too." He took in a breath, then finished it. "Bottom line, I dared to set foot in my parents' world and failed utterly."

"More like you stepped unknowingly into a pit of rattlesnakes and not only got out yourself but saved a lot of innocent people caught there while you were at it."

He shook his head slowly. "Why do you keep making me sound like some kind of hero?"

"Why do you keep denying what's obvious to anyone not as crooked as Witner?"

"I—"

"Are you stupid?"

"Not IQ-wise, but—"

"Do you really think your parents are right about you?"

"No, but—"

"Do you want to live the way they do?"

It was like getting peppered by Ray's shotgun loaded with bird shot. "No! But—"

"Do you value people who dump you because you did what had to be done?"

"You don't—"

"Are you trying to drive people away?"

It hit him then, hard. For all her kindness, for all her gentleness, Carly Devon was no pushover. And he realized he was seeing, for the first time, the tough, hammering cop she could be if she had to. She was questioning him like she probably did a suspect, trying to get him to trip up and let out the truth.

So I'll give her the truth.

"Just you," he said. It came out a little hoarse and he clenched his jaw. Lowered his gaze because he just couldn't look at those bright blue eyes any longer.

He thought he heard her breath catch. And her voice was entirely different when she said, very quietly, "Why?"

He'd given her all the practical reasons, and none of them had seemed to matter to her. So he dug down for an even deeper truth. "Because you...what happens between us...scares the hell out of me."

"Funny. It intrigues the hell out of me."

He drew back slightly, his gaze shooting back to her face. *"Intrigues?"*

"Because I've never felt anything like that so fast—" She stopped, gave him a wry smile, and he felt a sudden certainty that she was digging deep herself. And when she finished, her voice a bit rueful, he knew he'd been right. "Because I've never felt anything like it at all."

He sucked in the deepest breath he could and let it out slowly. "Neither have I."

"So that leaves us with one question."

His mouth twisted. "Only one?"

"One big one. What do we do about it?"

"Don't you mean, do we do anything about it?"

"Splitting hairs now?"

"No. Because the problem with what do we do is…I don't think there's any halfway here for me. Not when just a kiss about put me under."

The smile she gave him then, suddenly, was blinding. "Whew. Glad that wasn't just me."

He couldn't help smiling back. "That pizza delivery about killed me."

"Pizza," she said solemnly, "was not what I was hungry for just then." His smile widened. And then she added, softly, "Or now."

And he felt as if the sun had risen on a world that had been gray and grim for far too long.

But when her brow furrowed, he was afraid that sunrise had been a mirage. "I don't generally carry around protection," she said.

He could breathe again. "That's okay. Ray's not real subtle. He gave me a huge pack of condoms for Christmas."

To his relief, Carly laughed. Then she reached up and cupped his cheek. "Let's see if we can put a dent in it."

He kissed her again. And again, each time deeper, longer, sweeter. And it all seemed to fall away, all the doubts, all the questions, all the problems. Because right now nothing mattered but the woman in his arms and how she made him feel. Because she was kissing him back, fiercely, touching him as if she couldn't get enough. She couldn't have made it any clearer that she wanted him. He hadn't misinterpreted, not even that first moment he'd seen her and his breath had stopped in his throat.

He pressed her back on the couch, glad there would be no delivery interruption this time. He fumbled with her shirt, glad the neckline was wide enough he was able to pull it down to bare one shoulder, which he immediately had to, just had to kiss. He trailed his mouth up to her slender neck, all the while feeling his pulse start to hammer in his chest so hard he thought his heart might break free.

He felt a touch sliding over his abdomen, realized she'd slipped a hand under his shirt. She left a trail of fire with her fingers, and he smothered a groan as the ache in him ratcheted up another notch. Even the fact that it had been a while for him couldn't explain the inferno she kindled. He wanted to rush, because he wanted nothing more than to have her naked in his arms. But at the same time he wanted to savor every moment, linger over every inch of bared skin. The contradiction was driving the tension even higher.

But then she was pulling at his shirt, as if she were desperate to get it off. He pulled back long enough to shed it and toss it aside. Before he'd even let go of it, she was kissing him again, this time her lips tracing over his chest in a way that made it impossible to stop the sound that burst from him.

And then her hand slid downward to stroke over his

straining erection, and he broke. He clawed away her clothes and his own.

"Bed," he muttered.

"Too far," she said as she flicked her tongue over his nipple.

"Later." He gasped it this time as he slid his own hand between them. It was like another electric jolt when he found her slick and ready, more proof that this was real, she truly wanted him. He'd never realized how precious that was until now.

And when at last he slid inside her, when she arched up to him to take him deep, urging him on, he gave a heartfelt exclamation of incoherent sound he couldn't stop. Then he had to move, simply had to. He drove into her, savoring her gasps of pleasure even as he let out his own. This was real, this was true, and for the first time in his life, he understood. When she convulsed around him, crying out his name, he groaned hers out in turn, and the fall back to earth was long, slow and luscious.

For the first time in his life, Parker Ward understood what Ray had meant.

Usually Carly awoke at first light on Monday mornings, the detritus of her caseload and the general business of life tumbling in her head at the start of a new week. But this morning it was well past dawn, and it took the sound of her email notification to stir her out of a delicious dream. Sleepily she reached for her nightstand and the phone—and found instead solid, sleek male muscle.

Parker.

It wasn't her nightstand. And it hadn't been a dream.

She came fully awake with a start. Hastily reached the opposite way and grabbed the phone to silence it before it woke him. She knew from the musical tone, the one she'd assigned to that account, that it was work related. But she couldn't bring herself to open it this instant. She needed a moment to absorb, to process, and with a little echo of shivery amazement, remember the amazing night that had just passed.

And savor the amazing man who had given it to her. Because give he had, time and again.

Sometimes I get tired of being the one in charge. It had been a hint, and he hadn't missed it.

Then let me be the one.

He'd proceeded to do just that—take charge. Done everything with her and to her she could ever have wished. And had driven her completely, utterly mad.

He stirred, but didn't wake. She smiled at that, hoping it was because he needed the rest after last night. And she was glad, because it gave her the chance to look at him. To really appreciate the combination of strength in the masculine jawline, the cords of his neck and the breadth of his chest, and the softness in the twin sweeps of thick, dark eyelashes…and his mouth. That mouth that had driven her as close to madness as she'd ever been in her life. Until she'd begged, literally begged him, to stop teasing her and to slide back inside her, where he belonged.

Belonged.

You are a goner.

And darn it, Cutter was right. Again.

Of course, convincing the skeptical Parker of that might take some doing.

Finally she made herself tear her gaze away from the delectable sight of a naked Parker sprawled beside her. She sat up and looked at her phone. Frowned at the two voice mails from a Seattle number that looked familiar. But first she opened the mail app. Saw the sender's name and blinked. Doubled-checked the time, although she knew it was after seven, because she'd put her phone facedown last night to silence it until that time. For one of the few times in her life, she'd had much better things to do. Still, it was awfully early on a Monday morning to get a notification from the county lab. Usually it was midday before she heard anything.

And there was only one thing she'd personally sent to the lab in the last week.

"Carly?"

His sleepy voice came from behind her just as she tapped the message. He sounded like she'd felt moments ago.

As the email slowly loaded—Ray was right about the spotty cell reception out here—it much too belatedly hit her that this was Monday morning and even if she left in the next thirty seconds she'd still be late getting in. Because she wasn't five minutes from the department; she was at the other end of the county.

And then she felt a feather of fire ripple down her spine as he ran a finger down her back.

She wanted more than anything to toss the phone away— somewhere where it couldn't be seen or heard—and roll back over to him. She wanted to ride him again, feeling the rigid hardness of him stroking her from within. She wanted him to take her in a mad rush again, as he had in the middle of the night. She wanted him in ways she'd never wanted a man before, and with a ferocity that was almost frightening.

But this was also his case, although she couldn't call it that yet. At least, until she read this email, which her gut was telling her could change that completely.

So, reluctantly, she said, "I got something from the lab. The only thing I've sent them lately is that hat."

He blinked once, hard. And that quickly, he was wide awake. She tried not to notice that he was as ready as she had been to resume their night's activities, but it was difficult when the sheet slid down as he sat up.

Finally the message was loaded. She read it quickly. And let out a compressed breath. Everything had indeed just changed. Because the DNA on the hat had finally come back. Which explained the call and voice mails from the number that had looked familiar.

Because it belonged to a lieutenant from one of the most notorious drug gangs in the city.

Chapter 22

"So they know this guy over there?"

Despite the shock of the lab results, Parker stayed still to savor the sheer pleasure of watching a naked Carly get dressed, although he much preferred the other way around. But he'd have to settle for the memory of watching her as she sent a couple of long text messages, to Brett Dunbar and her boss, she'd said, while he had just admired her body, painted with morning light.

"All too well. I've gotten two calls from the gang division over there already, so we'll have more details as soon as we connect. But according to the match results, Ace Neuson—aka 'Noose,' if you can stand it—has a record as long as the Space Needle is tall," Carly said as she hooked her bra—no lace, but a pretty color that matched the sweater she pulled on next. The soft fabric hugged those sweet, full breasts he'd caressed and tasted and filled his hands with.

He tried to focus on something else as his body surged to readiness again just at the thought. The color of both bra and sweater was a blue green that seemed to turn her eyes the same shade. There was a word for that effect, when eyes took on the color of what was near them, but it escaped him at the moment. Because they hadn't gotten much sleep last night.

They.

Together. All night.

I should go.

Stay. Please. I want to wake up with you.

That wonderful smile. *You only had to ask.*

He gave himself an inward shake. He needed to focus, but it was difficult when he was still in that luscious haze from last night, from having her in his arms, under him, on top of him, beside him. He'd never had a night like that, never felt anything like the sheer, fierce, explosive pleasure of pouring himself into her.

He tried for coherency. "So he's a known gang member with a long record, but mainly in the city?"

"Exclusively in the greater metro area. He's never been popped anywhere west of the sound."

"Then why was he over here?"

"Maybe he wanted to rectify that."

His brow furrowed as he reached for his jeans and pulled them on. "You mean…expand his territory?"

"Or the gang's. Maybe the boss is getting greedy."

"Then Turner's kid…"

She watched him zip up with an almost regretful expression that threatened to turn him on all over again. It had been so long since a woman he liked, truly, deeply liked, had looked at him hungrily.

Hell, I've never liked any woman like that before.

Dressed now—sadly—she leaned over to pick up the weapon she'd set on the nightstand when they'd moved from the great room to his borrowed bedroom. And for the first time, he'd been glad of the smaller double bed in

Ray's guest room after the king-size he was used to, because it forced them closer together.

When she spoke, she was all business again.

"The guy with the hat could be his supplier."

Parker took in a breath. "This is starting to sound… official."

She clipped her holster to her waistband, pulled on her lightweight jacket and slid her phone into one of the pockets. Then she looked at him. "I think it's enough to justify digging into it to my lieutenant. A gangster slash drug dealer from the city over here, Turner's kid a user and what Ray saw…"

"And the kid's father lying about where he is, and putting that building up for sale the very next day… Ray was right from the beginning," Parker said.

"Starting to look that way."

"And the building sale is to get the money to pay a ransom. They should run some comps, see if maybe he listed that place for less than he could get for it, to move it fast."

Carly drew back slightly. "Now, that's a good idea."

"I have them now and then." He smiled slowly. "Like last night."

"That," she said with an answering smile, "was definitely a good idea." He could look at that smile forever. Not that he needed much to look at her again. And again and again.

Reluctant though he was, he finished dressing quickly. "I need to go tell Ray."

"That he apparently really did witness a kidnapping?"

"Yes, he—" He broke off suddenly.

What had hit him must have shown in his face, because she asked, "What's wrong?"

"What else besides dealing has that guy been arrested

for?" His voice was almost hoarse with the fear that had just swamped him.

"You name it." Carly was frowning now.

"Murder?"

"Arrested, yes. But not convicted. I don't have the details yet. But yes, it's occurred to me Turner's son could already be dead."

He felt a jab of self-reproach; he actually hadn't even made that jump. But right now he brushed it aside. And said only, "I lived under constant guard for over a year, coming up to that trial."

As he'd known she would, she got there instantly. "Ray."

"Witner was a bad guy, but he wasn't a killer. But I still got 24/7 protection."

"You're thinking maybe he really was seen?"

"I'm thinking I'm not willing to risk assuming he wasn't."

"I understand. I'll do what I can, Parker, but we don't have the resources for that kind of protection, especially when Ray insists he wasn't seen."

"Then I'll stay with him. They'll just have to deal. I'll sleep on the damn floor, if I have to." He grimaced. "How much trouble would I be in if I took his shotgun with me?"

"I'm thinking the rehab center wouldn't like it too much," she said. "And they have the right to—" She stopped suddenly.

"What?" he asked.

"We don't have the resources," she repeated slowly, "but we know some people who probably do."

He stopped in the act of pulling on the jacket he'd grabbed when he'd heard rain hitting the deck outside. Looked at her. "Foxworth?" She nodded. "They do…stuff like that? I mean, Quinn seems more than tough enough, but—"

"You haven't met Rafe Crawford yet," she said, and

her tone was rather dry. "He makes Quinn look like a pussycat."

Parker blinked; that was hard to imagine. But Carly seemed certain. And he trusted her. Admittedly he'd misplaced his trust before, but he didn't think he had this time. "I don't want Ray worried or scared."

"From what Brett has told me, they can do it so covertly no one would know." And then Carly was moving quickly. "Let's go."

"I need to see to Woof. Just let him out, then feed him and check his water."

She nodded. "Least we can do after he left us in peace last night."

Inappropriate as it seemed for the moment, Parker couldn't stop a quick smile from forming. "I don't think he liked what we were doing."

Her smile was wider. "I did."

His breath caught at her expression, and before he could stop himself, he was saying, "Enough to want a repeat?"

"More than one, hopefully."

She said it so easily it almost rattled him. Only half joking, he said, "You trust Cutter that much?"

"I work on evidence and proof, Parker. And I have the proof of Cutter's…skill in this area several times over."

He shook his head in wonder. "I think I'll go take care of just a plain ole dog."

She nodded. "Then call Foxworth. I'll drive. Time to put some official miles on that county car of mine."

Chapter 23

Cutter was out the door and running to greet them before Carly even turned the car into the gravel parking area.

"Is this where I admit I feel guilty leaving Woof at home?"

Carly smiled as she glanced at Parker. "It is hard, isn't it? But I think you were right. This might not be the day, even for a playdate with this guy."

"Yeah. Especially given that other car there."

She'd noticed it the moment they'd cleared the thick trees, and obviously so had he. "Turner."

"Yeah. How'd they get him here, and so fast? I only called and gave them the update an hour ago."

"They're definitely living up to their reputation," she said as she pulled in next to the vehicle that they'd seen before, at the vacant building.

"Especially given Turner's reluctance to talk in the first place."

"If what we suspect is true, not surprising."

"I guess." His brow furrowed as they came to a halt. "He's still worried about his kid, even though he's legally an adult now."

His rather puzzled tone made her ache a little. He was truly bemused by the idea. She shut off the engine and turned to look at him. "I'm thirty-two and my parents still worry about me."

"Well, yeah. You're a cop."

"That's only part of it. They worry not just about my safety, but whether I'm happy, whether I'm eating well, sleeping enough, where I live, all of it."

The puzzled look lingered for a moment, but then it was replaced by a rather startled look. "Where do you live?" he asked. She supposed it was a little odd that he didn't know exactly, given how they'd spent last night. "I mean, I know you're in the south county, but—"

"A couple of miles from the office," she said. "So I can run in or home almost every day, depending on my workload."

"So that's how you're in such great shape," he said. She gave him a raised eyebrow. He added hastily, "I mean condition, not...shape, shape."

"And here I thought you liked my...shape. You certainly paid enough attention to it last night."

That quickly, as if the memories were hovering as close to the surface in his mind as in hers, his expression changed to something hot and intense. "Your shape," he said almost fiercely, "is the most beautiful thing I've ever seen."

"Back at you, Mr. Built-Like-a-Superhero," she said and enjoyed his startled look and the little smile that curved his lips as he lowered his gaze.

The bark that came sharply then told her Cutter had run out of patience.

"The doorman calleth," Parker said wryly.

She laughed; she did like the way he put things. She got out, greeted Cutter with a scratch behind the right ear, then watched as he trotted over to Parker, who had come around the front of the car, for the same.

Then the dog backed up to where he could look at them both, and Carly would swear, crazy as it seemed, that he wasn't just happy to see them—he was happy to see them together.

As they reached the doorway Cutter had politely opened for them with a bat at the pad beside the door, Parker saw two men heading toward them. One he recognized as Liam, the sandy-blond guy with the Texas way with words and a penchant for naming inanimate objects. The man behind him, taller, darker—in more ways than one—he hadn't seen before. And he had a feeling he should be glad of that. Something in the man's eyes spoke of too much seen, and too much of it bad.

"Carly, Parker," Liam said. Then, with a nod back at the other man, he added, "Parker, Rafe Crawford. And you remember Carly, right, Rafe? Like what man could forget her," he finished with a grin.

"Indeed." Rafe's voice was deep, a bit gruff and as dark as the shadows that haunted his eyes. Then he looked at Parker again. "Good to meet the man who put a stop to some nasty stuff."

That startled him a little, but he quickly decided he would much rather be on the good side of this guy. "Thanks," he said and left it at that.

The man shifted his gaze back to Carly. "How's Brett?"

"Back home with Sloane, so I'm guessing delirious," she said.

A faint but definite smile crossed the forbidding man's face, and Parker felt a little easier. Or he did, until Rafe's gaze flicked to him and back to Carly. "I hear Cutter's up to his tricks again."

Carly blushed. He didn't blame her; they hadn't talked at all about going public with…anything. But it seemed with Cutter involved, it wasn't necessary.

"We're off to look after Ray," Liam said, graciously saving her from further embarrassment.

Parker's gaze shot back to Rafe. "We'll keep him safe," the intimidating man said. "Whatever it takes."

He watched the two men go, the quiet promise echoing in his head. And something about them, although they seemed unlikely partners, the cheerful Texan and the rather dour Rafe, made him believe they could likely fulfill that promise.

"He means that." Hayley's voice came from behind them and held the quiet sort of confidence he'd noticed all the Foxworths seemed to have. Well, except Cutter; he seemed to get a bit more impatient. "Rafe would die before he'd let another vet get hurt on his watch."

"Because he's one himself," Parker said, not quite sure how he knew. Maybe it was that same stubborn air Ray had.

"He is." She was looking from him to Carly and back, a little too speculatively. Almost as if… He gave himself an inward shake. There was no way she could know how he and Carly had spent the night. He made himself focus.

"Ray won't be happy," he said. "He won't like the idea of not being able to protect himself."

"Ray," Quinn said as he came up to them, "will never know. Unless he needs to." There was undeniable certainty in the man's voice, a certainty that made Parker wonder exactly what Rafe Crawford had done in the military.

"Thanks," he said, and it was heartfelt.

Then Quinn, too, glanced from Parker to Carly and then back, with that same kind of speculation in his gaze Hayley had had. "Cutter seems pretty smug this morning," he observed to his wife.

"That he does," she said cheerfully.

And Parker had second thoughts about whether they could somehow know. Because it hit him that perhaps Cutter could actually tell. Maybe he had some of that sweet scent of Carly's clinging to him that the dog's finely tuned nose could detect.

"Come on in. Carly, let him see you first."

Parker frowned at that as they walked into the welcoming big room, where the fireplace was doing a nice job of taking off the morning chill. The temperature had plummeted overnight, reminding everyone of the perennial battle between winter and spring.

Not that he'd really noticed. He hadn't noticed much of anything last night except the woman in his arms, in his bed. And it startled him how much that had changed... everything. Not just the physical gratification of having the fierce attraction he'd felt from the first moment he'd seen her consummated, but his entire outlook seemed to have shifted. For the first time in nearly three years, his life didn't look totally grim or debris-strewn. He didn't feel quite so hopeless, didn't feel like a failure.

Because Carly Devon admired him.

Because Carly Devon liked him.

Because Carly Devon wanted him.

She hadn't quibbled, hadn't played games. It hadn't been some elaborate give-and-take where neither party knew the truth about why it was happening. It had been the most open and honest connection he'd ever had with a woman, and he was beyond amazed at how much garbage it had cleared out of his mind.

"I like that smile," she whispered to him as they followed Hayley and Quinn. "Hang on to it."

He gave her a sideways look. "It's attached to you."

She smiled back at him. "As this one is to you."

He hesitated a moment before saying, "Do you get the feeling they…know?"

Carly's smile turned wry. "I think their scary dog told them."

That made him laugh, and the simple fact that he could laugh at all, in the middle of not just this but the mess his life had become, spoke volumes to him about how much he had changed, been changed, by having her in that life.

That he still had nothing to offer her, no future to speak of, was something he tried not to think about right now. But somewhere in the midst of that too-familiar morass was something that had been missing since the day he'd realized just what his course of action was going to cost him.

Hope.

Hope that someday, and soon, he would be able to—

"Hey! She's that cop! What the hell is she doing here?"

The shout ripped through the quiet of the room. Parker's head snapped around, his adrenaline spiking at the tone of the man's voice. In the same instant he heard Cutter growl a warning.

His every muscle tensed. If Turner made a move toward Carly, it would be a contest to see if he or the dog took him down first.

Chapter 24

"What is going on here, Foxworth?"

Quinn kept walking toward the man shouting, never hesitating. Carly started after him, then felt Parker tense beside her. Protectively. And that made her feel strange enough that it was a second before she was able to whisper, "Easy. Quinn wanted to see his reaction."

She'd known that from the moment Quinn had said to let Turner see her. And his reaction was one she recognized all too well. That of a terrified father. And to her that told her what she needed to know; this was simply a man trying to protect his son.

"Stay calm, Mr. Turner," Quinn said. "She's not here as a law officer."

"What the hell does that mean?"

"Play along," she whispered to Parker before saying brightly, almost cheerfully, to Turner as she waved toward the man beside her, "That means I'm only here because my fiancé is here." She felt the jolt as her words registered with Parker. "But if it bothers you, I'll go outside while the rest of you talk."

"I think it's a bit cold for that," Hayley said. "So shall we ladies adjourn upstairs?"

Carly's brow furrowed, but at Hayley's sideways look, she gave in and followed her upstairs to the third floor. She'd been up here only once, and that had involved a meeting around the large table next to the expansive windows that looked out toward the thick stand of evergreens. She'd never forgotten the moment the mated pair of bald eagles, the same ones that had put on a dramatic show at Quinn and Hayley's wedding, had lifted off from the large maple amid the cedar trees and swooped over the meadow before soaring skyward.

She was surprised when Hayley gestured her to the back of the room, where an impressive—and a bit intimidating—array of computer equipment was set up. She was more surprised when Hayley handed her one earpiece from a wired set, then settled the other in her own ear.

Carly blinked. Looked at Hayley, who smiled. "You were right. Quinn wanted to see how Turner would react to your presence. But he also wants your take on how he acts now."

She felt rather flattered. "I got the feel he was reacting like a very scared father."

Hayley nodded. "I agree. So let's see what we have here…"

Then she leaned over and tapped a couple of keys on the nearest keyboard. A monitor came to life and they were looking at the meeting downstairs. The sound went live in her ear just as Turner was saying, only a bit less stridently, "—then what's he doing here?"

He was pointing at Parker, who had taken a seat opposite the man and settled in as if he were content to wait him out.

"He's a client," Quinn said. "But we have business to discuss. Please, sit down, Mr. Turner."

The man did so, but warily. Then so did Quinn, although Carly noticed he was on the edge of the chair, ready to move quickly. The posture she herself would have taken, were she still in the room.

"Pardon my curiosity," Quinn said in a casual tone, "but I'm sure you know your price is below comparable market prices."

"Yes. I need the quick cash influx." He smiled, the businessman now surfacing. "And that's an advantage to you, Mr. Foxworth. If you can agree to the very short escrow I mentioned."

Carly looked at Hayley. "So that's how you got him here so fast. You offered to buy the building."

Hayley nodded. "We thought about going to him, but Quinn wanted to judge how desperate he was."

"By how fast he got here?"

Another nod. Carly went back to the screen. The camera must be in the flat screen, judging by the angle. And she had to work far too hard not to zero in on Parker instead of where she should be looking. But seeing him like this, able to watch him without him realizing it and getting self-conscious, was a pleasure. And revealing, as well; he might have that boy-next-door look, emphasized by that great smile and slightly disheveled hair, but those eyes of his were focused on Turner like a laser. And she realized she was seeing the man who had had the spine to stand up to an Olympic-level crook and call him out.

"We have no problem with a short escrow," Quinn said, and Carly snapped out of the reverie she seemed to slip into all too often around Parker. "But that's not the real issue, is it?"

"I—"

"Let's get to the real reason you're in a hurry to sell."

"Real reason? I told you, it's a personal matter. A... friend needs the cash," Turner finished awkwardly.

"A friend?" Quinn asked gently. "Don't you mean your son's drug dealer?"

Turner went so pale Carly felt sorry for him. His startled gaze went from Quinn to Parker and back. Then, stumblingly, he said, "I...don't know what you're talking about."

Quinn just looked at the man, and Carly could only imagine what it must feel like, with Parker's fierce gaze coming at him from one side and the steely gaze of a former Army ranger from the other.

"Do you know who we are, Mr. Turner?" Quinn asked, his voice still gentle.

"I've heard of Foxworth," the man said. "From the thing with the governor." His tone shifted, now tinged with a bit of anger. "That's why I agreed to this meeting. I don't know what you think you're up to. You want my building at an even lower price, or—"

"No, Mr. Turner. We neither want nor need your building. But we will buy it, to give you that cash infusion. If that's what you decide you want to do."

The man looked bewildered now. And for the first time, Carly heard the fear in his voice. "Want? I have no choice."

Quinn's voice went quieter still. It was a technique Carly knew, one she'd learned from Brett Dunbar; the lower your voice, the more the other person had to focus on you to hear you, and the more you could read the micro expressions that betrayed truth or lie, anger or fear.

"Because they kidnapped your son."

Turner jerked back. Stared. "How did— No. No, that didn't happen."

"In the alley right behind the building in question, last Tuesday at eleven in the morning."

Turner was gaping at Quinn now. It was a moment before he said, rather weakly, "That's not true. You can't prove that's true."

"Interesting that that's what he's concerned about," Hayley murmured.

"Kind of indicates it is true," Carly agreed.

"It was actually very smart of you, to tell him the only way you could get the amount he was demanding was to sell a building. Which would take time," Quinn said rather gently.

Turner looked confused, as if he didn't know how to feel about the compliment about something he was denying had happened. "I don't—"

"There was a witness, Mr. Turner."

"What? What are you talking about? What witness?"

And then, from behind Turner, came a quiet, steady, determined voice. Parker's voice. Speaking just one short word.

"Me."

Hayley blinked. But Carly understood immediately. And Quinn, bless him, never turned a hair, although his gaze flicked to Parker. While Turner had whirled to stare at the man who hadn't said a word before now.

Hayley glanced at her questioningly.

"Ray," Carly said. "He's protecting Ray."

Hayley's expression changed to one of complete understanding instantly.

Turner found his voice again. "You?" The older man's brow furrowed. "Wait. You're the one who called the cops?"

Parker nodded.

"Technically true," Carly said. "He did make the call when no one else would."

Turner shook his head slowly, as if processing all this was a tremendous effort.

"I can only imagine what he's been through since that day," Hayley said sympathetically.

"Have to forgive him for being edgy," Carly said. "I've dealt with a couple of kidnappings, and I wouldn't wish it on anyone."

Turner's eyes suddenly widened and he leaped to his feet, staring at Parker. Cutter was up in an instant, hackles rising as he let out a warning rumble. Quinn was moving before Turner was even completely upright, and Parker a split second later. Turner glared at Parker furiously, fists clenched. Quinn took a step toward the man whose back was now to him, but stopped when Parker's glance flicked his way and he gave a slight shake of his head.

"You brought her here," Turner said, his voice rising. "Damn you, you brought a cop here, when I promised I wouldn't call them. They'll kill him!"

"I brought…my fiancée," Parker said.

Hearing the words from his lips, even as part of a facade, sent a shiver of reaction through Carly. Seeing the smile that curved his mouth when he said them, the change in his eyes from cool to heat, kicked her pulse rate up as surely as if she'd just chased that rascal Cutter across the meadow.

"When we're through this bit of drama," Hayley said conversationally, "we'll have to have a little talk about you and Parker."

Carly couldn't look at her. "It's just…pretense."

"Mmm-hmm."

"It is," Carly insisted, wondering if it was as much for herself as Hayley, an effort to keep from jumping the gun.

"Sorry," Hayley said, her tone now so cheerful it was almost annoying. "Not buying it."

"I'm glad you're so sure," Carly retorted, her tone wry now.

"Not me," Hayley said. "Cutter. And you know as well

as anyone, when it comes to people who belong together, he's never wrong."

It was crazy. Impossible, even.

It was also undeniable.

And underneath it all, warmth expanded within her at that simple phrase.

Belong together.

Chapter 25

"That was a clever move," Carly said. "ID'ing yourself as the witness and thus deflecting any possible attention from Ray."

Parker didn't know what to say to that—he never knew what to say to compliments like that—so he merely shrugged. The meeting between Quinn and Turner continued inside, but they were outside the Foxworth building, where the sun had cleared the trees and warmed the morning air to a pleasant temperature for a stroll through the clearing.

"Of course," she went on in a casual tone, "now we have to make sure they don't come after you."

"Better me than Ray."

She smiled at him then, in a way that had him thinking things he had no right to think just now. He glanced back over his shoulder.

"I wonder why the dog didn't want to come out," he said as they walked; Woof would never, ever miss a chance to go outside.

"I think he was working," Carly said. Parker started to laugh, but then it faded away because he wasn't at all sure she wasn't exactly right. "He's one of their team, as much as, if not more than, any of them, Liam says."

And there it was again, back at the front of his mind. The clever dog's supposed other talent. "Liam. And his teacher."

"Ria, yes."

"And Teague and Laney, the groomer."

Her expression changed just slightly, but he knew she'd seen where he was going. "Yes," she said.

"Your detective and his wife."

"And Quinn and Hayley themselves."

A matchmaking dog. Who seemed to think he and Carly should be…matched. Even as his pulse kicked up in response to the thought, his mouth tightened slightly. Obviously the dog didn't take feasibility into account.

He tried to—had to—focus on something else. Anything else. He looked out toward the trees, wondering if perhaps the pair of eagles were around. He didn't see the familiar shapes in the maple where they usually were. Then he focused on the brighter, much more obvious aspect of the space around them. Parker didn't think he'd ever seen so many flowers in one place, strewn across the meadow in bright yellow profusion.

"Do you suppose they planted all these?" Carly asked, as if she'd noticed where his attention had gone.

Of course she did. She's a cop, and she never misses a thing. Even if she had to monitor things from another room, as she'd told him she and Hayley had done. He'd understood why, it only made sense, but it still had him wondering if he'd done anything stupid for her to see.

Since he'd grown up here, where the spring appearance was a known and welcome thing, he had an answer for her. "Daffs can spread on their own, if the conditions are right. Laura planted a few in one corner of their yard, and they spread all over the place." He smiled sadly. "She loved those things. I think she held on, at the end, just so she could see them one last time."

"I wish I could have known her, just from the way you look when you talk about her."

He looked at her then, saw the sincerity in her expression. "I wish you could have, too."

Especially since, for the moment, you're my fiancée.

He had to look away then, for fear the crazy tangle of emotions that had roiled through him when he'd said that aloud to Turner would show.

"Are they serious?" he asked abruptly. "About buying his building, I mean?"

Again she seemed easily willing to accept the shift in conversation. That seemed significant somehow. Perhaps because she'd already completely dismissed the whole "fiancée" facade.

"I think so," she said.

"At least the guy had the smarts to stall them off that way, saying he had to sell the building to get the money. That bought some time."

"Yes. He's clearly not stupid, just frantic. Terrified for his son."

They walked on farther, in an easy sort of silence he'd never experienced before. Like so many other things he'd never experienced before.

Like last night?

Before his mind could veer down that path, he scrambled for something else to say. "They've really done this before? Dealt with kidnappings, I mean?"

Carly nodded. "I don't know specifics, because they're not big on taking credit, but yes, they have. And were successful in getting the victim back alive each time."

And now they were out protecting the person who was

more important to him than anyone in the world. It hit him then that Ray might finally have some competition in that category. And that Ray himself would be delighted about it.

If I wish anything for you, kid, it's to find what I had with my Laura. If you have that, you can take on anything else in the world.

But caution rose in him. Despite his feeling like he knew her, it had been less than a week.

You thought you knew Witner, too.

He looked back toward the building. "It's…amazing, what they do."

"Kind of does the heart good, to know someone's truly out there fighting for the little guy—or the big guy, if they're in the right."

"Yeah." He grimaced. "Especially if you've seen the other extreme."

"Which you have. And actually, that's kind of what started them on this path, after the terrorist that killed Quinn and his sister's parents was cut loose in a back-room political deal."

He'd read the abbreviated version of the story on the Foxworth website, when he'd looked it up before letting them step in when it came to Ray. "That'd do it for me," he said wryly.

"Like innocent people losing everything did it for you?" she asked, giving him that smile again. That smile as if she were…proud of him. Which implied a connection. A caring sort of possessiveness that made him feel oddly warm inside. As just about everything about her did.

"Carly—"

A bark made them turn around. Cutter was racing toward them. When he saw them turn, he stopped, barked again, then turned and headed back toward the headquarters building. He paused and looked back over his shoulder.

"Ah," Parker said with a crooked grin, "the universal canine 'follow me' signal."

"With most dogs, I'd guess he wanted food or something. With this one, it's more like an order."

He laughed. Again. And he was seized with the urge to tell her how much she had done for him, to lift him out of that malaise he'd been in for so long. Then Cutter barked again, and he had the silly thought that it was to tell him the case took precedence at the moment.

But when they started to follow the clever dog, he reached out and took Carly's hand.

Chapter 26

"Quinn went with him to the building, to put on a show of looking at it to buy," Hayley explained when Carly asked. "Since he told him that to buy time, he—or they—might be watching."

"Will Turner be willing to wait the full time they gave him?" Carly didn't think so from what she'd seen, but they had spent more time with the man.

"Doubtful," Hayley said. "He's already panicky enough to do something stupid, so we thought it best he not be alone."

Parker gave the woman a wry smile. "Your husband would be enough to keep me in line."

"But you," Hayley said easily, "wouldn't panic. You'd just do what had to be done."

He blinked as he drew back slightly. Carly grinned at him. "And that is why Hayley is the people evaluator for the team. She's rarely wrong."

Hayley grinned, too, and Carly knew the woman had sensed Parker's state of mind and done her best to alleviate it. She made a mental note to call her parents and thank them for being them, as opposed to destructive forces like Parker's.

Armed with fresh coffee, they sat down in the main room again. Hayley set a cell phone on the coffee table and slid it toward them. "This is one of ours," she explained. "That red button on the top connects to a private, encrypted network only we have access to. Once we're under way, just push that and you'll be in direct contact with us, like a radio system."

Carly looked at the thing. "Wish our walkie-talkies were that compact."

Hayley smiled. "Ty could make a mint modernizing police systems. We're lucky he's happy where he is."

Carly smiled before asking, "Proof of life?"

"Next up," Hayley confirmed. Carly wasn't surprised. Foxworth knew what they were doing.

"Getting harder to find a dated newspaper to hold up in front of the guy, like in Ray's old movies," Parker said.

Hayley just smiled. "We prefer video anyway. Time-stamped, in a way we can verify."

Carly was sure Foxworth's technical people could do that; there'd been some equipment upstairs that she didn't even recognize.

"That's a big number they're demanding. You guys have that kind of money just sitting around?" Parker asked.

"We have an emergency fund for contingencies like this. Charlie sees to that." At his look she added, "Quinn's sister. Who sees to just about everything, when it comes down to it."

"Let me guess… She's the financial genius?" Parker asked.

"She is. She'll deal. Meanwhile," Hayley said as she looked at Carly sympathetically, "I know this puts you in a difficult place again."

"Not as tough as Turner's," she answered. "When a kidnapper tells you they'll kill your son if you call the cops, you tend to believe them."

"Yes. And he won't cooperate with you. He utterly refuses to have law enforcement involved at all."

"Directly," Carly said neutrally.

"There is that," Hayley agreed. "But can you maintain that step back? We have solid evidence of a felony now."

Carly nodded. "Yes, we do. I'd say it's time to clue Brett in. He's dealt with this before, where the victim's family refuses to cooperate."

"Agreed. Do you want to call him, or should we?"

"I will." She sighed inwardly. "I wanted to talk to him anyway." *About Cutter's accuracy rate in the matchmaking department.*

As if she'd read Carly's mind, Hayley gave them both a teasing look. "And that was a nice dodge, by the way. The fiancé thing." Carly's gaze shot to Parker, who was suddenly intent on petting Cutter, who had plopped his head on his knee. "It was a dodge, wasn't it?" Hayley asked, too innocently.

"For now," Carly said, knowing Parker wouldn't.

His head snapped up and their gazes locked. What she saw in those changeable hazel eyes both warmed her and warned her. Hope and doubt. She could work with that. Because she understood the doubt, because of the number his parents had done on him. And no one knew better than a juvenile detective that the damage done by parents when kids were young lasted a lifetime.

As she pulled out her phone to make an official call to Brett Dunbar, she had a moment to ponder the craziness of it all, that she, who had often been accused of being picky, overly particular and old-fashioned about relationships, was contemplating a serious future with a man she'd met less than a week ago. Because of a dog. Admittedly, a dog with a stellar record. Unbelievable, but stellar.

Well, Cutter plus the fact that Parker Ward got to her in ways no other man ever had.

Parker was pacing the length of Ray's small room at the rehab center when he came back from physical therapy.

"That son of a gun's a sadist," the older man muttered as he came in. "He delights in pushing the limits."

Parker stopped. "I thought you said you liked him."

"I like that he'll get me out of here sooner," Ray corrected. "Tomorrow would be good."

"Keep pushing." Parker knew he didn't need to say it; this man would never quit.

"I will." Ray sat down on the edge of his bed and stretched, lifting his right arm and flexing his elbow. "Plus a good amount of complaining. I figure if I keep griping he'll be sick of me sooner." Parker laughed. "Well, now, that's better. So what's eating at you that had you pacing the floor?"

Ray knew him too well. Read him too well. Just like Carly seemed to. But he wasn't ready to talk about that yet, not even to Ray. So he went for the other reason he was here. He pulled over the chair next to the small table by the window that looked out into the courtyard of the rehab wing and sat down. He leaned forward, his elbows resting on his knees.

"You were right," he began.

"Call out the trumpets," Ray said dryly.

"They'd complain about the noise even if angels were playing them," Parker fired back. Then they were both chuckling at the old, familiar exchange, and the easy rapport they'd always had was back.

Quickly, he explained what he could. "It was a kidnapping, although the guy was eighteen. Probably drug related."

"Those Foxworth folks involved?"

"They are. In fact, they're pretty much handling it." *Along with keeping you safe.* "Seems they've done it before."

"What about that pretty detective of yours?"

A quick denial rose to his lips, but he couldn't speak the words. Not when he wanted Ray's assessment to be all true, not just the pretty part. "You mean the smart one?"

"That, too," Ray agreed.

"She's in a tough place. She knows what happened, but the victim's father refuses to cooperate with law enforcement."

"What's she going to do?"

"Back off and observe, for now. When the victim is safe, then she'll try to go after the kidnapper."

"Alone?" Parker liked that Ray looked concerned.

"She's calling in some backup, their major crimes detective, and when the victim is safe they'll go wide, so between that and Foxworth…" He shrugged, trying to hide how worried he himself was.

"Good. Don't want anything to happen to her, now that you've finally found her."

Parker blinked. Straightened. "I…what?"

Ray snorted. "Please. Do you think I'm blind?"

"No, but—"

"I've watched you through a lot of—" Ray threw up some air quotes "—'relationships,' but you've never had that look before."

"What look?" Parker asked warily.

Ray seemed to hesitate, unusual enough for him that Parker caught himself holding his breath. And then the man who had saved him said quietly, "The look I wore whenever I looked at Laura. I've waited a long time to see you find the woman who could do that for you."

Parker sighed and lowered his gaze to his hands.

"Damn it, Parker, stop it. Don't let them do this to you."

His head came up sharply. For a crusty old salt, Ray rarely swore, so when he did it was a warning sign. And he knew better than to deny what the man had obviously seen. "She does make me feel that way." He thought about telling Ray about Cutter and his supposed skill at bringing people together. Decided the truth was preposterous enough without throwing that into the mix. "It's crazy. I've only known her a week—"

"I knew Laura was the one from the instant I saw her. Before we'd even spoken."

"I know."

The story had been Parker's ideal from the first time Ray had told him how he'd seen the fiery redhead standing up for a bullied kid his senior year in high school, facing down a boy who thought he was better than everyone else because his mother was on the school board. He'd masked his innate meanness with causes most thought worthy, but in that moment his true nature had been on display. And Ray himself had been on his way to intervene, but the petite woman got there before him, fearlessly facing down the much bigger bully. Some instinct had told him to just stand by, so he had, ready to take the guy out if he made a wrong move. But as most bullies did, he backed down, laughing to cover himself as he walked away, making borderline obscene comments about her as he went. The girl had turned to look at Ray, and the instant their gazes had locked, he'd known he was looking at his future.

"Don't fight it, kid. Trust me on this."

Parker wished it was that simple. Wished he could simply pursue what was between him and Carly, build something like Ray and Laura had had. But the truth had to be spoken. "I can't. I have nothing, Ray. No job, I'm broke, no prospects—"

"You know what my prospects were when Laura and I got married?" Ray asked sharply. "Grim and grimmer. I was eighteen and about to be drafted. The only thing I had to offer her was the likely prospect I'd be killed in Asia somewhere and never come back to her."

Parker stared at him. Ray had never told him this before. "I…didn't know that."

"Not exactly something I like remembering," Ray said, his voice quieter now. "But you know what Laura told me? That she'd rather be my widow, with the knowledge of how much I'd loved her, than someone else's wife."

"Damn," Parker said softly, unconsciously echoing Ray's oath in a much softer tone.

"You need to be as tough as she was, kid. Because in a way, the roles are reversed now. Your lady's the one doing the dangerous job."

Parker drew back at that, until the chair dug into his back. He hadn't really thought about it, other than being aware of her job and the weapon she carried, but Ray was right. Was he tough enough for that, to be the one ever waiting for potential bad news simply because of her work?

He knew that wasn't really the question. The question was, could he walk away? He was pretty sure he already knew the answer to that one.

But Ray wasn't done with him yet. "And don't give me this 'no prospects' crap, Parker. You're young, you're annoyingly smart, you're pretty—" Parker groaned at the old jab "—and you know who you are now. And you've been lucky enough to find a woman who looks at you the same way, no matter how short the time. Don't blow it."

It was a stern, uncompromising order, given by the one man in his life he would unquestioningly take it from. So he answered the only way he could.

"Yes, sir."

Chapter 27

"This feels wrong," Parker said as they sat together on the couch, the television tuned to a weather station as March seemed preparing to make good on the old saying about coming in like a lion. A drencher was predicted within the hour, and judging by the radar images, those predictions would play out.

"You want to elaborate on that so I don't get my feelings hurt?" Carly suggested.

He gave her a startled glance, then looked as if he were playing back what he'd said in his mind. The smile he gave her then was that crooked one she found so endearing.

"I really like that about you, that you ask instead of just going straight to the hurt feelings," he said, in the tone of someone who'd had a bit of experience with the other option. "Because I didn't mean what that sounded like at all. I just meant…there's a kid out there being held by this drug dealer and we know it, but…"

"Here we sit, warm and comfy?"

"Something like that."

"And I really like that about you. That you think about things like that."

He watched her intently, and for a moment she thought—hoped?—he might kiss her. She was just considering launching that action herself when the sound of rain distracted them. When they simultaneously turned back to the screen with the radar map, they both laughed.

"Gee, look at that. According to that, we're still high and dry."

"Looks like their radar needs to catch up."

He frowned suddenly. "The Foxworth guys who are watching Ray…"

"A little rain won't hamper them. Especially Rafe."

"Why especially?"

"He was a multidecorated sniper in the military. He's held his position under much worse conditions than this."

Parker blinked. "No wonder I got the feeling crossing him would be the stupidest thing a person could do."

"You're a good observer." He gave her a look that told her exactly where his mind had gone, as she thought it did far too often. How long it had taken him to realize Witner was a crook and a scam artist. So she went for diversion. "My parents would like to meet you."

He drew back sharply, clearly startled. "I… They… You…" He gave up and just stared at her.

"Let me clarify," she said with a grin. "They'd like to meet the guy who took down the scum that nearly stole a dear friend's future."

He half smiled and looked down at his hands. "Oh."

"Did I have you worried there for a moment?"

He looked up again, this time meeting and holding her gaze. "Hopeful," he said quietly.

Her eyes widened before she could stop the instinctive reaction. "Are you saying…? What are you saying, exactly?"

"That I'm starting to believe in a matchmaking dog."

It was all she needed to give in to her earlier urge, and she kissed him.

Don't blow it.

Ray's stern order echoed in Parker's mind as he lay listening to the rain hammer the roof and the deck outside. For the first time, he allowed himself to imagine a long, long string of mornings like this, waking up with Carly in his arms, her warmth somehow seeping into him, as if promising he would never, ever be cold again. In an unexpected way it was more precious, more tempting than even the undeniably hot, fierce moments during the night when they'd surrendered to each other in ways he'd never known before.

She was an open, tender lover, but at the same time fiery and demanding, and the combination had driven him to the edge of madness and then over, again and again. But right now, in this moment, he wasn't sure he didn't treasure this quiet togetherness even more. And that was a feeling he'd never had in his life.

Despite the late hour, he was nearly drifting back to sleep when the now recognizable ringtone of her phone went off. He smiled when he heard her sleepily protest. Especially since it was closer to noon than dawn. But she reached for the phone and turned her head enough to look at the screen.

"This better be good, Dunbar," she muttered before she answered.

He couldn't hear the other side of the conversation, but obviously it involved some teasing, because even in the cool, gray light of this rainy day, he could see her cheeks color.

"Been talking to Hayley?" A pause, then a rueful, "Yeah, yeah, I'm a believer."

It suddenly struck him what they might be talking about. What he'd been thinking himself. Cutter. A believer in his…other skill? His cleverness and manipulative abilities were obvious, but that sense of knowing when people were…meant for each other?

You've never had that look before… The look I wore whenever I looked at Laura.

"How mad is the LT?" she asked. "I've been a little scarce."

He guessed she meant the lieutenant, her boss. He didn't know that much about how it worked, but guessed she normally would have been in the office on a nine-to-five sort of schedule.

"Yeah, she's a good one," Carly said. Then her tone changed, and he knew they'd shifted to all business. She mostly listened, then said, "Copy." A moment and then, "No, I'll tell them, and Hayley can call Quinn, to keep us a step back. See you there."

She put the phone down, then turned back to look at him. At the first glimpse of her expression, all thought of perhaps another steamy session vanished. His body didn't get the message right away, and he had to shift slightly to keep his erection from nudging at her expectantly.

"Hold that thought," she said with a smile that made him even harder.

"Sure," he muttered. "Easy." He clenched his jaw for a moment, determinedly not watching her get dressed. When he was somewhat under control—he didn't think he would ever be completely around her—he got up himself and started to dress, asking her evenly enough, he thought, "You're not in trouble, are you?"

"No. Lieutenant Carter is a good sort. There are times when we work 24/7 on a case, so she cuts us some slack when she can. We were thankfully slow at the moment, but that DNA hit changed everything anyway." Carly smiled. "And she understands gut instincts. Especially since she's had Brett to deal with."

He managed a fleeting smile. "He had news?"

"He's been talking to some contacts he has on the other side. Turns out our DNA-match gangster got in a bit of a dustup with his boss."

"The…head gangster?" He wasn't really up on the terminology.

Carly nodded. "Then he seemed to vanish. The gang unit thought he was dead, until our DNA query came through."

"So he ran?"

"Rumor had it there was a price on his head."

"So if he'd stayed they'd be finding more than his hat under a dumpster?"

She smiled at that. "Exactly."

"Now they suspect he might be over here looking to start up his own operation."

The idea of big-city-style drug dealing invading this quiet county was repugnant to him. There was enough of it here already.

"I do not like this," she said, echoing his thoughts as she clipped her holster to her waistband. "We have busts for possession, small-scale dealing, the occasional meth lab. It's hard enough keeping that in check with our limited resources."

"Then throwing this guy in jail seems like a good idea," Parker said.

"An excellent idea. So I need to get over to Foxworth. Brett's heading there now."

He followed her out into the great room, where she grabbed her jacket from the hall tree just inside the door. Woof emerged from Ray's room, coming over to nose his hand. He let the dog out, trusting he'd stay close since Cutter wasn't likely to show up. The other dog was no doubt at Foxworth, doing whatever he did when he wasn't playing matchmaker. He gave a slight shake of his head at how… acceptable that idea was becoming.

"Won't Turner freak if another cop shows up?" he asked as he checked the dog's water bowl and put his morning food out for him.

She shook her head. "He's not there. Quinn's with him, going through the motions of getting the money for the ransom."

"They really think this guy is watching?"

"His former boss in the city was big on eyes everywhere. We're assuming he'll be the same."

"Makes sense," he said as Woof came back, heading for his bowls the moment he was back inside. "We'll go see Ray later," he told the animal as he went over and reached for his own jacket.

"Parker," she said. He looked over his shoulder at her. "You don't need to do this."

His brow furrowed. He turned back to face her. "Do what?"

"You can stay out of it now. We've got it from here."

He pulled back sharply, from what felt like a verbal slap. "What?"

"Between Foxworth, Brett and me, we have it handled. You did your part, more than most people would."

She was telling him to stay out of it. She thought he couldn't handle this, that he was as useless as his parents had always said he was.

"So that's it?" he asked stiffly. "Back off and let the pros handle this, you'll only be in the way?"

Carly crossed her arms and glared at him. "Right now there's this to deal with, so I won't give you the reaction that comment deserves. Which would likely involve physical violence. But one day very soon, Parker Ward, we're going to have a long talk about your damned parents and what they did to you."

He felt his own face heat a little as she brought up the very thing that had plowed, unwelcome, into his mind.

"Now that I have your attention," she said, much more gently, "I was only saying you don't have to do this, not that you couldn't. I was saying that you could go back to your life."

Only knowing how pathetic and pitiful it would sound kept him from saying, "I have no life." Besides, it wasn't true. Not anymore. Because… Carly. And realizing that was a powerful jolt.

"I thought you were…"

"Shutting you out?"

He nodded. "When I feel like… I'm in this now."

"I understand that. But you also have to know Brett and I—and apparently most of Foxworth—have some training you haven't had. And experience in dealing with this kind of scum. So forgive me for worrying about you."

Worrying? She was worried about him? Somehow that put it all in an entirely different light than her thinking he'd be in the way. And most of the pressure that had been building inside him eased.

"I just need to see it through," he said. "For Ray." *And myself,* he admitted silently. He needed this for reasons he didn't fully understand just now.

"All right. As long as you stay safe. And follow orders if necessary."

He gave her a crooked grin and a raised brow. "I did okay with that last night, didn't I?" Because a couple of times she had practically given orders, just as he had. And they'd both followed them eagerly.

The look she gave him then blew away the last of the tension. "Indeed you did." He leaned over and kissed her then, wishing they had more time. Then, as they headed out the door, she said pointedly, "I think you *need* to meet my parents. Soon. You need a serious dose of seeing what real, good parents are like."

"Little late at my age, don't you think?" he asked wryly.

She smiled at him then. "It's never, ever too late to see that kind of difference."

When they were in her car, with its trappings of her work, the radio, the computer, the gear, he grimaced. "I just got a taste of what it will be like, didn't I?"

"Like?"

"When you go off to protect and serve, putting your life on the line to do it, and leave me behind."

Something he didn't quite recognize came into her expression then, but she said only, "Worry more about the frontline people, the very first responders. I usually only get called in after the fact."

He shifted in the seat so he could face her. She noticed—of course—and turned to meet his gaze straight on. And he quietly repeated her words. "Forgive me for worrying about you."

"Why don't we accept it as a given that we'll both worry about each other and go on from there?"

He smiled. "I can do that."

And he realized then that what he'd seen in her face a moment ago had been not just acceptance but gladness at his assumption that, after this was over, there would still be that "we."

Chapter 28

Parker watched the tall, lean man in the chair opposite him. His dark hair, touched with gray at the temples, was still damp with rain, and the black coat he'd worn was hanging in the entry, drying. Cutter was at his feet, after greeting him with obvious delight when he'd arrived.

For a cop, Brett Dunbar looked pretty darned happy with life. And he was petting Cutter as if he truly did owe it all to him, as Carly had said. It was a bit disconcerting to meet the man who had been instrumental in taking down the governor, but somehow more disconcerting to realize that the man knew that the dog had zeroed in on another couple now.

Carly. His colleague and friend. And him. Which, he supposed, was behind the assessing looks Dunbar kept giving him. He wondered what would happen if he said or did something wrong, in the man's view.

"Turner is very antsy," Hayley was saying.

"Understandable," Dunbar said. "Worried about his son."

"He'd like to just hand over the ransom today, since

we have it in hand," she said, "but Quinn's keeping him reined in."

"Doesn't seem believable, that he could get his hands on it that fast after telling them he had to sell that building to do it," Carly said, just as Cutter got up and walked over to sit in front of her. She'd taken a seat beside Parker on the couch, close, but not as close as he would have liked. But then, this was business, not pleasure. Although any time spent with her was pleasure in his book. And Cutter's, judging by his blissful expression as she stroked him.

I know the feeling, dog...

"Agreed," Dunbar said.

Carly scratched behind Cutter's ears and the dog sighed happily. "And although the kidnapping makes his intellect suspect, we can't assume Neuson is too stupid to realize that. He may just be taking the gamble, going for the big stake to get started."

Dunbar nodded. "And he earned his chops under a guy who's been smart enough to maintain control of a big operation in the city for nearly a decade and stay alive doing it."

"The shortest escrow that's publicly on record in the county is three days," Hayley said. "Since we're not requiring any inspection, repairs or an assessment, we're going with that."

Dunbar gave Hayley a wry smile. "Only a name with the weight of Foxworth could get them to move that fast."

"We have some friends," she said.

"That you do," Dunbar said, and there was nothing but pure appreciation in his voice then. "Speaking of friends, Carly said you've got a full-court press on this."

Hayley nodded. "Liam's digging for any possible local connections on the suspect, and Teague's in the field checking the area and anything he comes up with."

"And the fearsome Mr. Crawford?" Dunbar said, and

there was nothing of humor in his tone or the description. He spoke it as if it were simply fact.

Hayley's gaze flicked to Parker for an instant, then back. "He's watching over our witness."

"He's safe as can be, then," Dunbar said. And somehow those words from a man he'd met less than five minutes ago eased what worry Parker had left about Ray's safety. When this was over, he couldn't wait to see Ray's face when he found out who'd been looking out for him.

When this was over.

He couldn't stop himself from looking at Carly. Where would they be, when it was? When there was no more case tying them together? When he would be face-to-face with his glum future, with the simple fact that he had nothing to offer her? Oh, he knew her well enough now to know she'd say he was enough, and she'd mean it. For now. He had a sudden vision of himself as some guy in the basement playing video games while someone else worked to support him, and he mentally recoiled.

In that moment, Cutter shifted, scooting over and plopping his chin on Parker's knee. Instinctively he reached out to pet the dog. And the moment he stroked the soft fur, the image faded, so quickly it was as if it had been pushed away. He stared down at the dog. Woof offered his own kind of soothing comfort, but it was simple, uncomplicated. The precious gift of unconditional love. What Cutter was giving was…something more. Crazily, it was as if those dark, amber-flecked eyes were telling him it would be all right. That everything would be all right.

"So, tomorrow?" Dunbar asked.

Parker snapped back to the room, thinking he'd better at least pay attention. Cutter settled down at their feet, as if he knew his temporary mission had been accomplished.

"Yes," Hayley said. "We'd like early, of course, but

Quinn thinks Neuson will push for midday, with more people around to hide among. So we're going for the waterfront park. Nice and public, and it shouldn't be too crowded if the rain keeps up as predicted."

Carly nodded. "Plenty of observation spots in the area."

"Yes."

"We can probably put some plain clothes in the area, too, if necessary," Dunbar said. "Neuson hasn't been here long enough to know us all."

"You got some who don't scream cop?" Parker asked, then wondered if he should have phrased that differently when Dunbar's gaze shifted to him. Gray eyes as cool as the rain outside narrowed slightly. It took everything he had to hold that gaze, and he thought the man must be a bad guy's worst nightmare.

"Carly doesn't scream cop," he said after a moment. "Just like you don't scream tough enough to take down the biggest con artist we've seen in decades."

That startled him. He suspected this wasn't a guy who threw out accolades carelessly. Just as Carly didn't. "Politicians aside?" he suggested.

And then Dunbar smiled, slowly. "Indeed," he said. And Parker felt as if he'd passed muster with the man, which he suspected was no small feat. He glanced at Carly, who was smiling and gave him an approving nod that he knew confirmed it. And given the respect she had for the man, it meant a lot to her that he had Dunbar's approval.

He had the fleeting thought that he'd run into a lot of people lately who thought of him in ways he himself never had. They couldn't all be wrong, could they?

Then Dunbar looked back at Hayley. "Proof of life?"

"Turner will demand it right before the drop."

"Good," Carly said. "Don't want to give Neuson too much time to think."

Dunbar nodded again. "I'll be around," he said. Then, with an amused glance at Parker, added, "Out of sight, of course, since I'm told I scream cop."

"Comes in handy sometimes, I imagine," Parker said neutrally. Dunbar smiled again, but before it really registered, Carly spoke and blasted away his equilibrium.

"Just like your boy-next-door thing does."

His gaze shot to her face. She wore nothing but the teasing expression he'd come to love. He fought down the memories. She couldn't know. Well, she could if she'd been at the trial, but he knew she hadn't been. Still, the words careened around in his mind, leaving him unsettled. Again.

And again Cutter seemed to sense it, and the dog came back to him to offer his unique kind of comfort. Parker stroked Cutter's fur, and it was as calming as before. He listened as they arranged a meetup time for tomorrow, checked in with Liam and Teague—and the laconic Rafe—and verified there were no new developments on their fronts.

It wasn't until Dunbar had departed that Carly got him alone and demanded, "What was that? You have to know... I can't be the first one who's ever told you that."

"That I look like the proverbial boy next door? Oh, yeah, I've heard it before."

"It's not a bad thing, you know." She smiled. "At least, not to me."

Normally her smile, that particular smile, would have made it all right. But not this time. "It's not you," he said.

He wished he could leave it at that. But this was Carly, and he knew he couldn't. She deserved an explanation. He wondered if it was the cop in her that made her say nothing, just wait him out. It probably worked with a lot of suspects. It sure as hell was working on him.

He let out a long, compressed breath. "During the trial, the defense spent a few days trying to...take me out. Claimed the scam was mine, and that I turned on Witner and tried to blame him when I knew I was going to get caught."

"Discrediting the star witness. Common tactic," she said.

"Yeah. But they didn't know how long I'd been talking to the police."

"I read it was long enough that their white-collar division set a few traps along the way, and he fell for them, so there was enough to discredit their claims instead."

Parker nodded. "He was a big fish. They took their time and did it right."

"And all that time, you were still working for him."

"Until they had enough."

"And you don't think you're a hero? If he'd found out, who knows what he would have done. He'd have been desperate."

"They were watching my back then." He grimaced. "I was worth everything to them alive—dead, not so much. And once they arrested him, they pulled me out."

"And kept you under lock and key until the trial?"

"And a fun time was not had by all," he muttered.

"Which brings us back to what set you off just now."

He sighed. "One of their accusations during that time was that…I used it. How I look. To lure investors in."

She stared at him. "Because that innocent face couldn't possibly be a lie."

"Exactly." He grimaced. "I spent a lot of time staring in the mirror, wondering what the hell it was they were seeing. Wondering if I'd be better off if somewhere along the way I'd broken my nose or acquired a couple of visible scars."

For a long, silent moment, she just looked at him. Then, quietly, she said, "For what it's worth, I like the way you look."

"It's worth…everything." He closed his eyes, for a moment unable to meet the clear, unwavering blue gaze of hers. She went on.

"But it's the man inside the looks, the man with the heart and mind you have, the courage to take Witner on and the loyalty to see to Ray—that's the man I fell for, Parker."

His eyes snapped open again. Fell for? As in…love?

She was watching him. Watching him as if she knew perfectly well where his mind had gone. "Carly," he began, but couldn't go on.

"We seem to have acquired the rest of the day free, assuming nothing changes. Why don't we go get Woof and take him to visit Ray?"

A soft, billowing sort of warmth swept through him. That sweet, simple offer seemed to sweep away his doubts, his worries. If this amazing woman wanted him, wanted whatever kind of life they would have, why on earth was he questioning it?

"I… That would be great. And Ray would love to see you. He likes you. And…" He hesitated, then took the plunge. "He seems to agree with Cutter."

She lifted one delicately arched brow. "He does, does he? I knew he was smart. The question is, do you?"

"I…"

She became suddenly serious. "I wasn't looking for this, Parker. But it's here, it's now and it's real. Very real, for me."

"Me, too," he said, thinking it sounded lame. "It's just that—"

She waved off his demurral. "The rest is just details we can work on. Unless you don't want to even try. But I can't believe the guy who did what you did would give up so easily." Her tone softened. "Not that you haven't earned a break, but life isn't real generous in handing those out."

He thought of all the things she'd probably seen in her work, kids trapped in awful situations, maybe even some who'd wound up dead because of it. And suddenly all his uncertainties, all his doubts and worries, seemed pretty meaningless. Petty, even. How bad could they be, if simply petting a dog—okay, a very unusual dog—could ease them? He wasn't a kid, even if he had been ridiculously naive for a while. And he was healthy, strong, and had done honest work before he'd succumbed to Witner's lure and his parents' pressure. He could do it again.

That hope that had sparked before expanded. It wasn't the kind he'd gotten familiar with during the trial, the hope that he'd get through the next day, even the next hour, but the kind that made the future, all of it, especially dreams he'd once discarded, seem brighter and, more important, attainable.

He looked at her, trying to find the words to tell her. And then, being Carly, she blasted his equilibrium all over again.

"And after Ray," she said with a sweet smile, "we can go see my parents."

Chapter 29

Carly gave a fierce hug to the man who had taken care of her and loved her since she'd been fourteen. "Don't go all cop on him," she whispered into his ear. "He's had enough of that just now."

"If he can't take it," David Devon whispered back, but then stopped. "Never mind. I forgot for a moment who he is, what he did."

Carly pulled back to look up at the man who had saved them all. "And that is why I love you so much."

Her dad's glance flicked to Parker, who was enduring a bit of gushing from her mother. "The question is, do you love him?"

"I think so. I know it's fast, but…I've never felt like this."

"Fast doesn't matter if it's real. Your mother knew with your father instantly."

It was one of the many things she adored about this man—that he spoke of her father so easily, never denying him or his place in their lives and memories. "He's got some things to work through. What he did cost him everything, Dad."

He met her gaze. "And yet he did it anyway, because it was right."

"Yes."

"All the recommendation I need, then."

Her mother had, of course, insisted on a full-on home-cooked meal. Which in Abby Devon's book meant more than anyone could possibly eat.

"Just like we used to," she said as she set Carly—and Parker—to work setting the table. Parker seemed a little stunned when he saw the food arrayed in the kitchen. When she started handing him silverware, he gave her a sideways look.

"Was it always like this?"

"Pretty much. She loves to cook."

"I meant what she said. Did you always sit down and have dinner...together?"

"A lot, especially when we kids were younger," Carly said. She met his gaze. "I suppose you never did?"

He shook his head. "I...usually ate in my room. They didn't want me bothering them."

Carly sucked in a deep breath in her effort not to say something about his parents that would be both foul and likely overheard by her mother, who had picked up yet another dish to take to the table, this one of Carly's childhood favorite cranberry salad.

"Some people," her mother said as she passed them on her way to the dining room, "simply shouldn't breed. But in your case I'm glad they did."

Carly saw his face redden. Realized it was part of that boy-next-door thing, too, that it sometimes showed when he was embarrassed. Considering how many people she met who had utterly lost the capacity to be embarrassed about anything, she found it charming. She smiled at him.

"I should have warned you she has parental hearing. She never misses a thing."

She sneaked looks at him over the meal, wondering how it must feel to go from remembering parents who hadn't even wanted him in the same room, let alone at the table with them, to now, with parents who weren't even his wanting to know everything about him, interspersed with frequent thanks for what he'd done to save those who hadn't been as quick as their friend to pull out of Witner's scheme.

Still, when the two men disappeared after dinner, Carly was a little uneasy. Until she heard the sound of hammering from the back of the house, where she knew her dad was working on expanding Mom's beloved sewing and craft room. Her mother turned from where she'd been putting the few leftovers in refrigerator dishes, cocked her head to listen, then looked at Carly. Who was smiling.

"He used to be a carpenter," she said. "And I think he wishes he'd stayed one. He loved building things for people."

Her mom smiled in turn. "A good, solid profession."

Then she fastened the lid on the small container of cranberry salad, hardly worth saving except that Carly suspected it was for her, put it in the fridge and turned to look at her daughter.

"For what it's worth, I approve. Heartily. He's a good young man, honey."

Carly enveloped her mother in a fierce hug. "It's worth everything, Mom. Everything." She pulled back slightly. "No lecture on rushing things?"

Her mother gave her an impish smile. "From the woman who fell for your father in the space of, oh, maybe twenty-three seconds?" Then, seriously, she said, "I've never seen you so happy, baby girl. Not even with James, and you were going to marry him."

Carly gave an intentionally exaggerated shudder. "And what a mistake that would have been."

A couple of hours later, as they were leaving, Carly found herself smiling inwardly at Parker's utterly bemused expression. "Thanks for helping Dad," she said after they got back in the car. "That project's important to him, because it's for Mom."

"It's going to be great."

"And," she added as she started the engine, "you survived."

"I… They were great."

"They are."

"Your dad is a great guy."

"Yep."

"And your mom is…"

"Great?" she suggested teasingly.

He gave her that crooked smile and her nerves fluttered. "I did get kind of one note there, didn't I?"

"But it's the right note. They are great, and I adore them both."

"I can see why."

"And that is why I wanted you there tonight. Not to run any parental approval gauntlet, Parker, but to see real parents. What they're supposed to be."

"I understand now why you're…who you are."

And that easily he turned it around on her; she thought that of all the compliments and accolades she'd collected in her life and career, none had ever pleased her more than that one, from him.

"I have to get back to see to Woof," he said as they pulled out of the driveway.

"I know," she said. "Headed there."

Then, after a moment, "Will you stay?"

They were pulling up to the stop sign at the end of the

block, so she turned to look at him. He was studying his hands, but as if he'd sensed her gaze, he gave her a sideways glance. "Careful there," she said. "Pretty soon I'll be bringing my toothbrush."

He smiled, that smile again. "I hope so." Then, in a rush, "I'll figure it out, Carly. Figure something out. I'm not a flake by nature, I swear."

"You think I don't know that? Doing the right thing sometimes costs, that's all. Right now let's get through tomorrow—then we'll go to work on the rest." She smiled. "Maybe we need a joint meeting with the man who knows you best."

He blinked. "Ray?"

"Of course."

And for the third time she got that smile, and she marveled at the thought that she would do a great deal to see it a lot more often.

They made a short stop—"All it's worth, trust me"—at her apartment so she could pick up some things. Including the toothbrush. When she saw him looking around the small place, she gave him a wry smile. "See why I love Ray's place?"

"It's nice," he protested. "I like the colors. And it serves its purpose—close to work."

"So tactful," she said.

"At least I'm not afraid I'm going to break something."

She wondered where he'd been where that might have happened, then decided she didn't want to know, given the circles he used to move in. The lofty circles he'd left because of that core of integrity even his parents couldn't destroy.

Woof was delighted to see them. After tending to the animal and assuring him they hadn't left because they didn't love him anymore—Carly's throat tightened as she

heard Parker explain that carefully to the loving dog—
Parker called to check on Ray, something she'd noticed he
did every evening to say good-night, which also tightened
her throat. If he'd turned out like this with the parents he'd
had, what would he have been if he'd had real ones like
hers? But then she looked around at Ray's warm, welcoming house and remembered he had had them, really—he'd
just had to borrow them.

"What?" he asked when he saw her expression.

"Just thinking you didn't really need tonight. You already had the perfect example right here, next door."

She hadn't expected him to react so instantly or strongly.
But he threw his arms around her and hugged her, hard
and fierce. And as it had before, it started as one thing,
but quickly morphed into another.

She'd never felt anything like what she felt with this
man. The sizzle along every nerve, places she'd never considered arousal points snapping to life under his touch,
his kiss. That he was obviously as hungry for her as she
for him fired her to an even higher pitch, until she was
a starving, grasping thing desperate for his next caress,
his next kiss, here, there, anywhere he wanted. And then
she had to, simply had to, reverse it. She wanted to touch,
to stroke every inch of him, including the several inches
the slick core of her was aching for. Then she wanted to
follow the same paths with her mouth. She wanted him
to feel as she was feeling, frantic, demanding, as if there
were nothing more urgent in the world than this moment.
She wanted to hear him groan out her name again, as if it
had been torn from hidden depths.

She got her wishes. All of them.

Given how long it was before they'd fallen into an ex-
hausted, delightfully sated sleep, she supposed it wasn't

surprising that it was late into the morning when she awoke. But she didn't move. Didn't want to move.

Carly had never had the experience before of wanting to linger like this. She wanted nothing more than to stay here, with Parker's arms around her. There was no urge to be up and about the day, and apparently not in him, either, because when she moved he just pulled her closer, into the curve of his long, strong body. The body that drove her to the edge of madness and then over. Again and again. Funny how she had never realized how wrong her previous relationships had been until this one practically screamed "Right!" in her mind. And she wanted to spend the whole day exploring every bit of it. And him, what few parts of that amazing body she might have missed.

But a glance at the time told her it was not to be today. And even as she thought it, Parker murmured in her ear, "Time?"

"Yes."

"Okay."

She stifled a grimace, wishing inwardly she'd never agreed to him coming along today. But she had, and she wouldn't take it back now. She'd just have to make sure nothing went wrong. She didn't want to have to explain to the lieutenant how she'd let an innocent bystander who technically had no reason—except his own principles and determination—to be there get hurt.

Not to mention that Parker getting hurt would tear her apart for entirely different reasons.

So she would just see to it that it didn't happen.

Chapter 30

The rain held, as they had hoped.

Winter had won the battle with spring on this day, and while there were a few die-hard locals out and about, the waterfront park wasn't nearly as busy as it would normally be. The scarceness of visitors had also netted them a parking spot just up the hill from the street that paralleled the waterfront. It was far enough to have a good view of the spot chosen for the drop, the huge ship anchor converted to a sculpture of sorts that was one of the features of the park.

"Nice and empty," Parker observed. They were here a full two hours before the time set for the drop. Quinn had recommended the early arrival, and Carly and her colleague Dunbar had agreed.

"Yes," Carly agreed, still scanning the area as she'd been doing since they'd arrived. "And I hope it stays that way. The fewer civilians out and about, the better."

"Was that another 'Stay in the car, Parker'?" She'd already cautioned him twice.

She shot him a sideways glance. "Seems you got the wrong message."

He blinked. "What?"

"The real message was 'Stay in the car because if you got hurt I'd never forgive myself.'"

He blinked. Grimaced inwardly. "Oh."

Just how was he supposed to be mad at that?

Carly went back to scanning the park. The sheriff's radio that hung under the dash of the vehicle crackled, then emitted two clicks. She reached for the microphone that hung on the side of the device. She didn't pick it up or speak, merely keyed the mic and sent a single click back.

"Brett's in position," she said.

"Code?"

"In case our guy is listening."

The clicks, he realized, could easily be mistaken for simple static. "What if you really need to talk?"

She smiled, but kept on scanning. "Phone. Unless it turns to crap. Then all bets are off."

"Will it?"

"Hope not," she said, and he could fairly feel the energy humming around her as she watched the target zone.

He was, Parker realized, getting another glimpse of Carly the cop, the professional. The woman who had gone with her gut and believed Ray when others blew him off. That alone had endeared her to him. Maybe he'd even fallen for her in that moment. Which was crazy.

Or was it?

...the loyalty to see to Ray—that's the man I fell for, Parker.

He wanted that to be true more than anything he could remember. Even more than he'd wanted that damned, seemingly endless nightmare of a trial over with. Which meant this had to be over. The sooner, the better. Not only because there was a guy being held prisoner out there, probably scared to death, wondering if his captor was going to kill him. No, he wanted this over with selfishly, so he and Carly could do that figuring out she'd mentioned, figuring out how they were going to make this work.

Make them work.

Meaning he had to figure out what he was going to do with the rest of his life. How he was going to pick up what pieces they'd left him and build something out of them. Something worthy of having this woman in his life. Right now that seemed utterly out of the realm of possibility, but then, so had getting through that trial.

He heard an unfamiliar sound, a signal tone. Realized it was the Foxworth phone Hayley had given them and pulled it out. Right now it wasn't the red button but only the screen flashing, signaling an incoming message with a video attached.

"This must be it," he said, feeling a kick of adrenaline. "The proof-of-life video they demanded. The text message says their guy already confirmed it was taken two minutes ago."

Carly's brow furrowed slightly. "And they only asked for it five minutes ago. He must be close if he's going to be here on time for the drop."

Parker tapped the screen and started the video playing. He held it out so they could both watch. It was clearly taken with a phone, with the familiar vertical format. The image was a bit shaky at first, probably as the holder hit the record icon. Then it focused on the subject.

If Chas Turner had been too much for his mother to handle, it wasn't apparent now. The guy seemed much younger than his eighteen years, probably because he looked utterly terrified as he begged his father not to hate him and to help him. He looked unhurt, however. At least visibly.

"He's not bloody," Carly said.

"Not yet, anyway," Parker said with a grimace.

Young Turner made a string of the kind of promises

terrified people did, including a couple Parker doubted he'd ever keep.

"Foxhole promises," Carly murmured.

Parker's gaze shifted to her as she put his thoughts into words even as they occurred to him. Then the voice on the video changed and his gaze shot back to the small screen. A rough, harsh voice from a person off camera made a promise that sounded much more like a guarantee, that if the money wasn't in place at the appointed time, they'd find only the kid's body.

The image blurred slightly as it shifted, almost panned, as if the holder had moved the phone before shutting down the recording. Then it ended. No more demands, no more threats, just an abrupt ending.

Parker let out a breath. "He means it."

"Yes," Carly agreed, but her brow was now furrowed even deeper than before. "Back it up about ten seconds and play the end again."

Parker hit the play arrow again and slid the progress bar down to near the end.

"Get ready to freeze it," she said.

She'd seen something? Parker moved his other hand, hovering a finger over the pause icon. He wanted to ask, but she was so intent on watching that he didn't. Whatever she'd seen—

"Now." He hit the screen. The video paused. "Can you enlarge that spot?"

She pointed at the upper left corner of the screen. It was amid the blur when the phone had moved, and while he saw something there, he couldn't tell what it was. He used his thumb and forefinger and swiped out to expand the spot.

"Damn," she said.

He stared at the thing that had been in the background

of the video. At the shape and size of the object in the un-focused image. "Is that…the sign?"

She smiled, and it was one he'd never seen from her before. The smile, he realized, of one of those profession-als who'd just struck gold. "It's the back of it. The wel-come sign."

The image flashed into his mind immediately, of the big welcome-to-town sign on the main road. It was hand-carved, legend had it, out of the first redwood tree felled in the area, used to make this sign even before they built the first buildings of the settlement that had grown into the town they were in at this moment. It was practically a monument to the locals. There was even a spot on it where it was slightly smoother and shinier because those locals tended to reach out and touch it if they were walking past.

It was also distinctive enough in size, shape and texture to be recognizable even from behind.

Something prodded at him and Parker closed his eyes for a second, trying to visualize the last time he'd driven by there. He'd gone to pick something up for Ray—a bag of his not-so-secret vice, candy-coated peanuts—at the small local market just up the street. On Saturday, before the meeting at Foxworth. It had been way out of his way, but Ray loved the darned things.

"Wait a second," he murmured, and he backed the video up even farther and played it again. "That backdrop, the ridged metal… It looks like a cargo container." He looked up and met Carly's gaze. She didn't ask, just waited. "There's one sitting at that self-storage place that's just down from the sign."

She went very still. "Right color?"

He nodded. "And they advertise twenty-four-hour ac-cess."

Perfect to stash a kidnap victim unseen. She glanced

back at the waterfront park, then at him. He could feel her
sudden tension. Quickly guessed the reason for it.

"You're not going alone."

"I'm not taking a civilian into what could be a dangerous situation."

That was all he was at the moment, a civilian. A useless
one at that. For a moment all the old feelings he thought
he'd finally gotten a handle on flooded back. And his voice
took on a bitter edge he couldn't help.

"I'll stay in the damned car, Carly. Unless I can't." *Unless you're the one in danger.*

She decided. "Hit that red button and tell Foxworth."

She had the car started and moving by the time he had
the first words out.

Chapter 31

Carly spent the entire drive to the city limits trying to decide if she hoped this was what it appeared to be or not. If it wasn't, if they found nothing, she just had to trust Brett and Foxworth to handle it at the drop. She did trust Foxworth not to mess up—with their reputation, it was impossible not to—and she'd trust Brett with a lot more than a simple takedown.

But if it was, if their destination was indeed where the kidnapper was holding Chas Turner, then she had at least a two-front situation on her hands: the kidnap victim and Parker, with the potential of a third if the kidnapper himself was still there. This was close enough, he could delay leaving until the last minute.

And she was in a position she'd never been in before, where nothing, absolutely nothing, mattered more to her than the safety of the man beside her. She'd been on protection details before. She'd so often been watching over kids in bad situations, and she'd done whatever she'd had to, to keep them safe. And would have been distraught if anything had happened to one of them.

But if something happened to Parker, she would be a lot more than distraught.

She would be devastated.

"Quinn says Turner is steady at the moment, now that they're finally moving," Parker said as he lowered the Foxworth phone. "He agrees we—" she felt rather than saw his sideways glance as he pointedly changed his wording "—you should check it out."

"Parker—"

"And they've told Dunbar where we're going," he went on, as if she hadn't spoken at all.

"They'll get him through it," she said as she turned onto the highway.

The question was, would they themselves get through it? It wasn't even the potential danger they could be heading into that was prodding her. It was what would be left after Parker had to sit by and watch her do her job. She'd known men who couldn't deal—had dated a couple—which was one reason why so often cops dated other cops, or at least other frontline types.

But wasn't Parker in fact one of those? Hadn't he been the man who had stood his ground for the truth and integrity when no one else would? It had just been a different kind of risk, and one he'd taken with full understanding of the cost. The cost he was still paying, a load he was still carrying.

And isn't that one of the reasons you fell in love with him?

She no longer tried to deny it, even to herself. What she felt with him was what she'd been waiting for, hoping for, what had been missing from every other relationship she'd had. It didn't matter that it had been only a week, it didn't matter exactly what his future prospects were or weren't, because she loved the guy.

Her parents approved of him. So did Brett. And if that wasn't enough…well, Cutter.

When it comes to people who belong together, he's never wrong.

She nearly laughed aloud, despite being headed into a possibly perilous situation, at the absurdity of it all. This was insane. And she, careful, well-trained, cautious Carly Clark Devon, was going along with it. And loving it. And the man beside her.

"Working out a plan of attack?" Parker asked, making her realize they were almost there and she hadn't spoken since they'd hit the main road.

"Actually," she said with a glance at him, "I was thinking about you. I do a lot of that."

He practically gaped at her. And she vowed in that moment that one day he wouldn't be so astounded at the idea.

"Carly," he said and stopped, as if her name was all he could say. Or wanted to say. Either one was okay with her.

Fortuitously, there was room to park off the highway right behind the sign that had brought them here. She pulled in and stopped the vehicle. Unfastened her seat belt and turned to face him.

"This is going to have to be a play-it-by-ear situation," she said, "depending on if we're right or not. And if we are, whether he or the victim or both are there."

"Look, I know you don't want me—"

"—hurt. Yes. Bottom line for me."

"Back at you," he said. "I don't want you hurt, either. But…at least let me be there to call for help if need be."

She studied him for a moment. "No heroics?"

His mouth twisted wryly. "Not hero material."

She raised her eyebrows and gave him a purposefully astonished look. "And how am I supposed to trust your judgment when you can't even get that right?" He lowered his gaze, but he let out a little laugh at the same time.

"All right," she said briskly. "If I know Foxworth, they're in the area in force. Brett says they never do anything halfway. So keep that Foxworth phone handy, and if it goes sour, hit that red button and yell for help."

"I'll send up a flare," he promised. "Going in on foot, since this—" he gestured at her official vehicle "—is a bit recognizable?"

"Yes," she said, silently hoping she wasn't, as well. But unless the guy had been watching the alley after the grab, he wouldn't have seen her. And it was much more likely he was guarding his main asset, his victim. He was a stranger here, too new a presence to have gained followers. And if he had the money to recruit help, he likely wouldn't be doing this in the first place.

Just as she was about to say it, he used the Foxworth phone to let them know they were here. He listened for a moment, said "Okay" and ended the call.

"Quinn said backup is standing by." He gave her a wry look. "And to hit the red button and yell for help if we need it."

Carly couldn't help grinning back. "I knew I liked that guy."

They got out of the plainclothes car into the rain. Almost simultaneously they both reached for the hoods of their jackets and pulled them up. Carly caught herself thinking that was too bad, because she quite liked the look of him when drops of water were trailing over his skin.

You are so gone, girl.

They headed down the street. And she didn't miss that Parker reached out and tapped the sign as they went by.

* * *

Parker was beyond thankful she'd let him come with her, because he didn't think he could have just sat there and waited. Even having Foxworth instantly at the other end—and his faith in them was huge, given the short time he'd been dealing with them—wouldn't have been enough to ease his mind with Carly walking into a completely unknown and quite possibly dangerous situation. Sure, it was her job, and she was trained while he wasn't, but still, if nothing else, he could make that call for help or distract the bad guy, something. Anything but sit and wait safely out of the way.

It struck him that that was something he was going to have to learn, if they were going to be…a *they*. And as they neared the self-storage place, he wondered how anybody who loved a cop stood it.

Wondered if he could stand it.

And he had about half a minute to process the fact that he hadn't even turned a hair at the silent acknowledgment of the simple fact: he loved her.

He suspected he'd known it for a while—that was, if you could count any part of the week he'd known her as a while—but it just seemed too fast, too impossible, no matter what she said about the Foxworths' dog's other… talents. But then he thought about Ray and Laura, and how he'd known in mere moments that she was the one for him. And how he'd said after she'd died that despite the wrenching, consuming pain, he wouldn't have traded a minute with her to avoid this agony.

They stopped at a spot where they could see the shipping container from outside the property. For several minutes they simply watched, but there was no sign of movement. A single car left from the other end of a row of storage units, but it was otherwise quiet on this rainy day. A thought occurred and Parker moved slightly. Scanned what he could see of the entire place.

"I don't see the silver car anywhere."

She nodded. "Could mean he's not here, or simply that he's got the car hidden out of sight."

"Or that we're entirely wrong," he said sourly.

"I can't deny it's a possibility," she said. But then she looked at him and he saw that gleam he'd noticed before in her blue eyes. Those beautiful blue eyes that had looked at him last night as if he were the most amazing thing she'd ever seen. And she smiled a smile that matched it. "But I don't think we are. I get now what Brett means about trusting his gut. Because mine's screaming right now that we're right."

"Then maybe we should go see about a storage space." As he said it, that little voice in his head jeered at him, reminding him he didn't own enough anymore to fill even the smallest storage space, but he quashed it. He'd come up with something. Somehow.

The man who did what you did can do anything he puts his mind to.

Carly's words, spoken with such certainty, echoed in his mind. And for the first time, he really, truly believed them.

Chapter 32

"You start," Carly murmured to Parker barely a moment after they'd stepped into the office. Parker gave her a startled look, but she hadn't missed the way the woman taking off her coat as if she'd just arrived had reacted to him as soon as he'd shoved back the hood of his jacket. "And you'd better be my brother. Use it, boy next door."

He rolled his eyes at her, but by the time they got to the counter, he was smiling. And so was the young woman. Flirtatiously.

"Thank you for coming in," she said. Looking only at Parker. "What a nice way to start my shift."

Carly winced inwardly as she realized the woman probably thought Parker was about her own age, which appeared to be early twenties. But she was distracted from that thought as Parker spun a sad and, thanks to that innocent face, utterly believable story about them looking for someplace to store their late parents' things.

Never let it be said the guy can't think on his feet.

"There's a lot of stuff," he said ruefully. "We'll probably need something like one of those cargo things," he added, jabbing a thumb over his shoulder in the general direction of the huge orange container.

"Oh," the woman said, looking a little crestfallen, "we only have the one and it's rented."

"We know," Carly said with a smile. "I think a friend of ours rented it."

The woman blinked. "He's…a friend of yours?"

Carly's mind raced, wanting to conclude that the woman doubted the friendship because the man who rented the container didn't seem like their type. Maybe more like a gangster type. But they had to be sure. She put on her best expression of sudden doubt. And Parker, quick as ever, kept quiet and let her run with it.

"I think this was the place he said." She pulled out her phone, called up the mug shot of Neuson and surreptitiously enlarged it so the details—like the arrest and case numbers—didn't show. She said nothing more, just turned the phone so the woman could see and watched for her reaction to the image.

"I… No, I don't know him," she said, but her eyes widened and darted away.

"It's okay," Carly said soothingly. "I know he probably told you not to tell anyone he'd been here. He's been having some problems. But he told us about the container, since we might need something that big."

"He didn't mention the pretty lady who worked here, though," Parker said, smiling at her again. The woman blushed and looked up at him from under lowered eyelashes, and Carly had the uncharitable thought that she'd practiced that in a mirror. And in that moment it hit her.

Jealous. Good grief, she was jealous.

And the darned smile worked, because the woman said, "Then I guess it's okay to tell you that he only took out a short-term rental. Just a month. Would that work for you?"

"It might," Carly said, shoving aside her decidedly un-sisterly thoughts. She looked up at Parker, who was, darn him, still smiling. "Why don't we go look around, bro? Make sure it's worth the extra drive?"

"Sure," he said easily. Then, to the woman who was still watching him closely, he added, "You'll still be in here, won't you?" as if that was his primary concern.

"I'll wait right here," she promised.

"That," Carly said to him the moment the door had closed behind them, "was a little too well done, Mr. Ward."

To her surprise, he lowered his eyes and shook his head. "I…haven't done that in a long time. Tried to…"

"Charm a woman?" He nodded as they stood under the eave of the building and contemplated stepping out into the rain again. "It didn't show. And I think it was the best approach. You could see he'd put pressure on her. You played it just right."

He still didn't—couldn't?—meet her eyes. But he said, "Those defense attorneys weren't entirely wrong. I remember when I realized, way too late, that that's why they hired me. Besides my parents' asking, I mean."

"For your charm?"

He shrugged. "For the fact that there were people—mostly women—who were…susceptible to it." He let out a wry, short laugh. "Witner used to take me to gatherings, meetings and parties, and just say, 'Go make nice. Be yourself.' And I thought it was a good thing. A compliment. And thought how amazing it was that I was there, among the glitterati, me, with no college degree, no real experience in big-money situations."

"And," she guessed, "that was probably what attracted people. Because if someone like you, so obviously a straight arrow, was working for Witner, he couldn't be a bad guy."

"But all the time it was just...me being stupid."

Carly stopped in the act of pulling her hood up as the rain intensified. "I hate your parents," she announced. "You may have been inexperienced, but you were what? Twenty-six? In that world?"

He nodded. "Still—"

"Why are you so determined to blame yourself?"

"I should have known it was all fake. There was no reason for him to hire me, if he was for real."

"Except your charm. People have made it to the top with a lot less than you've got." He finally glanced at her, and she added, "You sure as heck charmed me."

His head came up sharply, and now he was looking at her directly. "I never tried to. Even though the first moment I saw you knocked me for a loop. But I wasn't trying, wasn't looking for that. I didn't feel like I had the right to, not the way things are right now."

"I know," she said.

"But things aren't going to stay that way," he promised, fervently enough that she sensed he'd turned a corner somehow, that he was looking forward at last.

"I know that, too," she said softly.

They started walking, making a show of looking at the standard storage units but heading in the general direction of the container. Once they were out of sight of the office, they picked up the pace. And Parker reached out and took her hand. Squeezed it. She glanced at him.

"Thank you," he said quietly.

She knew he meant for her faith, her trust that he would right the ship that had been sent wildly off course through no fault of his own, except perhaps the need to please parents whose own values were highly suspect.

She squeezed his hand back, and they kept going. Now that they were a little closer to the container, they could see it had been there a while, and that since it was close to the outer security fence, some debris had piled up on that side, caught between the ridged metal and the chain-link. The paint looked oxidized, but she doubted they'd bought it new, so that could have been from a few years of transit, maybe by sea.

"That lockbox looks new," Parker said.

Carly looked at the box that likely held a side-secured shutter lock on the end of the container. It was indeed shinier, and even from a distance looked much newer than the door it was securing.

"Yes," she agreed. "And it doesn't match." It was a darker orange than the more faded exterior of the container.

"So did they add it so it could be locked, or did he? He'd only need the box and a few hand tools."

"I'd go with them," she murmured. "They'd need it to be securable." She glanced at him. "And I'm thinking he's not a particularly handy sort." *Unlike you. At many things.*

They walked farther, got close enough to see more clearly. Then both of them stopped dead. And spoke simultaneously. Both of them whispering as if their subconscious had already put the pieces together.

"There's a silver sedan parked over there, out of sight," Carly said.

"That lock isn't fastened," Parker said. "You can see it hanging down."

They looked at each other. This was too much coincidence to ignore. And they both knew what it meant.

He was here.

"Victim's safety—" *and yours*, she wanted to add but didn't "—comes first, catching him second," she snapped out.

"Good," Parker said simply.

And before either of them could speak again, before she could even tell him to use that Foxworth phone and let them know, one of the doors to the shipping container began to swing open.

Chapter 33

Carly.

Parker's brain snapped into high gear. If the guy really had been watching the alley, he'd be most likely to have noticed Carly. Any man would. Even if he hadn't guessed she was a cop, seeing her here would rouse suspicion.

So he couldn't see her.

In the split second this took him to realize and decide, he saw a foot step down to the asphalt, in the space between the bottom of the door and the ground. And from the corner of his eye he saw Carly reach back for her weapon. Then he turned swiftly, nudging her back against the wall beside them, and pinned her there so that his back was to the container and his body was shielding her from the man's view.

"What—"

"Shh. I'm just going to…make out with my fiancée. Hopefully that's all he'll see."

"And if he doesn't?" she hissed out.

"Then try not to shoot me, please."

The moment his lips touched hers, he had to contemplate whether this was the wisest move. Because what

flared between them—what always flared between them—
did not contribute to clear thinking. His brain always went
a little foggy. But then, it usually did around her anyway.

But then she was kissing him back, and suddenly they
weren't just acting. The taste of her, the heat of her, alerted
every nerve, and the fire she lit in him raced along newly
relearned paths. He tried to hang on to the thought of why
they were doing this, but he wasn't having much luck. The
rest of his body, especially points south, didn't much care
about the situation and came to life so fast it nearly made
him dizzy. And the way he was pressed against her, there
was no way she couldn't know that.

Even as he thought it, he realized that he wasn't the
only hard thing between them; he felt an unyielding hori-
zontal ridge against his belly. A ridge that explained why
Carly had only one hand cupping his face as they kissed.

The other hand was holding the gun.

That managed to chill him a few degrees. Enough to
take stock of reality. He reluctantly broke the kiss, then
tilted his head forward to rest his forehead against hers. He
felt her head turn, just a fraction. To get a look, he realized.

"Is it him?"

"Yes." Her tone that told him she was certain. If it hadn't
been for the bit of breathlessness in her voice, he would
have thought her entirely unmoved by the kiss that had
nearly put him on his knees.

"Do you think he noticed us?"

"He glanced this way. But only for a second." Then she
turned her head back until they were cheek to cheek. "He
locked the door and he's headed toward the car."

She said it as if the words were some sweet nothing
she was whispering into his ear. Hell, from her, a weather
report could be a sweet nothing—for him, anyway. He
shifted just slightly, as if only leaning in for another kiss,

but angled himself just enough to mask her from that direction.

"In a hurry?" he asked in a matching whisper.

"No. Cool as can be."

So they'd fooled him. For now, at least. "It's early."

"Yes." She shifted slightly, her hip rubbing against him, and his body decided it hadn't quite given up on those tempting thoughts yet. "He may be going to the drop site."

"Wasn't the deal that he bring Chas?"

"May be why he's going early. To check it out."

"Look for cops, you mean," he said dryly.

"Little does he know," she said cheerfully.

"Speaking of using your looks," he said rather pointedly. "Cop is far, far from the first thing a guy would think, looking at you."

"Sometimes you have to use what you have. And speaking of that—" she nudged him again with her hip "—hang on to that. I'll want to use it later."

He couldn't help it—he laughed. They were standing here within feet of a potentially lethal, drug-dealing kidnapper, and he was laughing.

Then, in the same instant he saw out of the corner of his eye the silver sedan emerge from behind the next row of storage units, she stretched up and kissed him. He would have thought it merely a diversion, a way to keep up the facade as the man drove by, had she not made that soft, low sound as her tongue slipped out to run over his lower lip.

The silver car turned to head toward them. Carly released his mouth as Parker went still. He felt her right arm shift just slightly between them. Or rather, he felt the unyielding edge of the pistol shift just slightly.

"Go to your right if I yell 'now.'" She didn't whisper it, but it was a low, harsh sound. And as much as he hated the idea, he knew she was right. And that he had to let her be who she was, no matter that the thought of her being hurt or worse made his gut churn.

"I love you."

It came out before he thought. Carly stared up at him, her eyes wide. "You surely pick your moments, Parker Ward."

He wasn't going to deny it now. But he spoke fast, because the car was getting closer. "I was afraid if something went wrong here and I told you then, you wouldn't believe me. You'd think it was just…"

"Adrenaline? Might have. But probably not. Because I love you, too."

His breath caught. He stared at her, his breath quickening. He wanted to kiss her again, so badly he started to lean toward her. But then he heard the sound of tires on asphalt as the car neared them.

And then it slowed. He could feel Carly's tension. "Your right," she reminded him, her voice back to a whisper.

He heard a low, familiar sound. A window going down? And then a voice. The voice from the video.

"Get a room!"

Then there was a laugh, and the silver car was pulling away.

Parker closed his eyes for a moment. He felt Carly relax against him, but he noticed she didn't holster her weapon.

"Well, that was pretty unruffled," he muttered as he reluctantly stepped back.

"Or cocky," Carly said as she shifted away from the wall, watching as the silver car slowed at the gate. "I'm hoping for that, because cocky often begets stupid."

Parker turned his head just in time to see the car pull out onto the highway. He frowned. "He's not heading toward the park."

"No, he's not."

Carly pulled out her phone and made a call. "Brett, he's on the move. In the silver sedan, southbound on Center Street from the highway. Solo." Whatever her colleague said back was short, and Parker hoped not sweet, because the phone was back in her pocket immediately. "He'll put it out, but what units we have in the area are down by the waterfront."

"The only things that way," Parker said, nodding in the direction the car had taken, "are a gas station, a tire shop, a fast-food place and a local market." Where he picked up Ray's peanuts.

"Maybe he's headed for the food drive-through."

"For himself or the kid?"

"Either. Himself first, I'm guessing, if he's feeding the kid at all. I doubt he's staying in there with him, though."

Parker grimaced. "It's probably pretty rank by now, unless he's risking walking him to the bathroom."

"He might be," Carly said, gesturing toward the building closest to the container. "There's one right there."

They watched until the silver car was out of sight. Then they both started toward the container, Parker grateful she didn't tell him to wait safely out of sight. He pulled out the Foxworth phone, and she gave him a smile, as if she'd been about to suggest just that.

"Tell them we're about to see if we have our victim," she said.

A sudden thought struck him. "Do you think he's got a partner in there watching Chas? Maybe that's why he was so confident."

"Could be," she agreed as they reached the huge orange box. Then she lowered her voice again. "That's why you'll be staying out of the line of fire until we're sure."

"Carly—" He tried to keep his voice down, too, but it was difficult.

"Just stay clear and keep that phone handy," she said, not even looking at him now, clearly focused utterly on the task at hand.

The dangerous task at hand.

A furious whisper broke from him. "Damn it, Carly, you can't just barge in there without knowing."

"Wasn't planning on it," she answered, motioning him over to the side of the container, while she took a position just around the corner from the doors on the end, her weapon at the ready. Then she looked back over her shoulder at him and said softly, "Kick it, hard, twice, then put your ear against it and listen. I know it'll be hard to hear through, but if there is someone else in there, he should move fast enough to make some noise."

He blinked. Looked up at the container. Saw a row of silver gratings near the top. "What about the vents? Be able to hear a lot better." His whisper was calmer now. Something to do helped. He filed that realization away for future reference.

"A little high," she whispered back, looking up at the small condensation vent near the top of the container.

"Not if I get up there." She blinked. "Ready?" he asked, feeling a kick of that adrenaline she'd mentioned.

"I hope you know what you're doing," she muttered.

So do I. It's been a while since my high jump days.

But then, it had been a while for some other things, and look how that had worked out. He smothered a grin, wondered what the hell was wrong with him, backed up a few steps and leaped toward the container and up. He missed with his left hand but caught the top edge of the metal box with his right and held on. That alone had made a loud noise, and he pulled himself up to the vent to listen. It was a bit tough with one arm, so he was glad when he managed to get a grip with his other hand. After listening for a moment, he kicked the side of the container again, hard, twice. And listened again.

He dropped back down and looked at Carly. "Sounds exactly like someone trying to scream with their mouth taped shut. And that's all. Not another sound, verbal or otherwise."

She was giving him a rather odd look. Then, softly, she said, "You'd make a heck of a partner, Ward."

He had no words for how that made him feel. So he used her own back at her. "Hang on to that thought."

Her smile was dazzling. "Oh, I will."

Partner. The word echoed in his ears.

And Parker thought he could never be luckier than to have that true in every sense.

Chapter 34

Carly walked quickly around the end of the container, holstering her weapon as she went.

"What, you're not going to shoot it off?"

She glanced at Parker, saw he was grinning at her. "Smart-ass," she muttered, but her own grin broke loose a second later.

She reached into her inside jacket pocket and took out the case that held her badge and ID. This was one of the reasons she carried it instead of wore it visibly as some did, so she could keep some useful things handy. That, and it helped when she was trying to get information without the badge between her and whom she was talking to. It was true that *cop* was not the first thing people usually thought when they met her.

From behind the card identifying her as a sheriff's deputy assigned to the detective division, she took a small, flat folded plastic case. She opened it and took out two thin pieces of metal.

Parker's brows rose when he saw them. "Lock picks? Boy, they really teach you everything, don't they?"

"Actually," she said as she tackled the shutter lock,

which was even heavier than it looked, "Brett's the expert on this. He taught me the finer points."

It was a moment before Parker said, unexpectedly, "I'd like to thank his wife someday."

Carly glanced at him, puzzled that he'd said that at all, let alone at this particular moment. "Thank her?"

"For making him so married."

She suddenly remembered the instant when she'd been jealous of the woman in the office. Parker's tone had sounded exactly like she'd felt then. And that warmed her even more.

"He is that," she agreed neutrally. "Eyes for no one but Sloane."

"Good. Because otherwise I can't imagine working with you and not going head over heels."

Her throat tightened as she went back to work on the lock. "As I said, you pick your moments."

It took her longer than it should have, in part because she had to go at it from the bottom, where the protective lockbox was accessible, but even more because she was rattled by what they'd both just said in the last ten minutes. What they'd admitted. But finally the shutter lock gave, and she pulled the side bar of the lock downward. She lifted it clear, started to bend to set it on the ground, but Parker took it and shoved it in a pocket. Then he moved toward the door on the left, but glanced at her before he did anything else. Yes, a good partner.

And he would be in all ways.

Crazy how she could be so certain of that so fast, but she was.

She nodded to him. He flipped up the latches and pulled free the handles that put the pressure on the vertical bars holding the doors closed. The door started to swing open, but she stopped it at barely a crack, leaning in to listen carefully, simultaneously unholstering her SIG again.

What she heard was exactly what Parker had described, the desperate sounds of someone trying to yell. Not a cloth gag, she thought. The sounds were more muffled than that, as if they couldn't move their lips to form words. Maybe tape.

And now she had to trust the rest of what he'd heard, meaning nothing. And that he'd do what she asked of him.

"Stay back," she said and saw the protest flash in his eyes as he did so. "We need to make sure he didn't booby-trap the thing."

His eyes widened slightly but he said nothing, just tightened his jaw and nodded. She let go of the door and stepped back herself. It swung open under its own weight. The only thing that happened was the muffled screaming got louder. She leaned just far enough to take a quick glance inside.

She saw only a wall of crates about fifteen feet back from the door, some wood, some cardboard, stacked nearly to the top of the metal container.

"There's at least another twenty feet behind that," Parker whispered. "Behind them?"

She trusted the former carpenter's judgment of the space. "Must be. So you wouldn't think to look unless you knew."

They both took a longer look this time. Then she took a step inside. Parker followed, and she gave him a sharp look.

"Don't even say it," he warned, and she knew he meant it. She should never have let him come, let him get involved in this aspect. She'd let her emotions cloud her judgment, but if something went wrong, he might well be the one to pay for it. But he was here, determined, and they had a terrified victim almost within reach.

The muffled screaming grew in volume. Loud enough

that they had to up their own volume to hear each other. "That tall crate on the left is out of line," Parker said.

She hadn't even noticed. Again that carpenter's eye? "Empty, maybe. Easier to move. And just enough room to get by."

He only nodded.

"Check with Foxworth for an ETA," she said, still studying the masking wall of boxes and crates.

He did, putting it on speaker, and since the muffled yelling had become a wail, she had to lean closer to hear Liam Burnett's touch of a drawl as the answer, "Less than five," came back.

"We need to get the victim out while we can. We don't know how long we have before Neuson is back."

Liam acknowledged, then said, "Rafe?"

"Three minutes." The words came with utter calm.

Liam again. "Carly, three minutes and you'll have overwatch."

"Copy," she said, wondering if this would be the time she would learn firsthand of the most intimidating of the Foxworth people's reportedly uncanny skills.

"Overwatch?" Parker asked as he slid the phone back into his pocket.

"Means Rafe will have us in sight, from a good position."

"Good position to—" Parker stopped suddenly, and she knew he'd remembered the man's background and understood she'd meant a good position to take a shot if necessary.

Then he looked toward the back of the container again, where the muffled cries were starting to sound a bit teary. He grimaced. "Let's get him out of here."

"Assuming he's not the booby trap," Carly said sourly.

He blinked. "You think…?"

"Not really," she said. "Brett's contacts say he's not that sophisticated. But they didn't think he'd strike out on his own, either."

"So don't assume anything."

"Exactly. Let's move. We're eating time we may not have."

They went quickly over to that slightly out-of-line crate. He pushed at it, and it moved slightly. He put a shoulder to it and it slid sideways. Much more easily than she could have done it. Even empty, the big wooden crate was heavy. Sometimes power and weight truly were the only answer. And a glance at his face, at his look of satisfaction, told her he knew it.

"Points to you," she said, and he smiled. They stepped into the back of the container.

The young man truly did look more like a scared kid right now. Hands and ankles tied and with another rope snugged around his neck—it was amazing he got enough breath to wail—and through a metal bracket obviously used for securing cargo, he was pretty efficiently helpless. His face, with his eyes wide as he stared at them—no, at the weapon in her hand—was tearstained. But the duct tape with its dull silver sheen had held despite the torrent; his mouth was still sealed. With the tears, it was lucky he could still breathe.

He might have brought this on himself, but right now all Carly felt was pity. Especially when he said, for the first time understandably, "Please."

"I'm a deputy sheriff, Chas," she said.

The identification and her use of his name did it. His eyes rolled closed in obvious relief. She put his threat level at about one, and only that because he was so scared he could do something stupid, which was sometimes worse than evil intent.

"Chas, you need to focus for a moment. Is he alone?"

The reddened eyes opened. A nod.

"Partner? Helper?"

A shake this time. She felt a little pressure ease; they were at least dealing only with Neuson, it seemed.

She reached to pull her small folding blade from its pocket on the side of her holster. She flipped it open and handed it to Parker.

"Let Foxworth know he's a single operator. Then cut him loose. I'm going to go watch for—"

Crack!

Carly shoved Parker to one side just as the wood of the crate directly behind them splintered. Almost simultaneously the metal of the back wall of the container clanged piercingly.

A shot.

It was too late. Neuson was back.

"Stay here," Carly hissed, and before Parker could even answer, she was moving toward the crate he'd shifted. For an instant he stood frozen, unable to quite believe, but knowing in his gut it was true. She was who she was, and who she was was the person who headed into the danger, not away from it. She was also the person who had shoved him out of the path of the incoming bullet. The bullet that had hit the back wall in a spot that told him just how near a miss it had been.

It also told him Neuson had likely been aiming for his captive, no doubt to make sure the kid didn't talk. Chas started to wail again, and inanely all Parker could think was he was glad they hadn't taken the tape off yet.

He could hear that Carly had gone around the corner of the crate and stopped. For a long, tense moment, during which he was unconsciously holding his breath, nothing happened. Then he heard more steps, quiet, light. Suddenly two shots. One different from the others. And a foul oath.

Then a third shot. And a yelp of pain.

Carly. That had been Carly.

Parker didn't think. He ran. Cleared the wall of crates. The front of the cargo container was empty. Outside. They had to be outside. He raced that way. Barely three strides on, he saw her feet. She was down. Still. Too still. Another stride and he saw the man standing over her. Pistol in one hand. Her badge in the other.

Neuson. Bleeding from the arm that held her badge.

"Say goodbye, bitch cop," he said.

And aimed at Carly's head.

Chapter 35

There was no decision to make, no hesitation. Parker hit top speed. Neuson heard him coming. The man straightened. He stared, clearly startled. In an instant Parker realized he'd thought the racing steps were Chas Turner. The kid he thought harmless.

Think again, scum.

He used the lip of the container doorway to launch. He flew at the man, almost horizontally. Hit him at the knees. The arm with the weapon flailed upward. Another shot, wild. Neuson swore viciously. Swung the weapon. Clipped Parker just above the ear. Then again. It felt like hammer blows.

His whole head rang. Everything hummed for a moment. His balance felt off. But then it steadied. Neuson twisted, trying to get free. No, trying to get his arm turned. To get the gun in a position to fire.

He had no choice. He drove upward with Carly's knife. Somewhere into Neuson's abdomen. He felt the heat of blood flowing over his hand. The blade was small, hardly lethal, but it made Neuson recoil and swear. He wanted to recoil himself but he couldn't. Wouldn't. Not with Carly's life at stake.

For a split second, everything seemed to freeze. Neuson had gotten purchase with one leg out to the side. He wrenched back from the attack enough that Parker could see the crazed glint in the man's eyes. The knife, slick with blood, slipped out of his grasp. The gun came around. Parker stared down the barrel.

The cliché barely registered because, crazily, the world seemed to slip into slow motion. His only conscious thought was that he'd be damned if he was going to die here, not when he'd just found the reason to live.

He vaguely felt the dig of something in his back pocket. Remembered. Dug out the heavy shutter lock. In the same motion, he swung it with all his strength. Connected with the side of Neuson's skull. The man flinched to the side. Parker started to reach for the pistol, to make sure he couldn't aim it again.

Neuson jerked suddenly, as if he'd been kicked by a mule. The gun went flying, hitting the container with a loud clang before bouncing into a pile of that debris caught next to the fence.

Then the words came, a string of harsh curses, as Neuson looked around wildly, almost in panic. An instant later, he fell back, hitting the open door of the container with a loud thud. He was clutching at his upper right thigh, just below the hip. Parker saw the bloom of a much larger patch of blood there.

He looked around. No one in sight. It took him a moment to process.

Foxworth. Rafe. Overwatch.

Sniper.

He rolled to his feet and scrambled to get to Carly. Saw the bright red patch on the side of her head, staining the golden hair. "Carly," he pleaded, reaching to touch her neck. After a moment he felt a pulse and remembered how to breathe. But it was too fast. Was that a symptom of blood loss? Or maybe shock? He didn't know and cursed his own ignorance.

His brain tried to grapple with the situation, to process. He'd being going to shoot her in the head, so he couldn't have already. Right? He brushed at the stained hair and saw only a gash in her scalp. Maybe he'd hit her with the gun, as he had Parker. Then he saw the other damage. A blooming red stain, low on her side. And more blood, pooling beneath her.

Fear gripped him, more, much more than he'd felt during the struggle with Neuson. If he lost her, if this new, precious part of his life vanished, he didn't think he could take it this time.

He found the place where she'd been hit, right below her rib cage, and pressed on the wound with one hand. It wasn't enough. The blood kept coming, too quickly. He yanked off his jacket and tossed it aside, knowing the rain-repellent material would do no good. He yanked off his shirt, swiftly folded the cloth and used it to apply pressure. He held it there with one hand and reached for the Foxworth phone with the other.

She moved. Made a faint sound. "Carly," he said again, and it was almost prayerful this time.

He heard a loud string of barks from the direction of the gate. Cutter. He wasn't sure how he knew, but he did. He dropped the now unnecessary phone and grabbed Carly's hand. He squeezed.

"Hang on, Carly. Just please hang on. Help's here. You'll be fine. You have to be."

Carly's eyelashes, those long, soft lashes that had brushed over his skin, fluttered. Then lifted. And he saw the most beautiful sight he'd ever seen, those beautiful blue eyes looking back at him. A bit dulled with pain, but looking at him.

"Hey, partner," she said, a bit weakly but understandably. His throat was too tight at just hearing her voice for him to get out another word. And then she reached up and touched his bare chest. "Well, that'll give the girl in the office a thrill. It does me."

And that simply, in the craziest of circumstances, she had him laughing. "I love you," he said fervently.

"Love you, too."

And then the racing Cutter was there. Parker had the vague thought they must have let him out of the car the moment they were close. Hell, the crazy dog probably demanded it. Seemed he practically ran the show anyway. And Parker admitted silently that he seemed to be doing a fine job of it, too.

The dog nudged him in a passing greeting but was clearly intent on Carly. He seemed to inspect her for a moment before he gave a quick canine kiss to her cheek.

"You were right, dog. Again," Carly whispered.

Parker's gaze shot to her face, and everything she'd told him about the dog's...other abilities came racing back.

"Yes," he said softly. "He was."

Cutter spun around and went to Neuson, who was still where he'd fallen, quietly groaning as he clutched at his leg. Cutter sat within easy reach and growled at the downed kidnapper in warning, clearly now in guard mode. Parker had the thought that this was an entirely different dog and Neuson would do well not to cross him.

He heard tires on asphalt, more than one vehicle, but didn't look up. Then vehicle doors opening and he still never took his eyes off Carly.

Dunbar, and the rest of the Foxworth contingent, was

here. Minus the man who had ended it all with a shot from who knew where.

Still keeping his gaze fastened on the woman he loved, he called out, "Kid's in there. Behind the crates." Liam went over to where Cutter was watching Neuson, and Teague went into the container, while Quinn came their way.

"Medics are on the way," Dunbar said, kneeling beside him and smiling at Carly. "You'll be okay, Carly."

"Not giving up now," she said. Her voice was a little weak, but the look she gave Parker was full of the spirit that made her who she was. The woman he'd fallen for in the space of a week.

"No, not now. You've got too much ahead of you now," Dunbar said. With a glance at Parker, he added, "Nice work. Thank you."

"Sorry we couldn't get here fast enough," Quinn said as he crouched beside them as well, then shifted his gaze to Parker. "But clearly you did what had to be done. Again."

Somehow that quiet approval from these men meant more than all the accolades the prosecutors had piled on him during the trial.

"That your blood or hers?" Quinn asked, and Parker realized the man was looking at the side of his head.

"Mine, I think." He swiped at the wet stream that tickled his face in front of his ear. "He caught me one with the gun."

"Doesn't look too bad."

"It's fine," he said shortly. "She's the one who matters."

"So Cutter says," Quinn said.

Parker looked at him. "He was right."

Quinn gave him a rueful, amused smile. "He always is, when it comes to that."

Parker heard Liam's slow drawl. Glanced over and saw

he was speaking into his own Foxworth phone, with a grin on his face. "—a little bit high, buddy. At least an eighth of an inch."

Parker heard Rafe Crawford's rough growl making a physically impossible suggestion, and Liam laughed. Then he looked at Parker. "He says thanks for shoving the guy clear for the shot."

Parker grimaced. "Wish I could say it was intentional. I just didn't want to get shot myself." *Or let him get another try at Carly.*

"End result's the same," Liam said with a grin.

And then Parker heard sirens approaching.

It was really over.

Chapter 36

Parker made the turn and paced back across the hospital waiting room. His head was aching a bit, but there had been no more dizziness, and his balance seemed fine again. They'd told him he didn't have a concussion, had put a couple of stitches in the split above his temple, and cut him loose with a warning not to drive for a week. So now here he was, on the other side of more hospital doors, and hating it.

Just the thought of Carly in surgery made him beyond restless. The blood loss, at least, had been rectified fairly quickly. Even though they wouldn't let him give blood for her. Hell, he would have given half of what he had if it would help her. Maybe more. Crazily, he'd found himself making a mental note of her blood type, for future reference. But now they were in an operating room, finding out what other damage had been done.

He avoided the cluster of people on the far side of the room, Carly's colleagues, in uniform and not—and many of them with bandages on their arms after donating blood for her—because at the moment he was tired of being thanked. He didn't know what Dunbar had told them before he'd left to get Carly's parents, but it was obviously good, and the man's word clearly carried a ton of weight.

He turned again, and again glanced toward the gathered group. At that moment a woman, not in uniform, headed his way. Maybe it was a friend of Carly's. It had all happened so fast he hadn't met any of her friends. She wore jeans and a green sweater, had light brown hair past her shoulders, with bangs that looked long enough to cover her right eye if they weren't pushed to the side. She was pretty, but not as pretty as Carly. When she stopped before him, he saw her eyes were a distinctive light green. Again pretty, but not as pretty as Carly's clear blue. Which he wanted to, had to, see again. Soon.

"Hello, Parker. I'm Sloane Dunbar, Brett's wife. I wanted to thank you. Carly is a sweetheart, and she's become a good friend."

Dunbar's wife. Thanking him. He must be still off balance, because all he could do was smile a little lopsidedly at her and say, "Funny. I was telling Carly right before it all went to hell that I'd like to thank you someday."

She gave him a puzzled look. "Thank me?"

"For making him so very married."

She got there very quickly. More quickly than he would have at the moment, he was still so scrambled. And the slow smile that curved her mouth made it very clear both that she understood and why Brett Dunbar had fallen for her.

"She is indeed a very attractive woman, in so many ways."

"Yes."

She was still smiling. "And I hear Cutter can chalk up another success."

That made him focus a bit. "It's true? He...brought you two together?"

"He did. Literally led Brett right to me. We had him at the wedding."

He nearly laughed at the image that put in his mind. And suddenly everything seemed a little clearer, a little less tangled. And the relentless pressure in his chest eased a little.

And then things got chaotic again as Sloane's husband—maybe he'd just think of the guy that way from now on—arrived and Carly's parents rushed over to him. Her mom hugged him fiercely, and her dad put a hand on his shoulder and squeezed, both pouring out more thanks. Brett had apparently told them that Carly would likely be dead if not for him. He didn't quite believe that, but this wasn't the time to argue the point.

"I guess I'll forgo the third degree about you being good enough for my girl, since you've proven that pretty dramatically," said the man who had the same look as the others gathered here. That look law enforcement seemed to give you.

"I—"

"And Brett agrees," her mother said, "so that's recommendation enough. Not that I hadn't already decided, mind you," she finished with a smile.

He smiled back. And decided he wouldn't even try to explain about a certain matchmaking dog.

Carly had never been much good at being still. It was, her mother had always said, how she had determined how sick she really was as a kid. If she stayed in one place or position for more than half an hour—unless she was engrossed in a book—she knew she truly wasn't feeling well.

She wasn't moving much now. From the waist up, it hurt her head; from the waist down, it tugged on the stitches—or maybe staples, she hadn't steeled herself to look yet—in her side. They'd told her—at least, she thought it was real and not a confused dream—that she'd been lucky, her concussion was mild, and the bullet hit had been more deep gouge than puncture wound. The damage, for a gunshot wound, was fairly minimal. But she still had a lot of healing to do and was ordered to stay still, as much as she could. And she dozed a lot, which she wrote off to the lingering bits of anesthesia still in her system.

Usually that dozing off happened when she managed to quit thinking about how she'd been too wide with her shot and hit only Neuson's arm instead of center mass. That she'd been dodging his own fired round was no excuse. No target except a paper one ever stood there and simply waited for you to aim at it. There would be some range days in her future. Lots of them.

Whenever her mind went down that already tired road, she tried to yank it back. The only thing powerful enough to keep her off that track was Parker. How many times had she awakened to see him sitting there beside the bed? It was so frustrating that she was too out of it to talk much, but he'd simply held her hand and told her to rest.

He'd simply been there for her. As he had been at the storage yard.

Parker, risking his life for her.

Parker, unarmed except with her pocketknife, tackling an armed gunman who'd already tried to kill.

Parker, pleading with her to hang on.

Because he loved her.

And that worked where nothing else could, and sent her off into more pleasant dreams.

The first time she awoke feeling almost normal, a couple of days later, her parents were there. She endured the tearful "Welcome backs" of her mother and told her dad ruefully she was already planning on those range visits.

"I blew it, Dad. If I'd hit him where I should have—"

"We'll talk about that later. Probably at the range. Right now I'm just glad you're all right."

"Only because of Parker."

"Yes." Her dad smiled then. "He's a good one, honey."

"I know."

"He's also very polite," her mother said, and Carly smothered a smile. Mom set great store by manners. "He wanted to be in here, I could tell, but he thought we should have time with you alone, family time."

Carly swallowed and looked up at the two of them, the woman who had loved her since she'd brought her into the world, and the man who had stepped up when her father no longer could, who had loved her as much as if she were his blood.

"How would you feel about…that family expanding?"

"To include Parker?" Her mother gave her a wide smile. "Already counting on it, sweetie."

As if the mention of his name had summoned him, the door to the room swung open, and Parker stepped in. The doctor—she wasn't sure which one, there had been a few in and out—was with him.

She didn't even realize she'd been doing it until Parker stopped dead and, smiling back, said, "I've been waiting to see that smile."

"The one that says I want out of here?"

"That's the one," he answered, grinning now.

"Luckily," the doctor said with her own smile, "that's what I'm here to discuss. First warning—you'll need to take it very easy for at least a week."

She followed that up with what Carly had expected, a long string of cautions and warnings about what she could and couldn't do, one of which included being alone for extended periods for a couple more days.

"I don't expect any complications from the concussion,

but they are still nothing to take lightly. So if you can adhere to all that, we should have you out of here tomorrow."

Her instructions given, the doctor went off to file the paperwork, although Carly had noticed there wasn't much paper involved these days.

"I'll take time off," her mother said.

"Or I will," Dad put in. "Or we'll trade off."

Parker started to speak, then stopped. And somehow Carly knew he'd been about to say he didn't have to take time off, but stopped himself because that was tantamount to reminding them he was unemployed. He looked at her, and she saw the old, familiar ache in his eyes.

"Mom, Dad, could you give us a minute?"

Bless them, they didn't hesitate. Dad gave Parker a very male shoulder hug, while her mother's was much more engulfing and fierce. Then they stepped out of the room. And Carly considered tactics.

"Don't worry. I don't expect you to take care of me," she said after a moment.

His eyes widened. "But…" He lowered his eyes before saying quietly, "I want to. But they're your parents, and you're close to them, and… Isn't that how it works?"

"You mean with real, loving parents?"

He met her gaze then. "Yes," he said simply.

"My mother once told me the easy part of being a parent is holding on. That part comes naturally. The hard part is knowing when to let go." She gave him the same smile she had when he'd come into the room. "I've made them wait for it, but they know it's time now. Because they know how I feel about you."

He let out a long, audible breath. Then, very neutrally, he said, "Your apartment's a little small."

"It is," she agreed.

"Ray's place is more peaceful. And has more room."

"And Woof," she said.

He smiled at that. "Him, too. He's a good comforter." He swallowed. "So...?"

She was feeling just contrary—and energetic—enough to want to hear it. "Was there an invitation in there somewhere?"

"I'd make it an order if I thought you'd listen."

"Like you listened to my order to stay clear?"

His gaze turned cool and unwavering. "He hurt you. All bets were off."

Oh, yes, there was a spine of steel beneath those boy-next-door looks.

"I don't know," she said casually after a moment. "I take orders all right, if I respect the giver." Her voice went soft; she couldn't help it. "And I certainly respect the man who saved my life and took down an armed felon in the process."

He looked startled, as if he hadn't thought about it quite that way.

"Especially," she added, "when he's the same guy who took down one of the biggest scam artists this state has ever seen. That puts him right into hero territory."

"I'm no—"

"Don't even try, Ward. All you need is the cape."

He let out a small laugh. He reached out and lifted her hand from the thin hospital blanket. She waited. It was a moment before he spoke.

"Blue."

She blinked. "What?"

"Blue. I want a beautiful blue cape. The color of your eyes."

Carly let out a delighted laugh, and she didn't even care about the tug on her injured side.

Chapter 37

Parker had the feeling he should be glad of the chaos that ensued when it turned out both Carly and Ray were released on the same day at nearly the same time. Not so much because of the logistics involved, he could have handled that, but because he was soon going to be face-to-face with the simple fact that his situation hadn't really changed. But he didn't have time to think about it much, although thanks to Foxworth, everything went off smoothly.

"Are you sure Ray's okay with this? With me…moving in on you two?" Carly had asked, showing a bit of anxiety for one of the first times since he'd known her. Which was, he had to remind himself, still less than two weeks.

"Are you kidding? He lit up like a Christmas tree," he'd told her. "He was just worried that we didn't spruce the place up for you."

She'd smiled at that. "I like it just the way it is." And insisted he not worry about her. Foxworth would get her there. He needed to see to the already antsy Ray.

She'd been right about Ray—*antsy* was indeed the word. "Laura would have a fit," the man muttered as he raced around the house, picking up this, hiding away that.

Woof was so close on his heels Parker was half-afraid they'd get tangled up and Ray would go down again. But the man nimbly dodged the dog, or was so used to him he knew which way the dog would jump, and everything seemed back to normal. Parker was so glad to see how well he was moving and using his injured arm, he didn't even try to stop him or point out that Carly had been here often and had, as she'd said, liked it just the way it was.

And then, suddenly, Ray stopped. He turned to look at Parker, who'd been wiping the kitchen counter as instructed.

"You two should take the master."

Parker blinked as he drew back sharply. "I… We…"

"If you're going to try to tell me you two aren't sleeping together, don't. So we'll trade rooms."

"Ray, no. Carly wouldn't want that, and neither do I."

The older man studied him for a moment. "Hmm. I'll think on it."

Parker wasn't quite sure what Ray was up to. He was, however, sure the man was up to something.

When the Foxworths pulled up in the driveway a little later, Cutter was—as always, it seemed—the first one out of the SUV. Woof went slightly delirious at the sight of his buddy, and after Cutter greeted Parker and Ray, the two romped off.

"Funny," Parker muttered. "Now he seems like just a dog."

"That's because his job is done," Hayley said cheerfully as she got out of the back seat, slinging a backpack over her shoulder. She didn't specify which job, and Parker didn't ask, because he was utterly focused on Carly, who had been in the front passenger seat, no doubt because it had been more comfortable for her.

He wanted to pick her up and carry her inside, so she

didn't have to walk. She would have none of that, although she did allow him to lift her out of the rather high SUV so she didn't pull anything.

The process of getting the things they'd stopped to pick up at her place arranged, and going through the rather detailed directions for wound care the hospital had sent home with her along with a scheduled appointment for follow-up—and Hayley smilingly delivering a reminder that the doctor had said intimate relations were not on the list of approved activities at the moment—ate up the rest of the afternoon. But finally, with a promise to check on them regularly and come back by midweek, the Foxworths and their uncanny canine companion were gone.

"Good people," Ray pronounced as they drove off.

"Yes," Parker said. "Kind of restore your faith, don't they?"

Carly, who had gotten off the couch to say goodbye to them, put an arm around his waist. "Kind of like you did for a lot of people."

He started to protest, but at her steady gaze, he said instead, "I hope so."

The smile that got him warmed him more than the fire Ray had started in the fireplace.

"'PCKL,'" Carly had quoted at him as she'd watched, and Ray had grinned broadly.

"Taught him well, didn't I?"

"That you did, sir," she had said respectfully.

"Now, now, none of that 'sir' stuff," Ray had blustered, but Parker had seen how pleased the older man was.

Looking after Carly's wound wasn't the most pleasant thing for either of them, but he did it despite hating causing her pain, and she did her best not to show he was hurting her. Nights were more interesting, even with sex being off the menu at least until that follow-up appointment, because it was so natural to him already to pull her close even in his sleep and he couldn't do that right now.

The rest of the time was…well, amazing. Parker had never been happier, having the two people in the world he loved most with him under one roof. Even the fact that it wasn't his roof wasn't bothering him at the moment, not in the still powerful relief that Carly was going to be all right. Her headaches had stopped, and her side wasn't quite as sore.

"Wait'll it starts to itch," Ray told her dryly. "You'll wish it was back aching again."

Carly grinned at Ray, and Parker grinned at them both. The three of them were like the family he'd never had, and he loved listening to Ray and Carly talk, getting to know each other. She listened to his stories with obviously genuine delight, and to Parker's surprise, he even delved into his war experiences, which he almost never did. It was a tremendous expression of trust, and later he'd been about to tell her that when she said it first.

"I'm honored. That he felt he could tell me about that time."

Parker had no words for how he felt in that moment, that she understood…everything.

And one evening after she'd been there a couple of days, both she and Ray said aloud almost simultaneously that they quite liked each other. Parker grinned more widely than he could remember doing in his entire life.

The next morning the rain finally let up, and Carly insisted on taking a walk, at least around the backyard, saying her muscles were starting to twitch with disuse.

"I'm feeling much better. Much steadier," she assured Ray when he gave her a look of concern. "I'll take Woof out."

"You take care, girl," he warned. "That dog can get a little clumsy."

"He's just...enthusiastic. Aren't you?" she asked the dog who'd been dancing around her feet ever since she'd said his name.

Parker got to his feet. "I know you don't need an escort," he began, tactfully.

She gave him an understanding smile. "But I'd like one."

They made a circuit of the big space, Parker watching carefully until he was certain she'd been right, she was much steadier.

"This is such a beautiful place," she said, looking at the thick stand of evergreens that marked the border of Ray's property. "So peaceful. You could stay sane no matter what the world threw at you, if you had this to come back to."

"Yes," he agreed simply. Then, tentatively, he said, "It's a bit far from your work, though."

She smiled. "I think that's part of what makes it so nice."

"Worth the drive?"

"Definitely."

They were dancing around what he wanted to ask, but he hadn't even talked to Ray about it yet, so he didn't feel he could. And then, as if the suddenly friendly fates had read his mind, he didn't have to.

"You know," Ray said over the breakfast table, where Carly had insisted on contributing her mother's French toast, which lived up to the advance billing, "I could get used to this."

"Me, too," Parker said, wondering if people could get sore muscles from smiling too much.

Ray leaned back in his chair and looked at them both. "I could get used to having you two here all the time."

Parker's breath caught. "But Laura… This was your home with her."

"She'd love it, kid. Nothing would have made her happier than if we could have had you from the first day we found you hiding under our deck." Ray took in a long, visible breath. "Having you both here makes this house feel…healed."

He glanced at Carly. She was looking at Ray, and he knew he hadn't mistaken the sheen of moisture in her eyes.

"That's the most wonderful thing I've ever heard said about a home," she said, and Parker also knew the change from house to home wasn't an accident. "And I could get used to it, too."

Did she mean…? Parker was afraid to finish the sentence even in his mind.

"We'd have to do some things," Ray said. "Like maybe take down that wall between your room and the back room, give you more space. Add a private bath. Private entrance, too, if you wanted, off the deck. You'd have a nice view of the yard and trees back there."

"So this is what you meant when you said you'd think on it?" Parker asked.

"Got it worked out in my head and started on paper. And I know you could build it. It'd get your hand back in, too."

He could. He knew he could. He looked at Carly. "It sounds perfect," she said. "But if you expect me to decorate it, think again. You've seen my apartment."

Parker was too stunned that she'd so easily agreed to… living with him. Them. Here, in this place he loved. The thought of days on end here with these two most precious people seemed…too much to even wish for.

"I was thinking," Ray said to her, "that maybe, being a county Mountie and all, you could deal with them. The county, I mean. And all those damned permits they make you get."

Carly grinned at him. "I know a guy who knows a lot of those folks."

By the time the Foxworths arrived, they had a remodel sketched out on paper, showing Ray's engineering skills hadn't lost a step. They told Quinn and Hayley the plan, and both of them grinned.

"You don't think we're crazy?" Carly asked. "I mean, we only met two weeks ago and—"

"Cutter knew from the first moment he saw you two in the same room," Hayley said blithely. "Didn't you, dog?"

The clever animal, who'd been playfully tussling with Woof over a rather ragged toy, stopped and looked at her. He gave a short yip, and Parker told himself it hadn't really sounded like "Yep!"

They took advantage of the spring sunshine and sat out on the deck while the Foxworths updated them on the case. The Turners wanted to thank them—especially Ray, Quinn said, which made Ray smile—and Charles felt bad that Carly and Parker had been hurt rescuing his son. That son had been so shaken Quinn thought there was a chance he might actually turn his life around for real this time.

"Oh," Quinn added to Carly, "Brett says thanks a lot for getting yourself shot and leaving him all the paperwork."

"I'll have to remind him of the messy cases I caught while he was off on his honeymoon," Carly said with a laugh. Then, "What about Neuson?"

"He's recuperating. They'll milk it to delay things, but he's looking at kidnapping, attempted murder, assault on a deputy sheriff and a few other charges. He's going to be, shall we say, busy for some time."

Parker said glumly, "I guess I've got witnessing at another trial in my future. And Ray, too."

"Afraid so," Quinn said. "But you'll have backup this time, someone who doesn't have a stake in the outcome."

Parker blinked. "We will?"

Hayley grinned. "I love this part," she said. "The name Gavin de Marco ring a bell?"

"Of course," Parker said. His mouth quirked. "One of the Witner prosecutors said in a pretrial meeting the defense attorney thought he was Gavin de Marco but wasn't even close. What about him? He quit, didn't he?"

"He works with Foxworth now."

Startled, Parker glanced at Carly. "You didn't include that when you mentioned him before."

"Didn't expect it to come to that," she said.

Hayley went on then. "Gavin will be there every step of the way, to make sure you and Ray and Carly are treated properly by all concerned."

"Well, well," Ray said, leaning back in his chair and looking pleased. Woof and Cutter trotted back, Woof planting his head in Ray's lap as if to reassure himself his beloved master was truly home. Cutter walked over to where Carly and Parker were sitting together on the wooden bench Ray and Parker had built together when Parker was twelve. He looked at them both for a moment, his tail wagging.

"Mission accomplished, dog," Carly said.

Parker would swear the dog nodded, although surely it was just a coincidence of motion.

"So now," Quinn said, "you can get back to those future plans."

"And I really like the idea of the three of you here, with each other to count on," Hayley said as Cutter walked over to her for a scratch behind the ears.

"Yeah," Parker said, feeling a jab of that old uncertainty. "All I need is a job. That remodel's only going to take a while."

Cutter's head came up then, and as the dog looked at him, Parker wondered what had been in his voice. But then he turned and trotted off around the corner of the house and Parker decided he'd been imagining things. Hard not to, when everybody seemed to accept as a matter of course that the dog was…different.

"Or you could be a kept man," Carly said cheerfully. "At least until you figure out what you want to do."

Ray laughed at that. "He'd be lousy at that. He doesn't even like me paying for things."

Parker heard a rustling from around the corner where Cutter had gone. Odd—the only thing there was the shed that Ray had opened this morning to get out some of his old drawing tools. And then the dog was back, carrying something carefully between his teeth. Parker stared. A hammer? What was the dog doing with a hammer?

The animal walked over to Quinn and sat. The other man's brow furrowed, and Parker felt a little better that it apparently made no sense to him, either. Apparently impatient, Cutter dropped the hammer at—or rather on, judging by Quinn's wince—Quinn's feet.

And then, suddenly, Hayley yelped a name, one Parker had never heard. "Drew Kiley!"

Quinn's expression cleared immediately. "Of course," he muttered. "Sorry, dog. Missed the cue there." Then he stood up. "Excuse me," he said, taking out his phone and walking out into the yard.

"What was all that?" Carly asked.

"An idea" was all Hayley said, but she was smiling lovingly at her dog. "You see, Cutter doesn't just demand we fix things. He sometimes shows us how to fix things."

"Are you sure that's just a dog?" Ray asked.

"Nope," Hayley said. "Not at all."

They watched as Hayley thanked her clever dog with some pets and kisses that left the dog looking like any other dog—blissful at all the attention from his special person. And Parker thought of Carly and Woof, and how the dog had been stuck to her like glue since she'd arrived, as if he'd sensed she was hurt and thus needed his attention. And Carly had accepted it in the spirit with which it was given, and more than once he'd come across her snoozing with Woof curled up beside her like some sort of clown-spotted guardian.

And then Quinn was back. He looked at Ray. "Can you look out for Carly in the morning?"

"My pleasure," the man said, clearly meaning it.

"I'm fine," she protested. "But I'd love to spend the morning with Ray. We can work on his brilliant idea some more."

The two smiled at each other, which got a smile out of the formidable Quinn Foxworth.

"There another shoe to drop here?" Parker asked, wondering what he was supposed to be doing while this bonding was going on.

Quinn shifted his gaze. "You," he said, "have a job interview in the morning."

Parker felt his jaw drop, couldn't help it. "I what?"

"Drew is a local contractor we helped out once. He's one of the best around, and he's been working to expand his business."

"I think I've seen his name," Ray said. "Didn't he build that house on West View? That's some nice work."

"He did," Hayley answered. "But he and his wife also just had a baby five months ago, so they have two kids now. He's been looking for some good people to work with him so he can have a home life, too."

"He's also a guy who knows something about tough times and doing what had to be done," Quinn said. "The job's already yours, unless you hate each other on sight, which isn't happening. I think you'll get along just fine."

Parker was still feeling a little stunned when the Foxworths left. Carly and Ray just grinned at him. "Well, now, son," Ray said, "I think I'll go busy myself on those remodel plans."

Parker knew he was just leaving them alone together. Carly was still smiling. "How's it feel?" she asked.

"I…I'm not sure."

"A little dizzying, isn't it?" she admitted.

He met her gaze, looked into those beautiful blue eyes he'd been afraid he might never see again. "You're sure, Carly? I'll understand if it's all been too fast, if—"

"You forget, I've been hearing Cutter success stories ever since Brett connected with the Foxworths over a year and a half ago. Brett's the most skeptical guy around, but he doesn't even try to deny that dog is…special." She raised a brow at him. "Besides, how else do you explain that bit with the hammer?"

"I can't," he admitted.

"You know something I can't wait for?"

A parade of heated images flashed through Parker's mind of everything he wanted to do with her as soon as her doctor gave the all clear. Which would hopefully be in just two more days.

"Besides that," Carly said, and her voice had taken on that low, husky tone that sent shivers up his spine and heat arrowing to other parts of him.

"Sorry," he muttered. "But when I think about that, I can't think of much else."

"Oh, I know the feeling. And I have a whole list of

things I want to do with you, Parker Ward, so you'd better save your strength."

He was pretty sure he visibly shivered then. And didn't care.

"I want that most of all," she went on. "But I also can't wait for this to all come out and know your parents are seeing you've been a hero all over again."

And Parker had no words for how that made him feel.

By the end of the month, his life had changed forever. The interview with Drew Kiley had been different from what he'd expected; the man hadn't asked many questions, but had taken him to a job site and put him to work while he watched. And after an hour, he had the job. Carly's follow-up appointment had gone well, and they'd spent that night—carefully—getting reacquainted. And that made Parker decide that having her on top was his preferred position, since it meant he got to look at her, all of her, more. And it felt so damned good.

Yesterday, Saturday, had been spent preparing for today, and as he looked around at the woman he loved chatting happily with her parents and Ray, who had hit it off as quickly as he and Carly had—"You're filling my life back up, kid," he'd said last night, and for the first time the grief in Ray's eyes had retreated—he marveled at it. A woman he loved more than life, the man who had saved his life, a home that was truly a home and a job he already knew was right.

He wouldn't trade one bit of it—even Woof—for the glamorous job he'd once had, even if it had been real.

Because this *was* real. More real than anything had ever been.

And if this was his reward, then it truly had all been worth it.

Thanks, Cutter.

He grinned inwardly at himself and walked over to join the family.

His real family.

* * * * *

Catch up with everyone at the
Foxworth Foundation with previous books
in Justine Davis's
Cutter's Code miniseries:

Operation Mountain Recovery
Operation Second Chance
Operation Hero's Watch
Operation Notorious

Available now from Harlequin Romantic Suspense!

COMING NEXT MONTH FROM

HARLEQUIN
ROMANTIC SUSPENSE

#2159 COLTON 911: SECRET ALIBI
Colton 911: Chicago • by Beth Cornelison
When Nash Colton is framed for murder, his former lover, Valerie Yates, must choose between proving his innocence and putting her mother's fragile mental health at risk. As they fight to rebuild their relationship, they must learn to trust each other—and find the person trying to kill Nash.

#2160 DROP-DEAD COLTON
The Coltons of Grave Gulch • by Beverly Long
FBI agent Bryce Colton has dedicated the past year to finding serial killer Len Davison. When Davison becomes obsessed with Olivia Margulies, Bryce believes the man may be within reach. But the obsession turns dangerous, and Bryce takes the ultimate risk to save the woman that he loves...

#2161 THE LAST COWBOY STANDING
Cowboys of Holiday Ranch • by Carla Cassidy
Marisa has been waiting to kill a man who kidnapped her. When she hires Mac McBride to care for an abused horse on her ranch, she thinks there might be some good in the world after all. But Marisa's past isn't finished with her—and Mac may not be enough to protect her.

#2162 MATCHED WITH MURDER
by Danielle M. Haas
When multiple murders are connected to users on Samatha Gates's dating app, Detective Max Green knows she'll have information he needs. Neither of them expected Samantha to become a target—and now she has to share her secrets with Max to find the true culprit.

Samantha dropped her head in her hands. "I had the
same thoughts. I called the Department of Justice this
morning, and the woman I spoke with said I needed to
speak with the warden. I didn't get a chance to call before
Teddy stormed in. But I…I can't believe Jose is behind
this."

Max stared at her with hard eyes and an open mouth.

She wrapped her arms over her middle, not knowing
how to explain the conflicting emotions Jose still stirred
in her gut.

"I have to go." Max strode toward the doorway of the
kitchen that led to the foyer, his strides fast and furious.

She staggered off the stool and followed behind him
as quickly as she could. Her mind raced with a million
possibilities. Her bare foot touched down on the wooden
floor of the foyer.

Crash!

She whipped her head toward the broken window that faced the street. Glass shattered to the floor and something flew into the newly formed hole.

"Get back!"

Max's yell barely penetrated her brain before he scooped her over his shoulder and ran in the opposite direction. He reached the carpeted floors of the living room and leaped through the air. They crashed behind the couch and pain shot through her body.

Boom!

A loud explosion pierced her eardrums. The lights flickered and plaster poured down from the ceiling. Max's hard body crashed down on her. Silence filled the heavy air and Samantha squeezed her eyes closed and waited for this nightmare to end.

Don't miss
Matched with Murder *by Danielle M. Haas,*
available December 2021 wherever
Harlequin Romantic Suspense
books and ebooks are sold.

Harlequin.com